THE ADVERSARY CHRONICLES

THE LUCIFERIAN PLAGUE

RANDY C. DOCKENS

Carpenter's Son Publishing

The Luciferian Plague

©2023 by Randy C. Dockens

Published by Carpenter's Son Publishing, Franklin, Tennessee

Published in association with Larry Carpenter of Christian Book Services, LLC
www.christianbookservices.com

Edited by Robert Irvin

Cover and Interior Layout Design by Suzanne Lawing

Printed in the United States of America

978-1-954437-73-9

CONTENTS

FOREWORD

This book is not about a particular Bible story. It shows how the Adversary is still alive and well in our world today, just as he was during biblical times. Bible prophecy indicates that he will continue to influence mankind until God puts a final stop to him at the end of days.

This book uses some of the main characters, including the archangel Mikael and fellow angel Raphael, who have been featured through the Adversary Chronicles series.

I want to convey that the Adversary was not just a concern for those who lived in ancient times, but is very much a concern for us *today*. We have the same struggles as did those who lived in Old Testament and New Testament times. Sides have been drawn, and final destinies will be determined by where one stands when one's life is called to give an account.

Where will you stand?

CHAPTER 1

NEW ASSIGNMENT

Raphael looked at Mikael as they appeared in the laboratory. "Are you sure this is where we are meant to be?"

"This is where Ruach specified," Mikael said.

They walked around numerous lab benches filled with various chemicals, flasks with colorful liquids mixed with the use of magnetic stirrers, and some benches filled with microscopes and other equipment. Petri dishes were displayed next to the microscopes, apparently ready to be viewed by someone.

Fume hoods lined the back wall; each had some type of experiment in progress. Some contained metric balances, others distillation apparatuses, with a few in use, and others were closed with their lights on, but vacant of activity for now.

"And what does Lucifer have to do with this place?" Raphael asked as he investigated one of the microscopes briefly and then looked around at various items displayed.

"Ruach was not very specific," Mikael said as he also turned, intrigued by the scientific apparatuses in use.

Raphael turned and looked at Mikael, a grin forming. "Now, there's a shocker."

Mikael smiled. "Apparently all will become clear as we explore this place. Remember, as this is the twenty-first century following Yahweh's life on earth, there is much more technology for Lucifer to use in his diabolical schemes."

Raphael turned up the corner of his mouth. "Well, that definitely gives one something to contemplate." He shook his head. "Seeing all he has devised over the centuries with very little technology, I don't even want to think what he may be contemplating this time."

"Look at this side of the lab," Mikael said as he walked beyond the lab benches to what looked like three padded benches with a monitor at the head of each. "Looks like something one would see in some type of infirmary."

Raphael nodded. "Yes, it does seem out of place considering the rest of the room." He turned in a three-sixty. "Where is everyone, anyway? Should we look elsewhere, or stay here?"

Mikael shrugged. "Ruach was not too specific. He just said to observe."

"And we haven't encountered Lucifer himself yet either. Seems as though we're on a different type of mission this time."

At that moment the door opened, and two individuals entered the lab. One was carrying a beagle.

CHAPTER 2

UNEXPECTED MYSTERY

"Dr. Thornwhite, you didn't have to carry him," the woman said. "I could have had one of the lab techs do it."

"Oh, it's no bother." Iain was hoping this effort would win him brownie points. He set the beagle on one of the padded benches and ran his hand over the dog's head and neck, giving the animal a friendly pat. The dog pushed its head into his hand each time he gave a stroke with his open palm. "Plus, he's so affectionate. What's his name again?"

"Rocco." She also petted the animal, which was now looking from one of them to the other while panting contently.

"Sit, Rocco," the woman said.

The dog immediately obeyed.

"Good boy," she said as she took a small treat from her white lab coat pocket and held it up. "Lie down."

The dog immediately complied, and a monitor came to life. Mikael noticed various metabolic functions and vital signs for the dog were displayed. The woman fed the beagle the treat.

Iain chuckled. "Impressive."

The woman shrugged. "Simple, really. I find most males are guided by their stomachs."

Iain's eyebrows went up. "Dr. Sheridan, I feel you are typecasting."

The woman's eyebrows also went up, as if challenging him.

Iain laughed. "But pretty accurate."

The woman laughed with him. "Call me Kaitlyn. Just my attempt at trying to be funny."

"Well, if we're being informal, call me Iain." He gave a warm smile. "That will make conversations go better, for sure."

Kaitlyn smiled in return, but then her attention jerked to the doorway as a lab technician burst in carrying another beagle in his arms. "Bev! Something's wrong with Roxie!"

Kaitlyn gestured to the other bed next to Rocco's. "Place her here."

The technician gently laid the animal down and the monitor came to life. Kaitlyn glanced at it as she retrieved a stethoscope from a drawer in the side of the bench. She scrunched her eyes and pursed her lips as she viewed the monitor but didn't say anything. Iain could see that many of the dog's vitals were displaying as abnormal. Kaitlyn stroked the animal with her left hand as she listened to the dog's heart and lungs through the stethoscope while using her right hand to change its position several times.

Kaitlyn removed the stethoscope from her ears and stared at the monitor again.

"How is she?" Iain asked.

Kaitlyn shook her head. "Not good. Her heart rate is very rapid, and her lungs don't sound good." She continued to pet the animal to keep it calm, but then stared at the dog's tail, which was moving slowly side to side. Her eyes shot to the technician.

"Ted, where did you get this animal?"

The technician gave a confused look. "Animal? Get? Well, from Roxie's cage right next to Rocco's, of course."

Kaitlyn shook her head. "No. This is not Roxie."

"What do you mean?"

"The tail, Ted. Look at her tail."

The technician did, and his eyes grew wide. "It's all white!" His gaze shot back to Kaitlyn. "It should be brown." Shaking his head, he stammered, "I . . . I don't understand."

The monitor began to beep. Kaitlyn's attention jerked to it, and then she pointed to Ted. "Intubate her. She's starting to crash."

Iain held Rocco to keep him calm as he was now feeding off Kaitlyn's anxiety and increased activity. "Shh, shh. Just stay calm," he said as he continued to pet the animal.

Kaitlyn listened to the dog's lungs as Ted began intubating the beagle. "Oh, my goodness!" She looked up, eyes wide, completely stunned. "Her plural cavity is already filled with fluid."

"So fast?" Ted asked. "How?"

Kaitlyn shook her head. "I don't know, but we need to drain it immediately." She opened several drawers looking for the right instrument. She pulled out a package and removed a large syringe from it. Just as she began to insert the needle, the electrocardiogram on the monitor flatlined. Ted immediately started cardiac compressions as Kaitlyn began to pull fluid from the dog's chest cavity.

"Iain, put Rocco back in his cage and then come help Ted," Kaitlyn said in somewhat of a frantic tone.

"Sure." Iain scooped up Rocco, held him close to his chest as he ran from the room to the lab next door, put the beagle in his cage, and then burst back into the room he had just left.

"Here," Ted said. "You help her breathe as I do the chest compressions."

Iain attached a bag mask to the intubation tube and then squeezed the bag in a steady rhythm as Ted carried on with chest compressions.

Kaitlyn continued pulling out fluid with the large syringe. "If we get her back, we need the plural cavity empty of this fluid so she can breathe better."

After several more seconds, the ECG came back to life. Ted stopped his compressions and slowly smiled. "I think she's back." He came around to where Iain stood and unscrewed the bag, checked the dog's breathing, and then slowly removed the intubation tube.

Kaitlyn stepped back with the syringe now full. "There. Hopefully that will give her a fighting chance—whoever she is."

Iain gave a deep sigh and breathed some air out, causing his cheeks to expand. "Wasn't what I thought I'd be doing today."

Kaitlyn looked at him and gave a weak smile. "Nor I. But if we don't find out the underlying cause, this may happen again."

Ted nodded as if understanding Kaitlyn was making a request. He pushed a button on an intercom next to the monitor on the wall. "Mary. Jeff. Please come to the lab. Emergency diagnosis needed."

Kaitlyn looked at Iain. "Dr. Thornwhite, come to my office. Let's discuss the ramifications of this."

Iain followed her but turned solemn as he was unsure of her statement.

As the two of them reached the door, the other two technicians entered pulling on their lab coats. They looked at Kaitlyn, but she simply gestured to the bed where Ted was examining the dog further. The technicians nodded and headed Ted's way.

"What's going on, Ted?" the woman asked as they approached.

Ted began telling the lab techs what had happened.

Kaitlyn and Iain stepped from the room.

* * * * *

Mikael looked at Raphael. "What do you think is going on?"

Raphael shook his head as he glanced from the three looking over the dog to Mikael. "No idea."

Mikael motioned with his head. "Let's go see if we can find out."

The two angels walked out; they passed through the closed door in a phasing kind of transference.

CHAPTER 3

MYSTERY DEEPENS

Iain followed Kaitlyn to her office and sat as she took the seat behind her desk.

"So whose dog was that you just treated?" he asked.

Kaitlyn shrugged while giving a blank stare. "I don't know. I have no earthly idea where that dog came from. She definitely isn't one of mine."

"And Roxie?"

Kaitlyn returned another shrug. "Again, I don't know. She should have been the one in her cage."

"So, she was kidnapped?" Iain tilted his head back and forth slightly. "Rather, dognapped, I guess."

Kaitlyn gave a weak smile with a quick raise of her eyebrows. "Yes. But why?"

"Was she any different than Rocco?"

"Oh, yes. That was the main reason I wanted you to come by today. I know you want to repeat what we've done with Rocco in humans, but we've taken Roxie to the next level, so to speak."

Iain leaned forward, intrigued. "What do you mean?"

"Well, as you know, we injected Rocco with specially designed nanobots."

Iain nodded. "Which monitor bodily functions."

"Right. They can be programmed to monitor blood pressure, electrolyte levels, and basically give out a complete blood analysis without us having to take a blood sample."

Iain grinned and pointed to the placard on her desk. "Hence the sign here?"

Kaitlyn looked to where he pointed and laughed. The placard read, "Dr. Crusher."

"Ted gave that to me after the first successful demonstration of Rocco to our administration. He said I had brought them into the *Star Trek* era." She grinned. "That's when he started calling me Bev."

Iain squinted. "Yeah, I heard him call you that but didn't understand the context." He shook his head. "I'm still not sure I do."

"The doctor on *Star Trek* was Dr. Beverly Crusher. My middle name is Beverly. I only allow Ted to call me Bev. He and I go way back." She got a faraway look in her eyes and said, in a low voice, "He should have completed his graduate studies." After a few seconds she came back to the moment and looked at Iain. "Anyway, that's the answer to that mystery."

"You and he are tight, I take it."

Kaitlyn nodded. "Pretty much. We've been through a lot together." She smiled as she sat back in her chair. "He's like the brother I never had." She got a pained look on her face. "His graduate project was to make an app to display all the findings from the nanobots, but the administration felt he was taking too long and gave the project to a medical engineering firm instead. They named it the Tricorder. That was all his idea, but he got no credit for it, so he dropped out of the grad program."

She shook her head. "I hope he gets back to it. He could make the app so much better than it is."

"Sorry to hear that," Iain said. "Maybe he could help me with the human trials?"

Kaitlyn sat upright. "Hey, I think he'd like that. Mind if I suggest that to him?"

Iain's eyebrows went up. "Oh, that would be great." Plus, Iain knew such a move would give him reason to stay in touch with Kaitlyn. He didn't know if he had a chance with her, but he wanted to at least have the opportunity. Maybe Ted could help on both fronts. Iain hadn't known Kaitlyn long, but he found her smart, articulate, and good-natured. Plus, he thought her reddish hair and jade-green eyes stunning. He wondered if she felt the same about his dark hair and blue eyes.

Ted stuck his head in the door. "Sorry to interrupt. Bev, campus security is here. They have some questions."

"Sure," Kaitlyn said as she stood. "Oh, Ted, this is Dr. Thornwhite. I'm not sure you two were really introduced earlier."

Ted stuck out his hand. "Hi. Ted Jordan. Glad to meet you. You're from the Sloane Foundation, right? To start human trials on our technology?"

"That's correct," Iain said as he shook Ted's hand. He found Ted at least two inches taller than he—at least six foot, he guessed—and somewhat rugged-looking. Being tall did not make him lanky in the slightest. His hazel-colored eyes were penetrating. Iain definitely wanted to stay on this guy's good side.

Ted gestured for them to follow. The security guards were outside the vivarium. One of the two was taking notes from Mary, the technician Iain had seen earlier.

"Officers, this is Dr. Sheridan, the head of the project here," Ted said.

The officer with the notepad gave a slight nod. "Hello, Dr. Sheridan. I'm Officer Peters, and this is Officer Connolly." Connolly tipped his hat as Peters continued. "We've been trying to ascertain what happened here. What's your take?"

Kaitlyn stuck her hands in the pockets of her lab coat and gave a shrug. "I really don't know. Apparently, Roxie was taken and replaced with a dog which looks very similar to her but isn't her. And who is also quite ill."

Peters made a few notes. "Any idea why anyone would do that?"

She shook her head. "No idea."

"And the note?"

Kaitlyn developed a shocked look and glanced from Ted to the officer. "Note? What note?"

The officer handed her a piece of paper. "Officer Connolly found this attached to the back of the dog's cage."

Her eyes widened; she showed it to Iain:

Thanks for the loan. The mystery is a warning.
Dr. Thornwhite will be too slow.

Iain looked up and glanced from one individual to another. "What? No one else knew about this." He looked back at Kaitlyn. "Our contract was completely confidential."

"I know!" Kaitlyn said. "Only myself, Ted, and the head of our department knew."

Iain glanced at Ted.

He held up his hands. "Hey, I didn't spill any beans. I haven't even had time for your project to register in my brain. I was too busy with Roxie."

18

"Speaking of the dog," Officer Peters said. "What's so special about a dog?"

Ted looked at him. "It's not just a dog, but a beagle. They are very docile, so they're easier to work with than most other breeds. She's even more special because she has about half a million dollars of technology in her."

"Taken for ransom?" Officer Connolly asked.

"Without the note," Kaitlyn said, "that might be my conclusion. But based upon what the note says, I don't think so."

"We will likely need to bring in city police, Dr. Sheridan," Peters said.

"I understand," Kaitlyn said. "But please talk to Dr. Conway, the head of our department, first."

"Absolutely," Peters said. He looked at each of them. "I need you all to be available over the next couple of weeks while we get to the bottom of this."

Each nodded.

"Dr. Conway's admin, Ida, has all of our contact information," Ted said. "Follow me and I'll take you to the head office."

As they left, Kaitlyn put her hand on Iain's arm. "Sorry, Iain, but I have several things to check into. Can we meet for dinner? I'll bring Ted and we can go over everything."

"Sure. Just say where and when."

"I'll have Ida contact you this afternoon. Can you see yourself out?"

Iain nodded. She looked visibly upset, but he didn't know how to help her at this point. They turned in opposite directions and headed down the hallway.

* * * * *

"Well, that got interesting quickly," Raphael said.

"Indeed," Mikael said as he watched the two walk in opposite directions.

"You think Lucifer is behind this?"

Mikael raised his eyebrows. "Oh, most definitely. It looks like we may have our work cut out for us."

CHAPTER 4

DINNER SURPRISE

Ida called Iain around four in the afternoon to give him the time and place for dinner. Since the restaurant was only a block from his hotel, the location allowed him time for a short teleconference with his team at Sloane.

It seemed things there had encountered a hiccup. The plan was to use the nanobots to help diagnose and treat specific types of cancers, so it was difficult to know whether to categorize the study as a drug, a device, or both. His oncologist and study coordinator were on opposite sides of the fence on the issue. In the end, Iain had suggested the Regulatory Director set up a meeting with the Device Determination Officer of the Food and Drug Administration so this could be ironed out for the proper preparatory work to be done appropriately. The project vice president was not happy about Iain's decision as this further delayed getting started, but he finally convinced her it was better to err on the side of caution than try and push in one direction if the Agency might push back after their filing due to a deficiency in information. But he also knew additional delays would likely put him in the hot seat with his administration.

Yet Iain had to wonder if what happened today would do that anyway.

The "short meeting" went far longer than Iain anticipated. Glancing at his watch, he realized the time was already a little past six, and he was to meet Kaitlyn and Ted at six-thirty. Iain looked at the shirts he had brought with him and pondered which one to wear to dinner. It wasn't a formal business dinner, nor was it a casual dinner. Yet he wanted to impress. He chuckled to himself. Was a shirt going to be the factor that would turn Kaitlyn off from him? He chose a light blue shirt with a dark blue pinstripe. *At any rate,* he thought, *I'll look neat and well put together.*

Iain quickly dressed, brushed his teeth, and remembered to put on just a dab of cologne. He chose one possessing an oriental fragrance with just a hint of vanilla as the base note; he thought that would better blend with the ambiance of the evening and not be overpowering. He shook his head. *Why am I analyzing everything I do this evening?*

The restaurant was within walking distance, but Iain walked at a faster gait than normal. Being late would not make a good impression. As he stepped through the door of the restaurant, he glanced at his watch: 6:29. *On time.* He saw the maître d' seating Kaitlyn and Ted as he approached the hostess station. Kaitlyn's eyes caught his as she sat, and she gave a small wave. Iain smiled, gave a short wave back, and walked to their table.

Ted stood and shook his hand. Kaitlyn gave a polite smile as he sat. "You timed it perfectly," she said.

"Thanks for choosing this so close to the hotel," Iain said. "That allowed me time to get some needed work done. I was able to have a . . . short teleconference with my team."

"Well, we aim to please," Ted said with a grin as he straightened his silverware.

Kaitlyn chuckled and gave Ted a slight tap on his arm. "You know you chose this because you can't resist their scallops."

Iain gave a broad grin. "Well, a win-win for sure."

The waiter delivered menus. Not surprisingly, Ted knew what he wanted without looking. Kaitlyn ordered and chose the wine, giving Iain a little time to quickly look over the menu and order. They chitchatted about various things until their wine and entrées arrived.

As Iain cut into his steak, he looked at Ted. "So, what more did you find out this afternoon?"

After taking a bite of his scallop and giving a quick look of reverie, Ted shook his head. "Not much, I'm afraid. Mary's still working with the dog to keep her stable. Jeff is analyzing the blood work to see what the main issues are." He shrugged. "It's just a matter of waiting at this point."

"Do the police have any leads?"

"No," Kaitlyn said as she tore open a steaming roll and began to apply butter, letting it slightly melt and then using her knife to evenly coat the surface to a tantalizing yellow. Iain found himself mesmerized with every movement this woman made.

Kaitlyn went on. "They seem baffled because there was no evidence of a break-in or anything missing—except for Roxie, that is." She laid her knife down with a sigh and sat back. "You know, it's just odd that no one heard her bark or anything. Even at night, I would think one of the security guards would have heard something."

Ted nodded. "The whole thing is odd—not to mention the note."

"Yeah," Iain said. "And what am I 'too slow' doing? The clinical trial?"

Ted raised his eyebrows with a slight shrug. "That would be my guess. But what are they going to do, perform trials without proper authorization?" He shook his head. "I mean, who would do that? And who would even participate in such a trial?"

"Well, I don't know of any other trial of this kind going on," Iain said. "There's nothing in the online list of trials on the government's approved clinical trial list."

"If they're being this nefarious about everything," Kaitlyn said, getting that faraway look again, "then they likely wouldn't be advertising their trial. There's definitely something going on that everyone's in the dark about."

"Yeah, but . . . " Ted began, but paused as his phone rang. Pulling it out, he seemed to freeze as he looked at the caller ID.

Iain gave him a curious look. "Anything wrong?"

Ted glanced at him with a concerned look. "I don't know. It's Mary. Let me take this."

Iain nodded as Ted put his napkin next to his plate, rose, and walked toward the front of the restaurant.

"I hope everything's okay," Iain said.

Kaitlyn gave a pensive look. "If it's Mary, it's likely about Roxie."

Iain looked to where Ted was pacing next to the large window just past the hostess station. Ted would run his hand through his hair every so often and pause in his pacing before starting up again. His free hand also moved sporadically as he talked. Iain could tell this was not a pleasant message from Mary.

In only a few minutes Iain saw Ted put his phone away and head back to their table. Both he and Kaitlyn looked at Ted as he sat down. Ted had a pensive look but just kept staring at his plate without saying anything. Iain couldn't tell if the news was good or bad.

"Well?" Kaitlyn asked. "What was it?"

Ted looked up slowly. "Apparently Roxie isn't missing after all," Ted said. "She's been with us . . . the whole time."

Kaitlyn grabbed his forearm. "Really? Where? Where did they put her?"

Ted shook his head. "Nowhere."

Kaitlyn scrunched her eyebrows in confusion. Iain felt exactly the same.

"The dog in Roxie's cage was . . . Roxie."

"*What?*" Both Iain and Kaitlyn seemed to say it almost simultaneously.

"That's impossible," Kaitlyn added. "While this dog looks very similar to Roxie, it's not the same dog."

"But it is. Mary said Jeff confirmed it."

"How?" Iain asked. "Through GPS tracking or what?"

Ted shook his head. "No, we didn't have her chipped. The frequency of the global positioning system interfered with some of the nanobot frequencies."

"Well, we need to figure out how to accomplish that going forward. We can't afford to have someone take her," Kaitlyn said. She shook her head again. "But her tail . . . "

"Some of the nanobots were reprogrammed to destroy hair pigment in her tail. Well, not only those . . . but, apparently, almost all of her nanobots were reprogrammed."

Iain held up his hands. "Wait. So how did Jeff confirm this was Roxie?"

Ted shrugged. "Blood. Teeth. Matching code. Mary said they're waiting for the DNA results to come back to definitively confirm."

Iain wasn't sure he understood the full picture Ted was conveying. "Is she going to make it?"

Ted grimaced and gave a slight shrug. "Mary thinks so but isn't really confident about it. Jeff was able to reverse some of the coding to at least get her in a stable condition. It will take quite some time to get everything back to normal, assuming they even can."

Iain thought about that for a few seconds. He still didn't understand how something like this could happen. "I thought the nanobots were just monitoring vital and metabolic functions and reporting back."

Kaitlyn nodded. "Yes, for Rocco. But we went a step further with Roxie. Many of the nanobots were incorporated into some of her cellular structures."

Iain's eyebrows popped upward. "Incorporated? Really? I mean . . . how?"

"Got time for a trip back to the lab tonight?"

Iain sat completely upright. "For *this*? I have all night."

CHAPTER 5

SAVING ROXIE

As soon as Kaitlyn signed for the meal, Ted's phone rang again. Shortly after answering, he developed a worried look and motioned for Kaitlyn and Iain to follow him from the restaurant.

As Iain held the door open for his colleagues, Ted, still on his phone, suddenly said, "Whoa, whoa, whoa. Slow down. You're not making sense." Ted shot a panicked look Kaitlyn's way.

"What's wrong?" Kaitlyn asked.

Ted turned the phone away from his mouth. "It's Jeff . . . " He quickly spoke into his phone again. "Okay, Jeff. Okay. I'll be there just as quickly as I can." He paused, briefly shaking his head and then nodding to what he was hearing. "Yes. Yes, you're doing the right thing. I'll get the passwords changed as soon as I arrive." Ted's eyes began to tear up. He spoke with determination. "Not if I can help it. You're doing good, buddy. Just hang on."

Ted put his phone away, grabbed Kaitlyn's arm, and almost dragged her along with him in an extremely fast gait toward his car. "I'm going to zoom ahead to the lab. I'll meet you and Iain there. I don't have time to explain now. Just get there as quickly as you can."

"But, Ted . . . " Kaitlyn started to say, but Ted dashed away without turning back.

Ted wasted no time as he jumped in his car and sped out of the parking lot before Kaitlyn and Iain had time to assess what they were to do. Iain heard a couple of horns honk as Ted rushed onto the highway. He turned his attention back to Kaitlyn. She seemed befuddled as she fumbled in her purse for her keys.

"Want me to drive?" Iain asked, noticing she was somewhat shaken.

"What?" She shook her head. "No. No, that's okay. Hop in."

Kaitlyn didn't drive as quickly, or as recklessly, as Ted did in leaving the restaurant parking lot, but she drove over the speed limit to get back to the lab quickly. She seemed deep in thought the whole way, so Iain didn't try to engage her in conversation. He wasn't sure what was happening, but he knew it had something to do with Roxie. It was apparently bad for Ted to tear up like he did while on the phone with Jeff, but Iain wasn't sure of the issue.

Once they got back to campus and parked, they hurried to the building housing the lab. Ted's car was parked at the entrance with the driver's side door still open. The engine was off, but the keys were still in the ignition. Iain retrieved the keys and closed the door before heading in. Kaitlyn didn't stop with Iain but went inside ahead of him.

Once he got to the lab, Kaitlyn was already looking over Ted's shoulder; his hands were flying over a computer keyboard. Jeff, doing the same on his laptop, looked awful. His eyes were red and puffy, his curly black hair unkempt, and he had perspiration on his forehead and temples. Sweat had also bled through several spots in his shirt. Jeff was somewhat the contrast to Ted; he was shorter and pudgier in appearance. But the two seemed very much in sync as they engaged with each other and their computers.

Iain noticed Mary sitting with Roxie's head in her lap. The dog's eyes were open, but her eyelids drooped, and she laid still without wagging her tail. Mary's long blonde hair looked partially matted to her head from sweat, and her crying had caused her mascara to run down her cheeks. Her blue eyes looked extremely sad. She gave a slight nod to Iain as she gently petted the beagle. The dog was now almost entirely white, looking much different from what she had previously. Iain went over to find out more information from Mary as the others looked too engaged for questions.

"Hi, Mary," Iain said in a soft tone as he sat next to her. "What's going on?" He pointed to the beagle. "This isn't Roxie, is it?"

She nodded. "It is." Her eyes watered again. "The nanobots have depleted her of almost all pigment. And they seem to be doing something detrimental to some of her organs and systems."

"That's just awful," he said. "Poor Roxie." He gently petted the beagle a few times in between the soft strokes Mary gave her.

Roxie moved slightly with a small whimper as if trying to say hello.

"Jeff has been correcting nanobot code all evening. But as soon as he gets it corrected, somehow it gets changed back to its detrimental instructions."

Iain scrunched his face. "Come again? How does the code change once set?"

Mary shrugged and gave a tired sigh. "That is the mystery. I guess someone must be overriding it."

The note came to Iain's mind: *The mystery is a warning.*

"Got it!" Ted shouted as he stopped typing and looked at Jeff.

Jeff's posture froze for several seconds, his eyes scanning his monitor. He slowly began to nod. "Yes. Yes, I think that's it. The code is not reverting any longer." He looked up at Ted and slowly smiled. "Good job, buddy!" Their hands interlocked fingers in midair in a type of victory stance. They let go and slapped a hard high five with each other.

Both looked at Mary. "How's Roxie?" Ted asked.

Mary shook her head. "Too early to tell. But if you're right, she should start to feel better soon."

All three came over to where Roxie lay with Mary and Iain.

There was silence for a couple of minutes as they each watched the beagle's reaction. But she lay as still as she had previously.

After a couple of minutes, Kaitlyn broke the silence. "Mary, Jeff, have either of you eaten anything?"

Both shook their heads.

She looked at her watch. "It's getting late. Why don't you go grab something? I can stay and watch Roxie."

Both shook their heads again. "I don't want to leave her just yet," Mary said.

Jeff nodded. "I'll just grab something from the vending machine."

"Well, let me grab something for you and bring it back here," Kaitlyn said. "The vending machine has only junk, and half the time it just eats your money." She looked from Mary to Jeff. "What do you want? My treat."

"Well," Jeff said, thinking. "There is that new burger place only a couple of blocks from here that is really good. I ate there the other day. Their burgers are awesome."

Kaitlyn chuckled. "Okay. Done. Mary?"

"Yeah, that's fine," she replied. "I am a little hungry."

"Two burgers coming up, then."

Kaitlyn turned to go, but Ted grabbed her arm. "Let me go, Bev. You're better qualified to deal with Roxie if anything develops."

She paused, then shrugged. "Okay. Just charge it on your department card."

Iain stood. "I'll go with you, Ted."

Iain turned to Kaitlyn first. "I think the note left for us was even more diabolical than it sounded."

Kaitlyn nodded, but responded, "Not sure what you mean."

"Yeah," Ted said. "What does the note have to do with this?"

"I think this is the mystery that serves as a warning."

Ted cocked his head. "You mean to teach us that we were sloppy and need to password-protect the code directing each nanobot?"

"Maybe," Iain said. "Or maybe something even more sinister than that."

CHAPTER 6

IAIN'S DISCOVERY

As they left the building, Ted stopped and took in a deep breath. "Man, that was intense."

"Looked like you and Jeff made a great team," Iain said.

Ted glanced at Iain and nodded. "He's a great guy. A little nerdy, but a great guy. I get along with him fine."

Iain smiled. "I could tell. You both looked in sync there on your computers."

Ted laughed. "Yeah. Nothing like fear and adrenaline to create a good bonding moment."

Iain laughed with him. "I guess so." Tossing the car keys to Ted, he said, "You may need these. Lucky I was the one who stole them than some random stranger."

Ted climbed in the driver's side. "Anyone stealing this thing would send it back with a sympathy note."

Iain patted the dashboard. "Now don't go and hurt her feelings. She's probably sensitive."

Ted started the car and shook his head. "If you want a sensitive car, she's all yours."

Iain grinned. "Not the car bonding type of person, huh?"

Ted's eyebrows went up. "Oh, give me a Z06 Corvette convertible and I'll be gushing sensitivity." He grinned. "And while you're at it, eighty grand to buy it would be nice too."

Iain chuckled. "Well, you have the department card, not me."

Ted gave him a double take. "Yeah, and Bev would have my head. Hard to explain how two burgers were forty grand apiece."

"That's true," Iain said. "Friendship only goes so far, I guess."

"In her mind, committing me to an insane asylum would be the friendly thing to do."

Iain laughed again and decided he'd try to assess how tight Ted was with Kaitlyn. "How long have you known her?"

Ted gave a quick shrug. "Oh, we started graduate school together. Bev came from med school, and I came from medical technology, but we hit it off well and made a good team."

"No doubt about that," Iain said. "Pretty obvious." He paused, then added, "Anything more?"

Ted glanced at Iain. "More? You mean, as in, romantic?"

Iain shrugged. "Just curious." He held up his hands. "You don't have to answer."

Ted chuckled and shook his head. "We decided a long time ago that romance would destroy our friendship. Plus, she being married to my best friend made it seem dishonoring to his memory."

Iain cocked his head. "Oh, I didn't know she had been married. Mind if I ask what happened?"

Ted sighed and took on a saddened expression. "Dan was a gung-ho patriot, if you know what I mean. He was deployed to Afghanistan shortly after he proposed to her. Rather than waiting, they got married the day before his deployment. Although he tried to get back home to her, he was redeployed before he had the chance to even leave Afghanistan. He was able to get a three-day pass, so she met him in Israel, I believe. They had about two days and a night together before he had to go back to his unit in Afghanistan." Ted shook his head. "He never came home. Suicide bomber took him out with several others in his squad. She took it pretty hard."

Iain sat in shock. "Oh, my! That's . . . that's horrible."

Ted shook his finger at Iain. "Now don't you dare tell her I told you that! She doesn't talk about it much."

"Understood. So I guess that means she goes by her maiden name instead."

Ted nodded. "Yeah, she had already decided that due to her academic career and what she had already published, she'd keep her maiden name for most things. She tells everyone her 'Dr. Crusher' placard is about *Star Trek* . . . " He bobbed his head back and forth. "Which it is, to a certain degree. But her husband's name, and my best friend, was Daniel Crusher."

"Wow," Iain said. "That's quite the story."

"So, we're more than typical colleagues. I have deep feelings for her, but it's more like what one has for family."

"It's obvious you're tight."

Ted turned to Iain with a small smile. "So, you're not trespassing."

"What? I, uh . . . "

"Can I give you some advice?"

"Advice?"

"Look," Ted said. "It will be obvious to everyone else that you like her before she knows you like her. That's just the way she is: task-focused. She sort of swore off romance after Dan died, and devoted herself to her work. You'll have to guide her along if you want her on this same path with you." Ted looked over at Iain. "She's definitely worth the effort if you're good enough for her. I warn you, though, if you hurt her, you'll have me to answer to."

"Well, thanks for the advice . . . I mean, warning."

Ted chuckled and pulled into the drive-thru. "Speaking of warning," Ted said. "Tell me your thoughts on the note we received." He rolled down his window to order.

To Iain, it seemed as though Ted had switched subjects, and that was the end of that conversation.

"What can I get for you today?" came the voice through the speaker.

"Let me have two number ones, and . . . " He turned to Iain. "Anything? I'm getting a milkshake."

"Sure," Iain said. "Vanilla shake sounds good."

"Five vanilla milkshakes," Ted said to the attendant.

Ted pulled around to the window to pay and get the order. Iain collected the food and drinks after Ted passed them to him, and Ted pulled off. Iain continued their conversation.

"When I first read the note, I thought the loan to which it referred was Roxie."

"But Roxie was never taken," Ted said.

"Exactly. So that was not the meaning."

"What do you think of the meaning now?"

"Well," Iain said with raised eyebrows, "I think it likely means either your or Jeff's laptops were used to download the program you use to control your nanobots in Roxie."

Ted looked at Iain wide-eyed. "I had mine locked away, so I don't think they took mine."

"And Jeff's?"

"I . . . I don't know." He paused. "But that would explain how someone had control over Roxie."

Iain nodded. "So the 'loan' to which the note referred was likely Jeff's computer. Can just anyone get into the building?"

Ted developed a wry smile. "Well, they let *you* in, didn't they?"

"Hey," Iain said. "I was given a visitor pass and had to be escorted."

Ted laughed. "And that's how it should be for everyone. But if they have a university badge, they don't typically get stopped." He paused, then said, "I guess we need to talk with security about that policy. Our research is more sensitive than we ever thought."

Iain nodded. "And potentially dangerous."

Ted pulled into a parking space near the building entrance. He looked at Iain with a serious expression. "Dangerous?"

"Look what happened to Roxie. What if that were people— and not just a beagle? That's serious enough, but consider the population at large."

Ted's eyes got big. "We need to have a talk with Bev." He grabbed the bag with the burgers and handed the drink caddy to Iain. "Let's go."

They hurried to the building.

CHAPTER 7

THE GOOD, THE BAD, AND THE UGLY

Once they entered the lab, Ted handed the bag to Jeff as he looked at Kaitlyn. "How's Roxie doing?"

"Better," Kaitlyn said.

They headed to where Mary was still sitting with Roxie. Iain noticed Mary had evidently freshened up. Her hair no longer looked matted to her forehead but looked combed and neat. Also, the mascara streaks on her cheeks had been washed away. Roxie still had her head in Mary's lap, but she lifted it slightly when they came over. Her tail wagged slowly. Iain saw that as a good sign.

Jeff handed Mary a burger and then took a large bite of his. "*Mmm.* Man, that is a good burger. What do you think, Mary?"

She took a small bite and her eyes lit up. "Wow, Jeff. Good choice. That is *really* good." She chuckled. "Or I'm just extremely hungry."

"Could be both," Iain said with a smile as he handed each a shake. He also handed one to Kaitlyn. Ted reached for his own.

Kaitlyn looked between Iain and Ted. "Splurged, I see."

Ted shrugged. "Hey, when it's your dime, why not?"

Iain gave her a slight bow. "Thank you very much. Wine and a milkshake all in the same night." He shook his head. "Couldn't ask for more."

Ted put a hand on Iain's and Kaitlyn's shoulders. "You two clearly need to get out more." He nodded toward Roxie and then looked at Kaitlyn. "Now that Roxie seems to be bouncing back, can we go to your office and talk?"

"Sure." She turned to the others. "Jeff. Mary. We'll be in my office if you need us."

Jeff looked up from watching Mary feeding Roxie a small piece of her burger. "Okay, Dr. Sheridan. Thanks for everything."

Kaitlyn smiled. "My pleasure."

The three of them walked toward Kaitlyn's office, nearing the lab exit door. Just before stepping out, Iain recalled his and Ted's conversation about the computers. He turned back. "Jeff, did you lose or . . . misplace . . . your computer for a period of time?"

Jeff stopped drinking his milkshake and looked up in surprise. "What?" He shook his head with a furrowed brow. "No. I've known where my computer has been the whole time."

Iain cocked his head. That didn't seem to fit with what he knew based on the note left for them. "So, it was in your possession the whole time?"

Jeff nodded, then stopped. "Well, not in my possession the whole time, but mine or Mary's."

Mary's gaze jerked to Jeff. "I didn't use your computer."

Jeff looked confused. "Of course you did. You left me a note yesterday saying you wanted to use the computer for an hour or so in the afternoon. I dropped it off at your desk." He looked back at Iain. "She wasn't there, but I made sure her door was locked."

Mary slowly shook her head. "No, Jeff. I never left you a note like that."

"But . . ." Jeff cocked his head. "I saw you typing on it about half an hour after I dropped it off."

"Jeff, I had a doctor's appointment yesterday afternoon. I never saw, or used, your computer."

"That . . . " He looked from Mary to Iain and back. "That makes no sense."

"How did you get the computer back?" Iain asked.

"I stopped back by her office an hour or so later. She wasn't there, so I unlocked the door, took the computer, and left a note saying I had taken it back."

"Well, I saw the note when I returned," Mary said. "I assumed you meant my computer, but it was there, so I just assumed you had borrowed it and returned it and forgot to throw away the note."

Jeff looked at Kaitlyn. "I'm so sorry, Dr. Sheridan. I guess all of this is my fault."

Kaitlyn pointed at Jeff. "No. Don't you dare go there. This is not your fault. It's the fault of some deranged person. But if you still have that note, put it in a plastic bag without touching it with your hands. We'll give it to the police. Maybe that can help their investigation."

Jeff nodded. Mary put her hand on his shoulder to give Jeff comfort. Kaitlyn, Iain, and Ted went on to Kaitlyn's office.

She plopped in her chair; Iain and Ted sat in the other office chairs. "What a day, huh?" Kaitlyn said.

Iain nodded. "Both enlightening and concerning."

"That's one way to put it," Kaitlyn said. "I definitely see the concerning part, but what's the enlightening part?"

"Iain has deciphered the note," Ted replied.

Her eyebrows went up. "Oh? How so?"

"We know the 'loan' wasn't Roxie," Iain said.

Kaitlyn nodded. "We now know it was Jeff's computer."

"Right," Iain said. "Which gave whomever it was the ability to access Roxie's nanobots. Hence the warning mystery."

"And . . . they want to do covert human trials on their own because . . . your trials will take too much time?"

Iain nodded. "That's how I see it."

Kaitlyn looked at Ted. "You agree?"

Ted shrugged. "It's what makes the best interpretation as far as I can tell."

Kaitlyn sat back in her chair and let out a sigh. "So not only have we compromised our own research, we have given someone the ability to do in humans what we did to Roxie."

Ted raised his hands slightly and let them fall into his lap. "Yep. That about sums it up."

"Uh, Kaitlyn, no offense," Iain said. "But how did such a small university get such genetic funding?"

Kaitlyn looked at Iain as if she was unsure why he was asking the question.

Ted jumped in. "Bev has quite a few important journal articles on the potential future of genetics."

"Oh, I know," Iain said, "and you could have had any position anywhere. But you chose this small, obscure university here in New Mexico."

"Yeah," Ted said. "Most of the big universities are just power-grabbing bureaucrats. She—"

"We," Kaitlyn interjected.

Ted nodded. "Have much more control over everything here."

"Plus, Dr. Conway used to work at the National Center for Genome Research in Santa Fe. He has a lot of great connections," Kaitlyn added.

"So just what point are you making?" Ted asked while turning to Iain, looking a bit irritated.

Iain held up his hands. "Hey, I'm not accusing anyone of anything. I'm just saying that no one would expect something this monumental to come out of such a small university. There could be some who would be jealous."

"But how would they even know?" Ted asked. "Roxie has been pretty hush-hush. We even purposefully used vague language in the grant."

Iain nodded. "But those in the know would be able to put the pieces together—especially when you've been touting the success of Rocco."

Kaitlyn looked in thought, then turned back to Iain. "But would they do this just to get first credit for something like this?"

Iain shrugged. "It's possible. But if others knew, it could have leaked to others with less than honorable motives."

Kaitlyn sat back and sighed. "And we may have just opened Pandora's box."

Iain looked from Kaitlyn to Ted. "So, what exactly *did* you do to Roxie?"

"Well . . . " Ted said as he looked at Kaitlyn. She nodded, so he continued. "We injected four types of nanobots into Roxie. We have those that monitor metabolic processes and vital signs, like we did with Rocco."

Iain nodded and waited for the parts he didn't know.

"The second type were programmed to detect certain genetic deformities and then . . . repair them."

Iain nodded again. He knew this was similar to what he wanted to do in his study by detecting certain cancer cells, no matter where they were in the body, even those that had metastasized, and then providing a drug to only those cells so they could be killed. This was a different process, but one similar in design.

"The third were programmed to incorporate into certain carrier proteins and chaperonin proteins," Ted said.

Iain raised his hand to stop Ted. "So this was to do what, exactly?"

"Several things, more than likely," Ted said. "Our main thought was that this would give us the ability to block certain viruses without having to inject anything else into someone. If we knew the protein the virus wanted to make, we could shut down those carrier proteins or the chaperonin protein that would make it viable to build another virus for reinfection."

Iain's eyes went wide. "Wow. That's pretty ingenious."

Ted grinned. "We thought so."

"And the fourth?"

"It could be programmed to attach to a specific amino acid to block further synthesis of various proteins."

Iain got excited when he heard this. "Oh, those could be used to prevent certain cancer cells from producing specific proteins, like PARP-14, so their growth would not accelerate, and doing so could actually starve and kill the cancer cells."

Ted raised his eyebrows. "That as well as other uses."

Iain sat back. "All that is remarkable . . . revolutionary, even."

"Yes," Ted said. "All can be put to great good."

"Or great evil," Kaitlyn added. "And we have just delivered it to someone. While academically frustrating, it would at least be better if this was just a competitor trying to get published before we do." She put her hands to her cheeks. "But I fear we have just delivered the ability for someone to do great harm."

Iain shook his head. "'Great harm' is putting it mildly. It could be catastrophic."

CHAPTER 8

DISTURBING NEWS

Mikael and Raphael stood in Kaitlyn's office listening to the three scientists discuss what happened that day. Mikael shook his head and walked back into the hallway, phasing through the closed door. Raphael followed.

"Well, that's concerning," Raphael said.

Mikael nodded. "It certainly is. Lucifer will love this technology. This puts so much more into his grasp than even his creation of the Nephilim and chimera during the time of Noah. Or when he tried to advance human genetics during the reign of Gilgamesh when the ziggurat Etemenanki was built, which later became known as the Tower of Babel."

"I know," Raphael said. "This goes so much farther than just cloning. It's almost as if all that the Creator has done can be modified or reengineered. It feels . . . diabolical."

"Well, it's like Dr. Sheridan said. It can be used for great good or great evil."

"And we already know which side of that equation Lucifer will be on," Raphael said. "But the Master did put limits on him, remember? Those angels who helped create the Nephilim were placed in Tartarus. You witnessed that."

"True," Mikael said. "But back then, Lucifer and his angels were the ones doing the genetic manipulation. Now mankind understands genetics enough to do the manipulation themselves. Lucifer only needs to manipulate or control them, not actually do it himself."

Raphael's eyes widened. "The loophole he's been looking for."

"Indeed, Raphael. Indeed."

"What do we do?"

"It's time to seek Ruach's guidance. Let's head back to the angel dimension."

The two vanished from the lab hallway, reappeared in their dimension, and then headed down a walkway looking for Ruach.

Another angel approached. He was of lower rank but of noble character, and this one Mikael trusted wholeheartedly. The angel bowed every time he approached Mikael. "My captain. It is good to see you." He gave another slight bow. "And you, Raphael. I trust all is well."

"Quentillious. It is good that I ran into you," Mikael said. "Unfortunately, all is not well. It seems we may be in for some more turbulent times with our Adversary."

Quentillious's eyes widened. "What do you wish me to do, my captain?"

"Get together a contingent of angels. Get Uriel and Azel to help. See if you can find where many fallen angels may have gathered. Start where Raphael and I came back from and expand your search from there. Don't engage, but report back to me."

Quentillious bowed. "Certainly, my captain. I will go at once." He turned and walked away at a quick gait.

"What are you thinking?" Raphael asked.

"It's likely Lucifer is gathering and influencing to get something nefarious going, if he hasn't already started to do so," Mikael said as he pointed. "Let's find Ruach and see what our next game plan should be."

At that moment, Mikael saw something like a blur in front of him—humanoid-shaped, but looking like heat waves one would see rising from a hot surface. "Ruach! We were just on our way to find you."

"And you want to know your next steps," Ruach said.

"Absolutely," Mikael said. "We have seen some disturbing things and believe that Lucifer may be behind it or will use this discovered technology to do something even more evil than he has in centuries past."

"You are right to be concerned," Ruach said. "Lucifer wastes little time in getting new technology to try and achieve his schemes."

"What do you wish us to do, my Lord?" Raphael asked.

"For now, watch him. But protect the five scientists you were just with. They hold valuable information to coming events. Lucifer will try to stop them so they don't interfere with his plans."

Mikael bowed. "Yes, my Lord. Quentillious is already getting a contingent of angels together to seek out strongholds near where these five live and work."

"Very good, Mikael. Evil will be released upon the Earth. This will embolden Lucifer's courage, but also make him vulnerable. We can take advantage of his pride once again."

Mikael looked at Raphael, but it was clear his fellow angel was not sure what Ruach was talking about either. When he turned back, Ruach was gone.

Mikael sighed. "He seems to always exit before I wish him to."

"Apparently," Raphael said, "he feels we have enough information for now."

"Well, we have enough for our next steps. Let's go back and see what's going on and what Quentillious may have found out."

Both disappeared from the angelic realm.

CHAPTER 9

FIRST STEP

"I do think working from here in New Mexico is the best option," Iain said as he broached the subject with his boss, Bill Harmon, over a video call.

Bill had the final say, and Iain needed to get his boss on his side. Not only did Iain want to be around Kaitlyn, something nefarious was going on, so being here was important. Yet he couldn't tell Bill all of that.

"I think Dr. Sheridan and her team will be key for us to help interpret data, and Dr. Gomez at the cancer center in Albuquerque will be the lead investigator. Santa Fe is only a little more than an hour from there, so this is really the prime spot for me to be. Plus, the genome research center is here in Santa Fe as well. All three have worked together in the past, so they can really help lead this trial and help motivate the other sites—most of which are also in the western U.S."

Bill held up his hands. "Whoa, whoa! Uncle, uncle!" he exclaimed, then laughed. "Wow, Iain. You seem pretty adamant about this one."

"Sorry, Bill," Iain said with a chuckle. "I just want to start out on a good foot with this trial. I know we're already behind schedule, and I want to make it up as best I can. It's somewhat inconvenient for me to be away from Sloane for so long, but I think getting the study up and running smoothly is more important right now. This is a tricky trial, and I need close proximity to the experts on this one." Plus, Iain knew, there were no real ties for him anywhere. He had no siblings, and his parents had passed away several years ago. He was free to live anywhere. Telecommunication made being anywhere and working anywhere compatible.

"Well, you've made your case, and I'm supportive," Bill said. "If you can get this off the ground soon, then the extra expense to support you there will be well worth it." Bill pointed his finger. "But if you don't, I may just deduct all the extra expense from your paycheck."

Iain smiled. "Understood. I have a meeting with Marjorie tomorrow to discuss the regulatory aspects and when all supporting documentation regarding the trial can get filed. I'll also discuss the schedule for the Investigators meeting and when we can get sites initiated."

"Okay, Iain. It's all in your shop now. Good luck."

Bill's image faded as the link terminated. Iain sat back and sighed. That was one major hurdle now completed. He hoped everything else would go as well as this video call.

* * * * * * *

Over the next three months, things did fall into place, but Iain found himself in a whirlwind of activity: he met with his team every week; spoke at the Investigators meeting to go over the protocol, expectations, and patient recruitment strategy;

and worked with the pharmacists at each site to help them understand how to prepare nanobots for injection—with Kaitlyn's help, of course. Through all of this, he found the craziness of getting this trial off the ground brought him and Kaitlyn closer. He was with her at least each week if not twice a week. He also had many meetings with Ted as Iain had agreed to be his right-hand man in getting the trial off the ground since he had so much intimate knowledge in how the nanobots functioned, communicated, and reported their data.

Once the trial finally started, Iain found his insanely busy schedule finally starting to calm. He set up a dinner with Kaitlyn and Ted to brief them on next steps.

Iain booked their dinner reservation at the same restaurant where he had initially met them. He thought that was apropos since this was, in some ways, the culmination of that first night. He arrived first and was seated outside in the garden terrace seating area which had a nearby fountain and, this night, a string quartet playing softly. As Iain sat, the sun was just setting, and lights were highlighting the fountain and surrounding shrubbery. He ordered wine, and menus were left for entrée choices when the others arrived. In the air was a sweet yet delicate fragrance. Looking to his left he saw a hedge of sweet acacia blooming with its puffy yellow flowers and a few wrens hopping about through its prickly stems. Perfect ambiance, he thought.

He sat facing the restaurant so he could see when his colleagues arrived. He stood immediately upon seeing Kaitlyn and Ted step onto the garden terrace. Kaitlyn looked gorgeous with her hair pulled into some type of updo, wispy ringlets down in front of her ears guiding one's gaze to her dangling jade earrings. These were of the same hue as her dress and matched her eyes perfectly. Iain was glad he had chosen more formal attire this time.

Iain kissed her on her right cheek. "You look lovely, Kaitlyn," he said as he gestured for the two to take their seats.

He shook Ted's hand. "Thanks for coming."

Ted nodded but then chuckled and shot Iain a mischievous smile. "No kiss for me?"

Iain laughed. "When you look as gorgeous as Kaitlyn, I'll consider it."

Ted looked at Kaitlyn and then back to Iain. "I guess I have no chance."

Kaitlyn lightly slapped Ted's arm. "You two stop." She picked up the menu in front of her. "Let's order. I'm starved."

Iain waved for the waiter. They ordered, the waiter poured wine for each of them, and Iain held up his glass for a toast as the waiter gathered their menus. "Here's to our success," Iain said.

"Hear, hear," Ted said as they clinked glasses.

"Speaking of success," Ted said. "What exactly will we be doing tomorrow?"

After taking another sip, Iain returned his glass to the table. "We get to see the scans of the patients in the trial." He glanced between the two of them. "I want you both there so you can see if they look similar to what you observed with Rocco."

"I can't wait to see them," Kaitlyn said, "but I expect them to be somewhat different since we were not targeting specific types of cells as you're doing."

"Good point," Iain said. "But you two have the most experience with these nanobots, so having you there to help interpret will be super helpful."

Ted tilted his glass toward Iain before taking a sip. "Looking forward to it."

Their conversation turned to more general topics after their entrées arrived. Ted told about some of his hiking exploits in the nearby Sangre de Cristo Range. "You'll have to come with me some time," Ted told Iain. "Deception Peak and Raven's Ridge are not that difficult, but they provide some amazing views." He pointed toward the horizon. "You can just make out the peak where its dark silhouette blocks out the stars on the horizon."

Iain nodded. "Sounds wonderful. Maybe when this trial is fully underway, I'll have some free time for those types of things."

"Sometimes," Ted said, "you just have to make time. Otherwise, they just get away from you."

"That's true," Kaitlyn said. "I feel they certainly have for me."

Iain debated whether to explore that statement further, but the waiter returned asking for dessert orders. He and Kaitlyn ordered, but Ted declined. He assumed Kaitlyn's statement had been about the time since her husband died. She didn't say anything more, so Iain didn't go further.

Ted scooted back in his chair and set his napkin on the table. "Thanks for dinner, Iain. But I need to leave." He stood.

Kaitlyn looked up. "What's wrong?"

Ted touched her shoulder. "Nothing, Bev. I just want to gather some information that Dr. Gomez wanted to go over with me tomorrow about how to use the nanobots for chemotherapy. You two stay and enjoy yourselves."

Ted turned to leave but then looked back and gave Iain a wink. Iain couldn't help but give a small smile.

* * * * *

"You think this ties in with what Quentillious told you?" Raphael asked Mikael.

"Oh, most definitely. There are many demons congregating at the cancer center in Albuquerque. I think Lucifer is very much interested in the outcome of this trial. Likely even more so than Dr. Thornwhite."

"You think Lucifer himself will be there?"

"Probably not," Mikael said. "I think he has other work going on somewhere."

"What's our next move, then?" Raphael asked.

Mikael put his hand on his fellow angel's shoulder. "Go find Quentillious and have him get his contingent of angels to the cancer center. Something tells me the results Dr. Thornwhite finds tomorrow will be of vital concern to Lucifer. I'm sure at least one of his high-ranking angels will be there."

Raphael's eyebrows went up. "You think we will have a battle?"

Mikael tilted his head back and forth. "Perhaps. At least a skirmish." He shrugged. "Perhaps not. Yet we need to be prepared for whatever happens."

"And you?"

"I'm going to follow this man tonight and see what else I can learn."

Raphael nodded and disappeared. Mikael entered the restaurant to follow Ted as he was leaving. Mikael didn't use the door but simply phased through the large window that overlooked the garden terrace.

* * * * *

"Well, Ted's leaving was unexpected," Kaitlyn said, looking a little unsettled. "I wonder why he didn't take care of that earlier."

Iain knew Ted probably did, but that he had made this move as his way of saying he was okay with Iain getting closer to Kaitlyn. Ted's warning about not hurting Kaitlyn came back to him, but he had no intention of stringing her along just because he found her attractive.

"Well, it's a big day for all of us tomorrow, but especially for Ted," Iain said.

"Oh, how so?"

"You said the nanobots were originally his idea, right?"

Kaitlyn nodded. Her eyes grew wide. "Oh, of course. If these nanobots work out in your trial, they will become the prototype for all sorts of therapy uses."

"Not only for him," Iain said, "but a big boon for you too." He put his hand gently on top of hers. She glanced at her hand but didn't pull away. He thought that a good sign.

"It seems for all of us," Kaitlyn said, giving a small smile.

Iain dared not move, but he didn't really know the next step to take. As he was wondering about that, the waiter returned with their desserts. Iain instinctively jerked his hands to his lap as the waiter approached. He determined to eat as slowly as possible as he wanted this time with her to last. Ted said it would take time to get Kaitlyn's attention. Iain had taken the first step in letting her know he was interested. Hopefully, she would soon reciprocate.

CHAPTER 10

MALPHAS

Albuquerque had beautiful skies the next day—but not so much so in the spiritual realm.

Mikael and Raphael arrived at the cancer center where Quentillious and his angels were in position on the building's roof. Each had swords drawn waiting for action that might occur, but had not yet. Mikael looked up and saw hundreds of demons circulating; the effect was somewhat like vultures waiting for an injured animal on the ground to give up and die.

"What's going on, Quentillious?"

Quentillious bowed and shook his head. "Nothing yet, my captain." He glanced up. "That's as close as they have come since we posted ourselves here."

"Have you checked to see if they are only a distraction?"

"Yes, my captain. Azel and Uriel went inside to see if any were there." He looked around and motioned for Uriel to come forward.

Uriel did so; he and Mikael locked forearms in greeting. Uriel gave a nod to Raphael. "Tell me what you have to report," Mikael said.

"We only found two inside. Not sure why as yet."

"Did you engage them?"

Uriel shook his head. "No. Malphas saw me, so I came back here. He didn't see Azel, so Azel is still observing. He'll bring us in if necessary."

"Malphas!" Mikael exclaimed. "Why is one of Lucifer's top angels here?"

Uriel shrugged. "Unsure, but he seems to be guarding the other demon."

"Why?" Raphael asked. "What is he doing?"

"Azel is trying to figure that out. So far, it doesn't look like anything important, but with Malphas there, it likely is."

Mikael looked down and saw Iain, Kaitlyn, and Ted arrive and enter the building. He glanced up and saw the demons fly closer and yet keep their distance. He turned to Quentillious and Uriel. "Keep an eye on them. Raphael and I are going inside. Be prepared for whatever happens in there . . . " He glanced up. "Or out here."

Both bowed. "Yes, my captain," Quentillious said.

* * * * *

Iain, Kaitlyn, and Ted entered the conference room. Dr. Gomez stood. "Welcome, welcome. I'm so glad you all made it. Without incident, I hope."

Kaitlyn smiled. "Yes, the trip was uneventful, which is the way I like them."

"Indeed, Dr. Sheridan, indeed," Gomez said. He gestured to a credenza in the back. "Please help yourself to some coffee and refreshments."

Gomez approached Iain as the others went to get coffee. "Our scans here are complete, but we don't have scans from all sites. My assistant will be bringing in files from the other sites as he gets them so we can match up some of the data with the electronic files that are online."

Iain's eyebrows went up. "They don't have all the data entered yet?"

Gomez shook his head. "Some do, but not all." He grinned. "But it doesn't matter for today as we will have the necessary demographic data in hard copy in case we have questions." He gestured toward a chair at the head of the table. "This one is for you so you can coordinate the scans however you wish."

A young man, likely in his late twenties, Iain guessed, entered with a folder. He went to where the other files were stacked and placed it under the others.

Gomez waved him over. "Mr. Threaders, come here. I'd like to introduce you to Dr. Thornwhite."

The young man shook Iain's hand. "Nice to meet you."

"Same here," Iain said, then squinted. "You're the one I always saw in the corner when we did our video conferences, aren't you?"

The young man laughed. "Yeah, that's me. Just trying to stay in the loop. Feel free to call me Walt."

Gomez patted Walt on his upper back. "Mr. Threaders . . . Walt here, is finishing up his master's in medical technology. He's been a big help on this project."

Ted walked up to Iain with a cup of coffee and handed it to him.

"Oh, thanks. Ted, have you met Walt?"

"We've talked. Good to meet you in person, Walt."

Walt nodded. "Same here." Turning to Iain, Walt said, "I'll be in and out bringing in more files. So just ignore me as you talk. I'll have my chair next to the door to disturb as little as possible."

"Okay, let's get started," Gomez said, directing everyone to their seats.

Iain went to his and opened the first file. He scanned the page, found the name of the electronic file, and pulled it up on-screen. "This is patient 001-0101. It seems this patient has liver cancer. Dr. Gomez, as this is one of your patients, do you want to talk about this one?"

Gomez leaned forward. "Sure. This patient entered the trial with stage 1 hepatocarcinoma. We think it hasn't had time to metastasize, but this scan should confirm. Mr. Jordan, mind explaining what the scans are showing us?"

Ted rose and went to the screen. "We incorporated luciferase into the nanobots which are programmed to target the cancer cells and bind to them. The luciferase produces bioluminescence, and this allows us to visually see where the cancer is located. If it hasn't yet metastasized, we should only see the liver light up."

* * * * *

Mikael and Raphael entered the room behind Walt and a demon shadowing him. So far, the demon seemed to be following and doing nothing else. Mikael came to a halt when he saw Malphas in the corner of the room.

"Malphas, what is so urgent that one of Lucifer's top angels is here to supervise?"

Malphas puffed out his chest. "Oh, I do all sorts of things. I could ask you the same question."

"Our Creator considers all humans important. I'm never on a mission without importance."

"Well, look at you, going and making yourself more important than you really are—again," Malphas said. "None of this concerns you, so you can just go give the Almighty One your report that all is fine. We're within our rights being here."

"And what's with the shadow puppet you have here?"

Malphas developed a wicked grin. "Bothers you, does it?"

"Everything you do bothers me, Malphas. I know you're up to something. I'm just not sure what—yet."

"I know it's upsetting to be in the dark about things," Malphas said in a mock caring tone. His tone quickly changed to one of disdain. "Get over it!"

Mikael walked to the opposite corner of the room and stood. Raphael followed the demon back and forth as Walt entered and exited the room. Mikael noticed Walt always put the next file on the bottom of the pile that was growing in height next to Iain. Yet on the next trip in, the demon—in a blur of a move—put his palm on Walt's head. It was a quick and almost unnoticeable move. This time, after Walt put the file under the pile next to Iain, he took the one on top with him and laid it in his chair as he exited the room. Raphael glanced at Mikael with a slight nod indicating he had seen the demon's action.

Mikael kept looking at Malphas to be sure he did not suspect anything out of the ordinary. Yet he knew the folder laying in Walt's chair was something Malphas did not want the group of scientists to see. He had to be sure Malphas's plan did not succeed.

When Walt entered again, the demon repeated his action, and Walt repeated what he had done earlier. As the demon was about to leave the room, Mikael gave a nod to Raphael and, in one swift motion, Raphael unsheathed his sword and plunged it into the demon, who went catatonic. Raphael placed his palm on Walt's head, grabbed the demon's arm, and both Raphael and the dark angel vanished.

Azel then rushed into the room causing the folders in the chair to fall to the floor in front of Walt. Mikael saw Walt pause in thought as he slowly picked up the folders, acting confused as to why they had been in his chair. In a swift motion, Malphas struck out at Azel, who deftly deflected his blow. Malphas then jumped, turning in midair over the conference table with both hands on his sword's hilt to make the weapon come down hard and deliver a death blow to Mikael as he landed. Mikael effectively blocked the blow by raising his sword over his head horizontal to the other sword's downward thrust. He swiftly pushed his sword up and around to ward off the attack while attempting to take Malphas by surprise with a slash into his side. Yet Malphas effectively parried the blow by quickly bringing his sword vertical with its tip pointed to the floor.

"Azel, to the roof! Quickly!" Mikael said.

Azel cocked his head as if he thought that not a wise decision, but did as ordered.

"What have you done?" Malphas said with a tone of disdain.

"Evidently, prevented whatever you thought you were achieving here."

"You'll be sorry for interfering."

Mikael shook his head. "No. I don't think so." He stepped back, passing through the wall, and was now in the hallway.

Malphas did the same and came down hard with a blow to try to take Mikael off guard.

Mikael again effectively deflected the assault, then unfurled his wings bringing them to their full length, and took a defensive stance. He used his wings to help turn his body right and then left in swift, successive movements as he repeatedly brought blow after blow at Malphas. This took Malphas off guard and put him in a completely defensive position. Malphas was able to deflect each drive of Mikael's sword, but his reflexes became slower and slower as Mikael increased the speed of his barrage.

Malphas's eyes began to show doubt in his ability to keep up with Mikael's blows. After one quick slice, Malphas deflected a little too slowly, and Mikael delivered a deep cut into Malphas's side. The large angel went catatonic and stood in what looked like suspended animation, his sword falling to the floor.

Mikael glanced back into the conference room where everyone was in discussion about the scan displayed on the screen. Walt had a puzzled look on his face as he delivered the two file folders from his chair back to Iain, placing them on top of the stack.

Mikael teleported to the roof of the building while taking the catatonic Malphas with him. There he entered a frenzy of fighting between his angels and those Malphas had brought in reserve. Apparently, seeing Raphael bring the other demon to the roof had spurred them into action. A few dozen were already catatonic on the roof. One demon came from behind Mikael as he appeared, but Mikael easily deflected the attack. When this demon saw Malphas catatonic, his eyes grew wide and he stepped back, just missing a lethal blow from Mikael's sword.

"Fall back!" the demon said. "Fall back! Regroup!"

All remaining demons immediately grabbed one of their fallen comrades and flew off. Two had enough courage and drive to snatch Malphas from Mikael's grasp and then fly off with him. Mikael let them go; he just wanted to see these dark angels leave. They circled above for a few minutes, then disappeared one by one in rapid succession.

Mikael turned to his angel contingent, who were sheathing their swords. "Great job, everyone. Stay here a while longer until we have a better understanding of Lucifer's next moves."

There were several nods and acknowledgments.

Mikael turned to Raphael. "Let's go back and see what else we can learn."

CHAPTER 11

SURPRISING SCANS

When Iain opened the next file, he gasped, as did everyone else at the table. The bioluminescence was showing throughout this person's body.

"That's impossible," Gomez said, his eyes wide, as he glanced at Walt, then turned back to the screen. "A person with that extensive an amount of cancer would not qualify for this trial."

Iain turned to Gomez. "Was any other nanobot preparation used than what the protocol called for?"

Gomez sat up straighter. "No! Of course not." He glanced at the screen again and looked back at Iain. "Well, not that I know of." He turned to Walt. "Mr. Threaders, have the pharmacist come to the conference room."

Walt seemed lost in thought, as if he was trying to remember something.

"Mr. Threaders. Walt!"

Walt snapped his attention toward Gomez. "Yes sir? Sorry, I was focused on something else here."

"Have the pharmacist come to the conference room. We have a few questions."

Walt nodded. "Yes, Dr. Gomez. Right away, sir." He quickly left the room.

"You know," Ted said as he looked from Gomez to Iain, "this reminds me of one of Roxie's scans."

Gomez looked deeply confused. "Who's Roxie?"

Ted smiled and held up his hand. "I'm sorry, Dr. Gomez. That's a legitimate question. Roxie is a beagle we used to inject nanobots that bind to certain intercellular structures. Because almost all cells had that structure, the bioluminescence scan revealed something very akin to what we are seeing here."

Gomez rubbed his chin. "So you're saying rather than targeting the cancer gene, these nanobots have targeted something common to almost every cell?"

Ted cocked his head and gave a slight shrug. "That's the way it seems to me."

Kaitlyn jumped into the conversation. "Is there a protein that cancer cells produce that is common to all cells and not just cancer cells?"

"Well, perhaps," Gomez replied. "But these nanobots were specific for a certain protein produced only by cancer cells." He shook his head. "I don't see how . . . " He gestured toward the screen. ". . . this type of scan could be produced if we followed protocol procedures."

Kaitlyn shrugged. "Well, I'm stumped."

"I think we all are," Iain added. He turned to Ted. "Is there a way to discover how these nanobots are different from others?"

Ted grimaced. "It's . . . possible. Not easy, though."

"Why is that?" Gomez asked.

"It may not necessarily be another type of nanobot but controlled by a different program. I'll need to isolate these from this patient and see to which code they respond, and then take a tissue sample to see exactly where they've bonded."

Gomez sat back. "Man, this mucks up the protocol significantly."

Iain shrugged. "Well, we must get to the bottom of this. We'll write an amendment to allow us to do whatever it is we need to do. That will allow us to explain all of this in the final report and to regulatory agencies."

A young woman entered the room followed by Walt. Everyone looked her way.

"Ah, Tiffany," Gomez said. "I was hoping it would be you."

"Hi, Dr. Gomez. What seems to be the problem?"

Gomez pointed to the screen. "*That's* our problem."

She looked, then squinted. "That's from this study?" She shook her head. "That's only possible if someone with stage 4 highly metastasized carcinoma were allowed into the study."

"Or," Ted added, "if a different set of nanobots were administered."

Tiffany's eyes widened. "What?" She shook her head. "No. That's impossible."

"And yet . . . " Kaitlyn said as she gestured to the screen.

Tiffany held up her hands. "Look, I'll help in getting to the bottom of this, but I can say with high confidence that this is not a pharmacy malfunction."

Iain held up his hands. "We're not here to place blame— just to try and understand." He turned to Tiffany. "Please see what you can find out and report back to Dr. Gomez."

She nodded and stepped from the room.

Walt spoke up. "I'll go tell Quality and get them in the loop."

"Great idea," Gomez said. "Good thinking."

Before Walt could leave, Iain called to him. "Walt, let Ted go with you. We need to get an amendment and revised informed consent as well." He glanced at Ted and then back to Walt. "He can let you know what he needs so we can better understand what's going on here."

Ted stood. "Sure. We'll need a tissue sample from this patient and any others who may show this pattern as well."

"Good point." Iain patted the remaining folders. "We'll go through these as you and Walt get that started. Then we'll regroup so you know how much work is needed for this."

Walt and Ted nodded and left together.

Iain gave a big sigh. "Let's take a bio break, and then we'll get back to the rest of these."

* * * * *

As those in the conference room stood and stretched, got coffee, or went to the restroom, Raphael looked at Mikael as he pointed to the screen. "So, this is what Malphas wanted to keep from them?"

"Apparently so," Mikael said. "But I don't know why." He stared at the screen for a moment. "What could Lucifer be up to?"

"It must have something to do with his world domination initiative. You know that's what all his other schemes have been about."

Mikael paused and looked from the screen to Raphael and back. "That's true, but I can't see how this is tied to that."

"Well, I think I'll go follow Mr. Jordan and see what he finds out."

"Good idea," Mikael said. "Have Uriel go with you." He shrugged. "Since we don't know what to expect, better to have one other with you."

Raphael nodded and disappeared.

As Mikael stood and stared at the screen, he shook his head. He knew Lucifer was always shrewd, always clever, and he knew there was some type of diabolical plan in play. Yet Lucifer had Malphas here, and not himself, so that meant something bigger was going on somewhere else. It seemed the mystery was getting deeper.

As the scientists took their seats again, Mikael stood behind Iain; he wanted to see what they would find. He knew this one patient was likely not the only one with severe scan abnormalities, and he wanted to see just how many of these Lucifer had identified. He told himself he would check with Raphael and Uriel later to see what they discovered.

CHAPTER 12

BRICK BY BRICK

From his seat at the end of the long table in the conference room, Iain observed a beautiful sunset as he waited for Kaitlyn and Ted to return and debrief him on all they knew. The reds and golds were spectacular. He was thankful for this view as it was nice to experience something pleasant after this complicated, stressful day. Knowing they had more than an hour's drive to get back to Santa Fe, he massaged his temples to combat the stress. A long sigh emerged as he sat back. If Ted or Kaitlyn did not want to drive, he was going to vote to spend the night here. A bed was calling him, and the closer it was the better.

Ted and Kaitlyn came in together. They looked as exhausted as he felt. Both sat—rather, plopped—in chairs next to him and opposite each other.

Kaitlyn pressed her palms to her cheeks. "This day was supposed to be a day of triumph and vindication. It's just another chapter of the nightmare that started a couple of months ago."

Ted nodded as he sighed. "Yeah. I thought maybe it had blown over since we never heard anything more since then.

Just the time the police give up their search because of no further contact, no prints to follow, or any other evidence, we get something more. I think in the end the police felt it was all a practical joke someone pulled on us."

"Well, this *definitely* isn't a practical joke," Kaitlyn said. "I knew it then, too. The note made me nervous. This . . . " She waved her hand in the air at nothing in particular. ". . . makes me frightened." Her eyes began to glisten. "Has our brilliance led to something catastrophic?"

Iain put his hand on hers. She looked at him and he thought he saw a look of . . . thankfulness? But he knew it was more than that. Iain wasn't sure how to describe it, but he was glad to see it. "First of all, we haven't reached catastrophic," he said, then paused a few seconds. "Actually, we don't yet know *what* we've reached. I know it isn't good, but we first need to understand what we've discovered." He turned to Ted. "What *have* we discovered?"

Ted drummed his fingers a few times before answering with a slight shrug. "Not really sure yet. There are six scans we need to investigate as they don't fit the pattern we expected. Walt is requesting a tissue sample from each investigator. Dr. Gomez is in the process of talking to the two patients from his clinic and will talk with the other investigators tomorrow about those found in their clinics. There are five other clinics we don't yet have data from."

"When do you think you can look more into this?" Iain asked.

"My guess is that it will be three or four weeks," Ted said.

Kaitlyn's eyes widened. "That's a lot of wasted time."

Iain nodded and produced another sigh. "I agree, but I get it."

"Really?" Kaitlyn asked. "Why?"

"Well, to do this by the book," Iain said, "so we can demonstrate we followed protocol, we must have the protocol amendment approved and the informed consent signed by the patients before we can get the tissue samples. The investigators need to schedule time for the patients to come in, and only then can we begin to see what's going on."

Kaitlyn shook her head. "And meanwhile, those who did this, I'm sure, are not waiting for all of this proper procedure before they start their next steps—whatever those are." Her tone was one of irritation.

Iain's hand was still on hers, and he gave a slight squeeze. "I know. I know. But what choice do we have? If we get sloppy, we lose on so many levels."

Kaitlyn's voice softened. "Yeah, I know." She closed her eyes and shook her head slightly. "Yet I feel our hesitancy to act swiftly could lead to something else to continue this nightmare."

Iain stood and began to pace in front of the conference window. The sun had set and there was only a slight hue of red on the horizon. He shook his index finger. "Maybe there's something we can do in the meantime."

Ted sat up straighter. "There is?"

Iain stopped suddenly and turned. "Yes. We have all the demographic data, vital signs, and chemistry lab data." His eyebrows raised. "What if we work to see if there is a common denominator between these patients?"

Kaitlyn looked from Iain to Ted and back; she looked a bit more hopeful. "Can we do that?"

"We can try," Ted said, not sounding confident. "But with only six, I'm not sure how well that will work." He shrugged, but with a hint of optimism in his eyes. "Worth a try, though. I'll start on it tomorrow."

Iain came back to his seat. "Okay, next question: who wants to drive home tonight?"

Ted raised his hands as if in a defensive stance. "Hey, I drew the short straw this morning."

Kaitlyn shook her head. "Let's just find a hotel here in Albuquerque." She gave a slight shrug. "We need to be here tomorrow anyway."

"Good," Iain said. "My thoughts exactly." He stood and gestured toward the door. "Let's go get some well-deserved rest."

As they headed to the front of the building to turn in their visitor badges at reception, Ted said, "Can we just go through a drive-thru somewhere? I really don't want to sit in a restaurant for another couple of hours."

"Sounds good to me," Iain said as he looked at Kaitlyn; she nodded. Iain patted Ted on the back. "Sure, Ted. Just for you."

Ted chuckled. "Thanks."

After informing the receptionist of their planned return visit the next morning, they grabbed some burgers at a local drive-thru on the way to a nearby hotel, checked in, said good night, and headed to their rooms.

Iain took off his coat and tie, plopped into the chair next to his bed, and took out his burger. He looked around at his room. He had been cooped up all day, and here he was cooped up again. While tired, he wanted at least a little fresh air. He glanced out his window and saw the lighted pool below looking like a turquoise gem in the dark night. He decided he would go eat by the pool, enjoy the night air, and then come back to bed.

Once outside, he used his room key to open the gate to the pool area which was flanked by two large overgrown Spanish broom bushes. The area looked deserted. *Good*, he thought. He'd have some solitude as he ate. He put his bag and drink on the first patio table he came to and began to stretch. It was then that he heard a chair scrape across the concrete surface of the pool deck. He glanced over and saw a female silhouette at a table on the other side of the pool. As his eyes adjusted to the low light, the person's features came into better view.

"Kaitlyn?"

"Iain, is that you?"

Iain chuckled, picked up his food, and walked around the pool. "I guess great minds think alike. Felt you'd been cooped up for too long as well?"

"Absolutely." She pulled out the chair next to her. "Please, join me."

Iain sat, and both took a couple bites of their burger without speaking. Iain could hear the faint sound of water being sprayed into the pool, felt the light breeze on his skin, heard the soft swishing sound of swaying palm branches from the trees around the outside of the pool fence, and could see several stars in the sky above the hotel roofline. It all led to, finally, a relaxed feeling.

Iain paused and breathed in deeply. "Such a beautiful night, isn't it?"

Kaitlyn nodded as she took a sip of her soda. "It really is. A nice way to end such a crazy day."

"Not the way I thought I'd be ending this day, but I couldn't think of a better way to do so."

She gave him a warm smile. He hoped she understood what he was really hinting at: being with her was a great way to end the day.

"I'm glad you decided to stay in Santa Fe to get your trial off the ground," she said. "It really shows your dedication to its success."

"Well, being close to the expert of the nanobots was very important to our success."

Kaitlyn smiled as she placed a strand of hair behind her ear. "Oh, being near me was key?"

Iain nodded as he returned the smile. "Oh, absolutely." He leaned in. "The closer the better."

"And why is that?" she said, her eyes scanning his face.

She didn't move, so he took that as a good sign. "It gives me the chance to do . . . this." He leaned in farther and softly kissed her. It was nice. She didn't resist, but didn't reciprocate, either, so Iain kept it short. He was glad to see her still smiling at him afterward.

She looked down in a coy manner. "Well, I don't remember reading that in the protocol."

"No?"

She shook her head.

"I guess I'll have to write an amendment."

She chuckled lightly, placing her hand on his cheek. She looked into his eyes and said, "Yes, you do that."

"I will," he said in a soft tone, wondering where this would lead.

She sat back and sipped her soda, looking content and satisfied. Following her lead, Iain sat back as he took the last bite of his burger. He assumed this relationship would have to be constructed one brick at a time.

Iain watched as Kaitlyn seemed to go into deep thought. After a short time, he said, "Everything okay?" He was wondering if she was having second thoughts about their kiss. Her next words surprised him.

"Are you spiritual?"

Iain's head jerked back slightly. "What? You mean, like believe in God?"

Kaitlyn bobbed her head back and forth. "Yes, sort of. I mean, when you were showing that patient whose scan lit up like a Christmas tree, I got a strange sense of evil in the room. Did you . . . feel the same?"

Iain tilted his head. "I was concerned, most definitely. But . . . a sense of evil?"

"Yeah." She sat up. "It was short-lived, though. Almost as soon as Walt dropped the files on the floor, it was gone." She shook her head and shrugged. "Maybe it just brought me out of my thoughts. I . . . I don't know." She looked back at him. "I was just wondering if you felt something similar."

"Well, not like that, exactly. I do feel something sinister is going on, though."

Kaitlyn developed a worried look. "I just hope we haven't unleased something horrible into the world."

"What?" Iain sat upright and took her hand. "Don't you dare think that. What you have done is something absolutely wonderful." He shook her hand lightly, forcing her to look at him. "Wonderful, you hear?"

She nodded but didn't look confident.

"You can't blame yourself for what some other deranged individuals may do. It's almost always true that what can be used for great good can also be used for great harm. We just need to put some more safeguards in place, that's all."

"You think so?"

Iain kissed the back of her hand. "Absolutely." He stood and helped her to her feet. "And since that is what we will do tomorrow, you need to get some well-deserved rest."

She chuckled slightly. "Yes, doctor. Whatever you say."

Iain put their trash in the nearby garbage can, and they walked back toward the hotel together. Even before they reached the pool gate, however, she put her head on his shoulder. He wrapped his arm around her shoulders and gave a small squeeze. Kaitlyn gave a quick glance up at him and smiled. Iain smiled back. Another brick had been laid.

He opened the gate for her, and she stepped through, then turned to say something.

"Iain, I want to thank—"

Her sentence was cut short as someone plunged a cloth bag over her head, evidently hiding in the shrubbery at the gate. Before he could react, Iain felt a sharp pain to the back of his head. He tried to reach for Kaitlyn as he saw her struggling and heard her muffled cries. But darkness enveloped him, and he was unconscious before he hit the ground.

CHAPTER 13

KIDNAPPED

Jerking awake, confusion immediately set in as Iain tried to understand why he was sitting outside. Large bushes partially obscured his view of the hotel. His head throbbed. He went to feel the back of his head, where it hurt most, but he couldn't move. His hands were . . . tied!? *What's going on?* The remembrance of what happened earlier suddenly flooded into his mind. *Kaitlyn. She's been kidnapped!*

Iain thought about yelling for help but realized tape had been placed over his mouth. Any attempt to free himself was unsuccessful and only caused the zip tie around his wrists to cut deeper. Standing proved impossible as his hands were tied behind him low on the fence surrounding the pool; he was below the crossbar that went perpendicular to the iron pickets composing the fence. Being this low and behind the bushes would make it difficult for anyone to see him, assuming anyone would even walk by at this hour.

What is the hour? It was still night. He tried to look at his watch, but that too proved impossible. Thinking back, he assumed it was likely around midnight when he and Kaitlyn had started walking back to the hotel, so . . . He looked around for any clue of the time—but saw nothing. Assuming he was out for no more than an hour or so, it couldn't be much past two in the morning. Anyone coming by at this hour, he reasoned, was a remote possibility at best.

Iain looked around on the ground for anything he could potentially use to help free himself, but there was only gravel and twigs. Nothing appeared substantial enough, or sharp enough, to cut through his restraints. He struggled in frustration again, but that did nothing but hurt his wrists even more. Maybe there was something behind him. He felt along the ground but again only felt rocks and twigs. Nothing helpful. He then hit something metal and pulled his hand away in pain. It was hot—extremely hot. Turning as best he could, he realized it was one of the lights shining into the palm trees for aesthetic landscaping. Feeling the sharpness of the metal casing surrounding the light, and its heat, made Iain think this could be enough to cut through the plastic zip tie.

The process worked, but not without pain. First he had to struggle to push his arms back far enough to reach the light. Then it was so hot he kept burning his fingers and palms, causing him to keep pulling away. He could be close to the light for only seconds in any one try. It took a considerable amount of time, but the strategy eventually worked—he felt his hands finally come free! He grimaced as he slowly moved his arms to regain their mobility, their ache slowly subsiding. After sitting and massaging his shoulders for several seconds to get them moving without producing severe pain, he removed the tape around his mouth, which was also painful, and stood. Looking at his watch, his eyes widened. It was almost three in the morning.

His first instinct was to find Kaitlyn, but he had no idea where to even start looking. Intel was nonexistent: no idea who took her, no idea where they went, and no real idea why they took her. He assumed it to be her knowledge of the nano-bots. Although he thought Ted would have been the more logical choice of the two for such an abduction, the people who took Kaitlyn probably didn't know that. At any rate, he didn't know what to do but get Ted and then reach the police.

Iain ran—more like stumbled—across the small parking lot between the pool and the hotel to the side door he had stepped through what seemed like a lifetime earlier. *Locked. Well of course it's locked,* Iain told himself. *It's the middle of the night.* After fumbling for his room key to unlock the door, he ran the one flight of stairs up to Ted's room on the second floor. Thankfully, he remembered Ted's room was only two doors down from his. Reaching it, he pounded on the door. No answer. He pounded again.

The door flew open. An angry Ted, wearing only boxers, stood in the doorway. "Iain! What on earth? What's so important for you to pound on my door in the middle of the night?" Ted then seemed to notice dried blood on Iain's wrist. "What happened? What's going on?"

"It's Kaitlyn!" Iain said. Only after he said those words did he admit to himself what he knew to be fact—she was gone, and this caused him to be overcome with sadness, making it difficult to complete his words. "She's . . . " His throat constricted, so he had to swallow before continuing. "She's been taken!"

Ted pulled him inside and shut the door. "What on earth are you talking about? Here, sit down. Tell me what's going on."

Iain shook his head. He didn't want to get weepy, but he felt a few tears trickle down his cheeks. "Somebody took her, Ted. She's gone!"

Ted raised his hands. "Wait. Gone? You mean . . . *kidnapped*?" He shook his head. "Why would anyone kidnap Bev?"

Iain put his palms to his cheeks and shook his head. "I don't know." He looked back up at Ted. "I went down to the pool to eat my dinner. To get some fresh air, you know. After being cooped up all day, I just wanted some air. Kaitlyn had wanted the same, because I found her already there. We sat, ate, and talked for a while. Then, while walking back to the hotel, someone grabbed her and knocked me out. When I woke up, I was tied to the fence." He held up his hands showing his wrists with the dried blood and a few burnt spots on his fingers. "It took me almost an hour to get free. I came straight here."

Ted began to pace. He picked up his phone.

"Who are you calling?"

"Iain, we have to call the police."

Iain nodded. "Yes. Yes, of course."

Ted punched in 9-1-1, took a deep breath, and let it out slowly. "Yes, I need to report a kidnapping. Yes, it occurred maybe an hour or so ago."

Iain heard Ted giving all the necessary information, but his mind was not really registering any of it. He kept reliving what had happened. Could he have anticipated, been more observant, even prevented this from happening? He knew he really couldn't have, but he still felt like a failure for allowing it. Already, at least a couple of hours had gone by, so they could have taken Kaitlyn almost anywhere and be . . . anywhere.

When Ted hung up, he threw his phone on the bed and put his hand on Iain's shoulder. "We're to meet the police in the lobby."

Iain nodded and went to the bathroom to wash up while Ted got dressed. As Iain washed dirt and dried blood away, a surreal feeling came over him. He knew it was true, but the realization of Kaitlyn being taken just seemed impossible.

Iain and Ted had to wait only a few minutes for the police to arrive. Within just a few minutes of talking with them, Iain felt he and Ted were the ones being given the inquisition. He explained all that happened. Looking over at Ted, he saw him going through the same experience with the other officer.

"Mr. Thornwhite," the officer questioning him said, "are you sure Ms. Sheridan didn't just leave?"

"What?" Iain cocked his head. Anger rose within him. The audacity! "What is that supposed to mean? I told you she was kidnapped!"

The officer cocked his head. "Yes, I know that's what you *said*. But lovers' quarrels often end with one person storming out and later returning. She'll likely come back on her own later today. They always do."

"Not if they've been kidnapped!" Iain's voice was sharp, arising from his clear anger.

"Well, she's not really missing until she's been gone forty-eight hours."

"Forty-eight . . . " Iain put his hands on his head and pushed out a sarcastic chuckle. "She could be *dead* within forty-eight hours."

"Now, Mr. Thornwhite, let's not be overly dramatic."

"And is *this* being overly dramatic?" Iain held up his hands to show his wrists.

"Do you have any witnesses to your statements?" the officer asked.

"Witnesses? Are there usually witnesses to someone being zip-tied to a fence in the middle of the night?"

The officer shrugged. "Would help."

Iain lifted his head and sighed deeply. This was going nowhere.

The other officer came over. "I looked in Ms. Sheridan's room. Empty. Looks as if no one was ever there. No suitcase, bed not slept in. Nothing." He raised his eyebrows and looked at Iain as if giving a dare. "Care to explain that, Mr. Thornwhite?"

"Look, it's like I said in the beginning. We have a clinical trial being conducted at the cancer center here in town. Our meeting went very late, so we decided to stay overnight. Therefore, no suitcases. We decided to eat at the pool right after we got here. And she was kidnapped, so no rumpled bed."

"And where is this zip tie you told us about?"

Iain shrugged. "Next to the fence near the light facing the hotel that highlights the palm trees around the pool."

The officer shook his head. "Not a trace of one there."

"That's . . . that's impossible."

"So, I ask you, Mr. Thornwhite, what really happened? Did you do something to Ms. Sheridan, and now want it to look like a kidnapping?"

"*What?!* That's completely ludicrous. Why would we call you if I wanted to keep it hush-hush. If the zip tie is gone, that means they were around to collect that evidence after I left it there, so it means they've been gone less time than I thought. You can likely catch them!"

"We called the precinct in Santa Fe. It seems this is not the first hoax you've reported."

Iain sighed. "That was *not* a hoax. And neither is this." He drew a breath, then said with firm conviction, "Something very bad is going on. Someone is planning something bad using our nanobot technology. You really need to take what we are telling you seriously."

The officer chuckled as he closed his notebook. "Watch many spy movies, Mr. Thornwhite? We'll continue to investigate. But if she returns, you let us know."

Iain watched the two officers leave, then dropped onto the nearest sofa in the hotel lobby. Ted came over and sat next to him, shaking his head and placing a hand on Iain's shoulder to give a small squeeze.

"Unbelievable," Ted said.

Looking at Ted and exhaling a weary sigh, Iain muttered, "It seems we're on our own."

CHAPTER 14

GENUINENESS

Mikael leaned back supporting himself with his hands behind him on the large boulder on which he sat. He had been here many times, to this very boulder next to this tranquil stream surrounded by such beautiful flowers, trees, and unique creatures. Other times he had come to this spot in Eden to clear his mind and help him think more clearly about his duty as leader of his Creator's army and about the greatness of his Master, the Lord of Hosts. Often the majesty of a new bird, flower, or creature would take his breath away by its beauty, uniqueness, and vibrancy. Being here always impressed upon him the right choice he had made in serving his Creator and Lord: someone so powerful, so unique, but also so loving— and even delicate.

This time he had come to gain perspective about . . . Lucifer. Often in the past, when he came to this spot, only his Lord's creation was in this place. He looked around and smiled. Now, ever since his Lord had gone to earth in human form, died, and was resurrected, he brought all the righteous from Sheol to dwell here in Eden. There was now a great deal of activity here, and all who lived here enjoyed the beauty of the Master's creativity as much as he did.

"There you are," Raphael said as he approached, moving at a quick gait. "Are you needing a contemplative break as you have before?"

"No," Mikael said. He paused. "Well, yes. I can always use a break, a time to think, but that is not the reason I'm here this time."

Raphael sat next to him. "No?" He smiled. "Well, that's a change." He laughed. "Just how many millennia have had to go by for me to hear that statement from you?"

Mikael jabbed at Raphael's shoulder. "Hey now."

"I'm just saying, I've never heard such a statement from you." Raphael turned more serious. "So, why *are* you here?"

"Now that the righteous from Sheol are here, I wanted to get some perspective from others."

Raphael's eyebrows raised. "About?"

"About Lucifer."

"What do you mean?" Raphael asked. "We've known Lucifer since before he rebelled. Don't you think you really know him?"

"Oh, we know him, for sure, but how others have experienced and characterized him could be helpful for us."

Raphael sat up straighter. "Okay, fair enough. So what have you found out?"

"It's been interesting to learn how these humans have experienced him, yet not physically seen him, as we have."

"That's true. I never thought about that."

"Noah said he directly experienced the wickedness of many of the Watchers and the Nephilim but could tell they held obedience to someone or something unseen. Many in his generation could not understand that, so they worshipped those they *could* see. But he could see through their wickedness because of his devotion to Yahweh."

Raphael cocked his head in thought. "We did observe that, but I never thought about it from that reasoning."

Mikael nodded. "And Daniel told me something similar. He said that even though he had many conversations with Nebuchadnezzar and others of the royal family, they could never seem to take that step to fully believe in Yahweh because . . . he was invisible to them."

Raphael shook his head. "But at that time, Lucifer and his demons were invisible to them as well. So why did they feel that way?"

"Lucifer empowered his priests by possessing them and creating visible signs that instilled fear." Mikael sighed. "It seems fear is a powerful tool that often overshadows the love our Creator bestows."

"I never realized that," Raphael said. "So we have to help humans get over their fear to experience our Creator's love?"

Mikael nodded again. "And right before you arrived, I finished speaking with Paul, whose letters became part of Scripture."

"He was very successful in getting others to understand our Creator, even in a time of great persecution for him and other followers of our Lord."

"Granted," Mikael said. "He was able to successfully implement what both Noah and Daniel understood, but then he also understood that Lucifer, in his day, made politics a form of religion being imposed on everyone."

Raphael looked at Mikael as if he had an aha moment. "So he helped people understand that religion by politics is only to generate fear and therefore must be false. Then they could better understand that this falseness was tied to the statues they would see, and this again reinforced the fact that these are false forms of worship. That then led them to ask what the true form of worship is, and he could then point them to our Creator."

Mikael smiled. "Exactly. So it helps us understand how humans experience Lucifer and not just how *we* experience him."

"All that is nice to know, but how is it applicable for our assignment this time? There are no Watchers, Nephilim, persecution, or statues."

"Yes, but what is the common thread to all of those?"

Raphael thought for a few minutes. "I'm not sure. I know all those things are not truth, but how do you get someone to not only understand truth but *want* it?"

"Genuineness, Raphael. Genuineness. All those things I mentioned are about selfishness in someone or something and not in the care of the actual individual. There is no sincerity to them."

"So, in our case, we help Iain experience the genuineness of our Creator and not the superficial nature of the world in which he lives."

Mikael stood. "That's it, Raphael. That is our mission. It is not just to repel the acts of Lucifer, but for Iain to experience the genuineness of our loving Creator."

CHAPTER 15

hope surfaces

Ted sat quietly the next morning as they ate breakfast at the hotel. After eating, Iain sipped his coffee and looked at Ted, who seemed to be in thought, a million miles away. Iain was glad for the hotel store since it had small travel packs of shaving cream with a razor and toothpaste with a toothbrush. That was all he needed to be ready for this day. Wearing the same clothes didn't seem like a big deal. They smelled okay to him, so he was fine with wearing them again. It seemed Ted felt the same. He knew if Kaitlyn was with them, though, a stop at a clothing store likely would have been in order before the day could begin.

"What are you thinking, Ted?"

Ted slowly looked up as if it was a struggle to come back to reality. "Just trying to rack my brain as to what we can do."

"Yeah, same here."

Ted made tracks with his fork in his leftover syrup on his plate and then looked up at Iain. "Should we talk to someone higher than the police?"

Iain's gaze shot to him. "Like the FBI?"

Ted shrugged. "Someone."

Iain thought about that. "Well, the police said they could do nothing for forty-eight hours—likely the standard for anyone else we would call."

Ted tossed his plastic fork onto his plate in frustration. "Yeah, you're probably right." He shook his head and sighed. "I feel like not going back to the cancer center today, but I know we need to understand the data, that it could provide a real clue for us to understand what's going on."

"I don't think we should tell Dr. Gomez about Kaitlyn—not yet, anyway."

"I was thinking the same thing," Ted said. "We don't want to derail any of their progress, as it's all vital to us understanding these discrepancies. Plus . . . "

Iain raised his eyebrows waiting for Ted to continue.

"What if someone there is part of her kidnapping?"

Iain cocked his head; Ted put his hand on Iain's forearm. "Think about it, Iain. She's kidnapped right after we find out about this discrepancy in the scans." He held up his hands. "I'm not saying there *is* a connection, but . . . " He shrugged. "Do we really know them?"

Iain nodded slowly. "You're right, Ted. We don't really know. All the more reason to not say anything right now." He sat up straighter. "We'll wait the forty-eight hours, and if we don't know anything more by then, we'll seek higher help."

Ted nodded and took a deep breath as if preparing for something difficult. "Ready to go?"

Iain nodded and walked to the car with Ted. As Iain got in the driver's side, a whiff of Kaitlyn's perfume hit him, catching him off guard. A sense of sorrow and dread overwhelmed him, and he had to fight his emotions to regain his composure. Both he and Ted were in their own thoughts most of the way back to the cancer center.

The receptionist gave them their visitor's badges and made a phone call. In a matter of minutes, Walt entered the lobby with a bright smile.

"Welcome back," Walt said. He looked around. "Where is Dr. Sheridan? I thought she was coming as well."

Iain forced a smile. "Not today. Something . . . unexpected . . . came up."

"Well, I hope nothing too serious," Walt said with a smile. He gestured for them to follow. "I have you set up in the same conference room as yesterday. Is that okay?"

Both nodded. As they walked, Walt went on. "I've had the data from the six patients with the unexpected bioluminescence scans put into a database so you can access and make whatever comparisons you wish."

"Thanks, Walt, that should prove helpful," Iain said.

"Oh, no problem. Also, the scans for the other five sites arrived early this morning. I'm going through them now. I've found three so far, and I'll have those added to the database within the next hour."

Once they stepped into the conference room, Walt set up Iain for his electronic exploration by supplying him all the access codes and passwords needed.

Walt turned to Ted. "Anything else you need?"

"I'd like to have access to the scans themselves. Is that possible?" Ted asked.

"Sure," Walt said. "What are you looking for?"

Ted shrugged. "I'm not really sure, but thought I'd investigate."

Walt's eyebrows went up. "Okay then. Follow me." He turned to Iain. "Anything else before I leave?"

Iain shook his head. "No. Thanks, Walt."

By the time Iain got his program up and running to compare all parameters between the patients to see if they had anything in common, Walt had been able to input the others from the additional sites. Iain was expecting three of the irregular scans from what Walt had said, but he found a total of four from the five sites. That put the total now at ten patients. That still wasn't a lot of individuals to do this type of population analysis, but Iain knew he had to start somewhere. He initiated the program and sat back to let it run.

Just a bit later, Iain took a bio break and found Ted coming down the hall to the conference room. Ted had a strange look about him, Iain thought.

"Ted, is anything wrong?"

Ted looked both ways down the hallway, then pulled Iain into the conference room and closed the door.

"What's going on, Ted?"

"I was looking at the scans Walt pulled for us when it occurred to me that although we have to wait for the tissue samples after the informed consents are signed, we do have residual blood samples from these patients here at Dr. Gomez's clinic."

"Yes, that's true," Iain said. "But I'm not sure where you're headed with this."

Ted gestured to the chairs. "Here. Have a seat. I've discovered two things."

"Okay. So, is this good or bad?"

Ted tilted his head back and forth. "Some of each, I think."

Iain cocked his head but let Ted continue.

"First, only the nanobots that bind to cancer cells respond to our programming."

Iain nodded slowly. "That means . . . someone injected additional nanobots." He shook his head. "But why just these individuals?"

"The additional nanobots are in everyone. Or at least I suspect everyone. I tested a blood sample from a patient with the heavy bioluminescence and one without. The same type of nanobots were in both."

"But . . . " Iain scrunched his brow. He was having a hard time comprehending what Ted was implying but not saying.

"The bioluminescence is exhibited only when the nanobots bind to their target."

"Right," Iain said. "So that means only some of these patients had the specific target."

Ted nodded.

"So what's the target?"

"Unsure yet. I need to do more digging."

"And the second thing?"

Ted grew excited. "This is even better. Bev may have taken a blood sample with her yesterday."

Iain sat upright. "What? Why? And why wouldn't she tell us?" He paused. "Wait. What do you mean by 'may have'?"

"Walt said Bev wanted to do some testing, but he wouldn't let her until an informed consent could be completed. But I noticed a twenty-four-hour blood sample missing this morning."

"How does that help us?" Iain asked.

Ted grinned. "Because I can hack the nanobots to give us GPS coordinates of their whereabouts."

Iain grabbed Ted's shoulders. "That's great!" He patted Ted's shoulders a few times in excitement. "That's totally awesome." He shook his head as his grin matched that of Ted's. "How can I help?"

"I need your computer access passwords."

Iain scrunched his brow. "Okay, but why not use the computer in the lab? It's likely more sophisticated and has direct access."

Ted's eyes widened. "I don't want anyone here to know."

Iain cocked his head. "You . . . know something?"

"No, and that's why I want to keep this hush-hush."

Iain gave Ted a confused look.

"Iain, someone put these unauthorized nanobots into the dosing solution. We don't know who that was, so I don't know who to trust. Therefore, we trust no one."

"But—"

Ted cut him off, giving him a hard stare. "No one."

"Okay." Seeing Ted continue to stare, Iain added, "Okay, Ted. I hear you. And I agree. You make a good point."

"Good," Ted said as he held out his hand. "Now, the access codes."

Iain handed Ted the information Walt had left for him and watched Ted's hands fly across his keyboard as only he could do. When it came to computers and nanobots, Ted was a whiz.

The door opened and Walt peered in. "Hey, guys. Ready for lunch?"

"Uh . . . " Iain looked at Ted, who shook his head. Iain grimaced. "Is it possible to have something brought here, Walt? We'd like to continue working if that's okay."

"Oh, sure. I'll have our caterer bring you something. Any preferences or allergies?"

Iain shook his head. "Anything you decide is fine with us. The simpler the better."

"Very well," Walt said. "Turkey sandwiches coming up."

"Sounds great, Walt."

As soon as Walt left, Iain's computer dinged, indicating the comparison program had finished. "Hmm," Iain said. "That's interesting."

Ted paused and looked at him. "What do you see?"

"There's only one thing all ten seem to have in common," Iain said.

Ted's eyebrows shot up. "And that would be?"

"It seems each of their medical history states that someone in their family was diagnosed with Tay-Sachs disease."

Ted gave Iain a blank stare. "And is that significant?"

Iain shrugged. "I'm sure it is. Just not sure what. It seems I have some more digging to do as well."

Ted waited until after lunch was delivered before displaying his findings. After taking a couple bites of his sandwich, Ted displayed the GPS locations for all nanobots on the screen.

"Wow!" Iain said. "That's a lot of points."

"These are all the nanobots delivered to all patients from all sites."

"I see. So that's why we see them outside New Mexico as well?"

Ted nodded. "If Kaitlyn took a sample from this clinic, we can display only nanobots in patients from this site."

When Ted did so, all the dots outside of New Mexico disappeared. The map then automatically expanded and showed only New Mexico.

"Hmm," Iain said. "I'm not sure this really helps us. There are many dots outside the clinic."

Ted held up his hands. "Patience. Patience. I'm not done yet."

Iain laughed. "Sorry. Okay, Mr. Genius. What's your plan?"

"Well, this is showing all nanobots in all patients from this clinic. The sample that Kaitlyn took—"

"If she took it," Iain interjected.

Ted nodded. "Yes, if she took it, it's in this sea of dots somewhere. Because her sample is a smaller number of nanobots compared to the total, I'm going to cut back the display to only show fewer and fewer totals."

"Any idea how many nanobots are in a dosing solution?" Iain asked.

Ted shook his head. "No, and that is another learning point for us, to be sure we know that in the future, but it must be several thousand." He shrugged. "Yet since these are from someone else, it's a guessing game even if we knew ours."

"So, what cutoff are you going to choose?"

Ted rubbed his chin. "Well, let's just go with simplicity. There's roughly five liters of blood in a human body, and let's say we administered one thousand nanobots. Then knowing that they replicate when the target is found and it takes about four hours to replicate once, and the sample potentially taken was about a day after dosing, that would be six replications or about sixty-four thousand nanobots as the replicants also replicate until all targets are identified. I think Walt said the blood sample was ten milliliters, so that would make the number of nanobots in the blood sample to be about one-hundred and twenty-eight." He looked at Iain and gave a quick shrug. "Let's try one-hundred and twenty."

Iain grinned. "Okay, Math Boy, go for it."

Ted put in the parameter and all the dots disappeared except for a select few.

Iain's eyes grew wide. "They're just outside of Santa Fe." He looked at Ted. "So, she evidently did take a blood sample. Can you enlarge the map?"

Ted did a few keystrokes as Iain walked closer to the screen. The map enlarged and Iain pointed. "Taos. Kaitlyn's in Taos?" Iain asked.

"I can do better than that," Ted said. The map enlarged again with the dots near the center of the screen.

Iain walked still closer to the screen. "VA hospital? Why would they be at a Veterans Administration hospital?"

"Don't know. But we've got to find out." Ted, in thought, turned to Ian. "Should we go to the police with this?"

Iain looked back at Ted. "They already think we're nuts. They'd just chalk this up to conspiracy theory as it would seem we're saying our government is against us." Iain looked at the screen and back to Ted. "Plus, they said Kaitlyn would need to be missing at least forty-eight hours before they can act."

"Maybe we can get her back even before then," Ted said.

"Maybe we can," Iain said. "Got any plans for tonight?"

Ted smiled. "None. This is the priority."

CHAPTER 16

DANGER DISCOVERED

Both Iain and Ted looked at the hospital across the street from their car in disbelief. There were several ambulances, police cars, and fire trucks around the hospital entrance, and people were scurrying around like ants.

"What on earth?" Iain looked at Ted. "What do you think?"

Ted shrugged. "No idea." He looked back at Iain. "But there's only one way to find out." He opened his car door and stepped out.

"What are you doing?" Iain asked.

Ted bent down and looked back in the car window. "Going to find out what's going on. You coming?"

Iain got out of the car. "Reluctantly."

As they started to cross the street at the crosswalk that led to a sidewalk leading to the hospital, the policeman directing traffic at the intersection stopped them.

"Sorry, guys," the officer said. "Can't let you cross here."

"What's going on?" Ted asked.

"It appears to be a gas leak. The entire hospital has to be evacuated."

Iain's eyebrows raised. "That serious?"

"Apparently so, sir." The officer then gestured toward the side of the road from which they had come. "Now if you will both go back to the other side of the street, please. It's for your own safety as well as not interfering with the hospital staff doing their duties."

"Oh, sure," Ted said as he turned and pulled on Iain's arm.

"Thank you both. Have a good day." The policeman's attention turned to a car that was attempting to turn into the drive leading to the hospital.

As they reached the other side of the road, Iain looked at Ted. "What do you think?"

Ted rubbed his chin while looking up and down the road they were standing next to. He pointed with his head. "Let's go down there and cross toward the back of the hospital."

Iain followed Ted in that direction. "Okay," Iain said. "What's your plan?"

Ted looked back at Iain and waited for him to come alongside. "Bev is in there somewhere. Either this gas leak is real and she's in danger, or it's fake and someone has her against her will, which puts her in danger." He shrugged. "Either way, we need to get inside and rescue her."

Iain nodded, but inside he was panicked. He had never done anything like this. But he also knew Ted was right. They had no one else on their side—yet—so Kaitlyn's rescue was up to them.

On the backside of the hospital property stood a row of Pinyon pine trees in front of the property fence; these allowed them to climb the fence unseen. They made their way around the building toward the front and to the side of a fire truck which was empty of anyone at the moment. Likely the firemen were assisting the hospital staff in getting patients out, or checking for the gas leak, if indeed there really was one.

Ted quickly checked the compartments on the truck and found two jackets, pairs of pants, and helmets. He handed one of each to Iain. "Put these on. While we won't look official, exactly, it will hopefully get us in without detection since no one should scrutinize us too closely."

"Where do we go once we're inside?" Iain asked. "Where do we even start to look?"

Ted shrugged. "My guess is to the basement—whoever took Bev doesn't want to be seen or noticed. Plus, I don't think a VA hospital would have a genetic wing from which they'd be working."

"But they would have a cancer wing."

Ted shook his head. "They won't be there. While *we're* targeting cancer, they aren't. Who even knows what they're targeting?"

"Okay. Good point," Iain said. "We'll find the nearest stairs and see if we can get to the basement."

They scurried into an outside alcove obscured by some trees and put the firefighter gear over their clothes as quickly as possible. They walked as inconspicuously as possible to the hospital entrance. As they got close, Iain saw an empty wheelchair and began pushing it as he approached the entrance to make it look like he had a patient to get to. Ted walked beside him. They received a few glances from others, but no one stopped them. Iain noticed several hospital vans parked alongside the parking garage entrance in the near distance. Once inside, Iain gave the wheelchair to one of the orderlies and kept walking. The visitors' desk was deserted, likely due to the lobby being in pandemonium as patients seemed to be backed up for transport. Iain saw Ted grab something off the visitors' desk and then point to a sign that read "Stairs." Iain nodded and followed him into the stairwell.

Ted looked at Iain and let out a long breath. "So far, so good." He cocked his head as if listening. "I don't hear anyone in this stairwell, so we should be okay for now."

Iain tapped his arm. "Let's get going then."

The next floor down read "Parking Garage." There were no more stairs, but there was a door which read "Employees Only." Iain tried the door. Locked.

Iain looked at Ted. "Now what?"

Ted grinned. "Good thing I found this." He held up a hospital employee ID card.

"So that's what you grabbed."

Ted swiped the key card across the lock access next to the door; they heard a click. The door opened with ease. Just beyond the door lay another set of stairs. Yet this stairwell was not well lit. At the bottom of the stairs was another door. They took off their firefighter gear, dumped it in the stairwell, and tried the door. It creaked upon opening. Iain cringed as the sound seemed way too loud as it echoed in the stairwell. He just hoped that wasn't true on the other side of the door.

The door led them into a long hallway, once again dimly lit.

"Why do basements always have to be so creepy looking?" Iain whispered. "Can't hospitals afford one-hundred-watt bulbs for their basements?"

Ted chuckled. "No suspense in that."

"I'm not looking for suspense. I'm looking for a steal and peel."

Ted gave Iain a blank stare. "That was a pathetic metaphor."

Iain shoved Ted forward. "Let's just execute the plan."

Ted shook his head. "Again, bad choice of words."

Their eyes suddenly grew wide as they heard a door shut somewhere down the hallway. Both froze. Iain found himself not breathing.

"Must have been down another corridor," Iain whispered. "I didn't see anyone."

Ted nodded. "Come on," he said, waving Iain to follow.

About two-thirds of the way down the hallway a cross hall-way extended. Ted slowly peered around the corner and then motioned for Iain to follow. After getting about a third of the way down this hallway, they saw a door open farther down. Iain and Ted looked at each other, eyes wide. Iain quickly tried a nearby door, but it was locked. Ted did as well; same results. These doors had no employee key card access. Iain stood in one of the door frames and plastered his back to the door, sucking in his gut as much as possible. Ted did the same on the opposite side of the hallway.

Iain heard a man talking to someone inside the room as he held the door open. "Doc said the hospital should be empty by five. You maybe have an hour after that."

There was a pause. Evidently someone inside the room was speaking, but Iain could only hear muffled sounds.

The man they could hear spoke again. "If it was me, I'd just leave once you have her secure. I value my life." Another pause. "Suit yourself, mate. I'm off."

The man shut the door. Iain plastered himself against the door behind him, praying he wasn't visible. Iain heard shuf-fling of feet; thankfully, the man's steps were traveling away from their position. Iain took a quick glance and then pulled back when the door opened again.

The other man stuck his head out and spoke. "Tell the doc not to count me out. I'll be there, so my cut had better be there too. Actually, mine should be larger than yours since you're abandoning me here."

Iain heard the first man laugh. "Aw, such a shame. It's mine if you don't show up." The man laughed even harder.

The second man slammed the door. The first man continued to chuckle, but this soon grew more and more faint as he continued walking off. Shortly, there was only silence.

Iain relaxed and stepped back into the hallway. Ted followed. They cautiously ventured down the corridor arriving at the door where the men had stepped out. They realized it was risky to open that door as they had no idea what—or how many others—they would find inside.

Ted tried the next door over. The knob twisted. Unlocked!

Iain grabbed Ted's arm. "What if it's the same room?" he whispered.

Ted shrugged. "Do we have a choice?"

Iain grimaced but shook his head. Ted opened the door just a few inches to peer inside and then swung it wider. It was empty, and completely dark, except for light that came through an inner door inside this room; evidently this room was connected to the one the men had stepped from. Iain closed the outer door as gently as possible. It produced only a light click.

Iain went to the inner door and looked through the glass pane which provided just enough light in their room for them to make out shadows. He saw only one guy sitting in a chair with a gun laying on a large crate next to him. Iain realized he and Ted were probably out of their league since they had no weapons. Ducking low, he scooted to the other side of the door to see through the pane to the opposite side of the room. When he peeked through the glass, he gasped.

There sat Kaitlyn! Her back was to him with her hands tied behind her. His heart wanted to rush in and rescue her, but his head knew that would be a foolish idea without a plan. He pulled Ted away from the door so they could whisper and develop some type of strategy. Knowing it was around four o'clock when they arrived at the hospital, he guessed they had little time left. He wasn't exactly sure what would happen around six that evening, but one didn't have to think too hard to put together "gas leak," "evacuation," and the words the man had spoken earlier to know they were likely planning to get rid of evidence—and very possibly Kaitlyn along with it.

CHAPTER 17

RESCUE PLAN

After Iain pulled Ted back from the door to a spot behind a large crate, he whispered, "We have to come up with a plan, and we don't have a lot of time." He pulled back his sleeve and tapped his watch, showing the time. "It's almost five o'clock already." He pointed toward the door. "He's likely to leave soon."

Ted cocked his head, then whispered in return. "But that's good, isn't it? The sooner he leaves, the more time we have to get Bev out of here."

"Yeah, but we need to know where he goes if we're going to solve any of this."

"But it's going to take both of us to get Bev out," Ted said. His tone sounded a little annoyed. "Her life is more valuable than us knowing where this guy goes."

"Of course it is," Iain said. "Both of us being here to get her out is definitely part of the plan."

Ted squinted. "So, what *is* your plan?"

"The blood sample. We need to get the blood sample into this guy's possession so we can track it."

"What!?" Ted's eyes went wide; he looked around nervously knowing that came out too loudly. Not hearing any response from the next room, he said, now much more quietly, "And just how do you plan to do *that*?"

"I don't know. Ideas?"

Ted rubbed the back of his neck. "Well . . . " He looked back at the door and sighed. "I'm not sure. He can't know we're here, that's for certain."

They both went back to the window and peeked in again. This time both were trying to visualize a working plan. Iain pulled Ted back to the large crate again.

"He has a backpack. I'm pretty sure he'll take that with him."

"He also has a gun," Ted said, eyes wide. "Plus, where is the blood sample?"

"Kaitlyn must have it on her somewhere—tucked in a pocket or . . . somewhere. I don't think these others know she has it. Otherwise, they would've discarded it before they got her here."

Ted bobbed his head back and forth a bit. "Likely that's true." He rubbed his hand over his mouth looking nervous. "We don't have a lot of time for this switch." He shook his head slightly. "And how will we get him out of the room to make the switch?"

"I'll lure him into this room," Iain said. "You sneak into the room with Kaitlyn, switch the blood sample from her into his backpack, leave the room into the hallway, then reenter this room."

Ted's eyes went wide. "Oh, sure. Piece of cake." He gave Iain a hard stare. "You know how crazy and dangerous this is, right?"

"I know, Ted, but what options do we have? I'm open to other ideas."

"What about the option of doing nothing and just letting him leave?"

Iain put his hand on Ted's shoulder. "I know that sounds appealing, but what happens when they find out Kaitlyn is alive? We can tell the authorities about the kidnapping, but nothing about their whereabouts or who they are. That puts Kaitlyn back in danger again with no protection."

Ted swallowed hard. "Okay," he muttered. He nodded again and whispered more forcefully. "Okay. Let's do it. How are you going to lure him in here and not have him find you?"

"I've been thinking about that. There's a partially empty crate near the outside door. I'll hide there, and you hide behind the inside door. I'll push this top crate over. The noise will lead him in here. Then you sneak into the room with Kaitlyn."

Ted shook his head. "Sounds pretty iffy." He shrugged. "But let's do it."

Iain first removed the light bulb so the room would remain dark. He then climbed into the crate after Ted crouched behind the inside door. Iain took a deep breath, then pushed the top crate off and onto the floor. There was a loud crash and intravenous bags spilled out on the floor. Iain crouched lower inside the crate. The nails in the crate's lid prevented the top from coming all the way down onto the crate itself, and this allowed a sliver of a viewport for him to observe the room.

The man slowly opened the door and flicked the light switch several times, but quickly realized the light was out. The darkness gave Iain and Ted a slight advantage—at least until the man's eyes adjusted to the darkness. As the man slowly entered the room with gun drawn, Iain saw Ted slip around the door and into the lit room before the door closed. Now Iain knew he had to give Ted as much time as possible.

"Who's there!" the man demanded. "I warn you. I have a gun."

Iain tried to remain motionless. He heard the man go deeper into the room, pushing the intravenous bags around with his feet and slipping a couple of times. Iain heard an *"umph!"* followed by an *"Ow!"* then heard a thud. He heard the man quickly scrambling to his feet. Catching a glimpse of the man's silhouette, Iain saw him limp slightly.

Afraid the man might give up and turn back toward the room with Kaitlyn, Iain slowly lifted the crate's lid. He hoped the man's eyes had not yet adjusted to the darkness so his movement would stay unnoticed. Being near the door allowed Iain to reach the doorknob and turn it slowly. Knowing opening the door would let light in, he waited until he saw the man's back facing him. Iain opened the door just far enough to grab its edge and fling the door open, then dropped back into the crate—all in one swift motion. The man whirled, ran to grab the door before it closed, and rushed into the hallway. Iain heard him swiftly walk a few steps in one direction and then the other. The door again opened, and the man entered, cautiously, evidently not sure if the potential intruder had escaped or not.

Breathing hard, the man leaned against the crate in which Iain crouched; the crate lid shifted slightly. The man paused and began pulling on the lid after realizing it was not sealed. Iain slipped under a thick layer of bubble wrap as much as possible, hoping that would be sufficient since the room was mostly dark.

The man suddenly dropped the lid of the crate upon hearing a crash from the other room. Iain saw the man ready his gun, walk cautiously to the inside door, open it slowly with gun drawn, and step into the lit room, the door closing behind him.

Iain was unsure what had happened. He strained to hear what the man said next but could not understand his words. Iain's mind told him to remain where he was, but he also had to know if Ted had been caught or not. As silently as possible, Iain stepped out of the crate and crept over to the door to peek through the pane. The man was righting Kaitlyn in her chair. Apparently, she had fallen over. Iain thought that strange.

"I wondered if you'd wake before I left so I could carry out doc's orders," the man said with something almost like amusement in his tone. He tightened the ropes around Kaitlyn. Iain heard her mumble something, but because of the gag her words were unintelligible. The man laughed. "Complain all you want, but it won't make any difference."

Going to his backpack, the man pulled out a small bottle and a rag. "I don't know why the doc doesn't want any drugs in your system." He looked at Kaitlyn and smiled. "It's not like anything will be left of you once this bomb goes off." The man looked at his watch. "Which is soon, so I have to get out of here." He doused the rag with something and held it over her mouth and nose. Kaitlyn struggled a little but went limp quickly.

It took all Iain had to remain where he was and not rush in to attempt a rescue, but he knew he had to wait. As long as the man didn't use his gun, Iain knew he had to wait and rescue Kaitlyn once the man was gone. But it was also clear: they were running out of time.

The man returned the contents to his backpack and threw it over his shoulder. "There. That should keep you out at least forty-five minutes." He looked at his watch. "And you'll be dead in less than thirty." He chuckled. "At least you won't know what happened. See, doc is merciful after all."

Before leaving, the man checked her bindings once more. For good measure, Iain assumed. The man then quickly headed out the door. Iain could hear his fast-paced steps going down the hall and then become more and more faint.

Iain rushed into the room and checked on Kaitlyn. Her head was hanging at her chest. He patted her cheeks. "Kaitlyn, Kaitlyn!" No response. He could see her slowly breathing, but she remained unresponsive. To his right, he saw Ted climbing out from underneath a tarp.

"I wondered where you went," Iain said with a slight grin. Then, with a somber tone, he said, "Help me with Kaitlyn. It will take the two of us to carry her out."

Ted scrambled over to help untie her. "What on *earth*?"

"What is it?" Iain asked as he continued trying to wake Kaitlyn.

"The knots have been glued!"

"What? That good-for-nothing . . . I wondered why he was checking her bindings before he left when he had just made her unconscious."

"Likely wanted to make sure that any intruder, if still here, would have a very hard time," Ted said.

Iain looked at his watch. "Ted, we only have about fifteen minutes." As he fumbled with the bindings around her feet, he sighed. "I think we may have to just carry her out in this chair."

Ted nodded. "I agree. Let's do it."

As they picked up the chair, Iain saw a wire. "Wait! Wait!"

Ted stopped. "What's wrong?" He followed where Iain pointed. "What the . . . ?"

"The chair is tied to the bomb! If we had moved the chair at all, it would have triggered it," Iain said.

Ted turned in frustration and panic. "What do we do? We don't have time to deal with this!"

Iain bent down for a closer look. "It's *also* glued." Iain thought quickly. "Here, lean her and the chair toward you."

When Ted did, Iain grabbed a chair leg and pulled with all his might. It eventually gave way, causing him to fall to the floor as he heard a loud *crack*.

Iain scrambled to his feet. "Now let's get out of here."

Iain grabbed the back chair legs and Ted the back of the chair. Ted flung the door open, and they shuttled down the hallway as fast as they could with the chair between them. Ted backed up the stairs as Iain held the legs high to hoist the chair up to the garage level. Once in the garage, they ran with everything they had to make it to the entrance, Kaitlyn still being carried between them. Iain knew that if the bomb went off now, they'd be buried under tons of concrete.

"Three minutes!" Ted yelled. "Faster! Faster!"

Iain ran with all his might, careful not to trip. He saw sunlight ahead and kept running. They made it to the top of the exit ramp and found a van, empty but idling, apparently abandoned. He assumed that, due to the chaos in getting all the patients evacuated, the van had been forgotten. Ted climbed in first and they laid Kaitlyn, chair and all, in the seat behind the driver. Iain hopped in the driver's seat, put the vehicle in gear, and gunned the accelerator. The wheels screeched due to the fast start just as . . .

. . . the bomb went off. Smoke billowed out of the garage and engulfed the van for a few seconds until its speed allowed them to clear the structure entirely and give them enough vision for Iain to get as far from the hospital as possible. Glancing into the rearview mirror, Iain saw the entire building collapse onto itself, sending a huge dust cloud in all directions.

CHAPTER 18

ANOTHER DILEMMA

Once Iain distanced the van from the hospital and its debris by several city blocks, he pulled to the side of the road near a bus stop and put the van in park.

"Man, that was close," Ted said, eyes wide and still breathing heavily.

"You can say that again," Iain, also breathing hard, said as he turned toward Ted. "After we get Kaitlyn free, let's put her in the back seat of our car and see if we can make a total getaway. I'd rather talk to the cops on our terms and not theirs."

"Agreed."

Both looked around in the van for anything they could use to help with untying the ropes holding Kaitlyn to the chair; the glued knots seemed next to impossible to loosen. Ted found a long, thin piece of nylon wire and used it to cut through the ropes. It took more time than Iain wanted, but they could do nothing else until Kaitlyn was free.

Once the ropes were off, Iain secured her in the van seat as Ted took the chair—after checking to be sure no one was around—and bashing it on the ground, breaking it into several pieces, looking around as to where to dump them.

Ted rolled down his window. "Let's keep those for evidence later, if needed."

Iain cocked his head. "Good idea." He then brought them back into the van. Iain drove back toward the hospital and parked a street over from where he had left their car. Police and fire trucks were all over the scene of the now demolished hospital.

Ted looked at Iain. "So what's the plan?"

"We have to get our car," Iain said. "We can leave the van here. Don't want to be caught stealing a hospital van."

Ted grabbed his chin and looked in thought. "Okay. I'll go get the car. You wipe down what you can, just in case, so they can't prove we were here." He shook his head. "I don't know for sure that we have to be that careful." He shrugged. "After all, we're not the ones who did anything wrong. But we'd probably better cover all our bases."

"Okay," Iain said. "Just be careful. Get back here and we'll get Kaitlyn in the car, and then we'll head back to Albuquerque."

"Why not just go home?"

"The crime occurred in Albuquerque," Iain said. "We need to let the authorities there know."

Ted seemed unconvinced. "We'll debate that when I get back." He glanced toward where the hospital used to be. "I need to get the car before too many onlookers block my getaway."

Iain watched as Ted quickly headed to the other side of the street and across the open lawn that stretched from where he parked to the street running next to the hospital. To attempt to look inconspicuous, Ted mingled with other onlookers who had started to gather. He made his way to where their car was parked, hopped in, and pulled away as quickly as he could, although he had to wade the car through several groups of onlookers. The police were occupied with the increasing number of people coming to gawk at the scene, so no one paid Ted any real attention. In only a few minutes, Ted pulled up behind the van.

Iain got out and looked to be sure no one was paying them attention—which they weren't. Everyone's focus was on the hospital debris and chaos. As he opened the car door, he noticed a thick layer of dust from the hospital collapse covering the car. "We need to go through a car wash before we get back," Iain said. "This car is a mess."

"Let's worry about that once we get safely out of here," Ted said.

Iain nodded. While it was a need, it was definitely secondary. He helped Ted carry Kaitlyn to the car's back seat, put the chair remains and rope in the trunk, and then climbed in so he could attend to her as needed. Ted hopped into the driver's seat and sped away, going as fast as the speed limit would allow.

Iain found a travel pillow Kaitlyn had brought with her on their trip and put it under her neck. He wasn't sure if that made her more comfortable, but it certainly made her look that way with her head propped more securely. He tried to wake her, but to no avail. Evidently, whatever the man had used was quite potent.

"I still think she would be more comfortable at her own place in Santa Fe," Ted said, restarting the debate from minutes earlier. "Plus, it's closer."

"Yes, but this all started in Albuquerque," Iain countered.

Ted made eye contact with Iain in the rearview mirror. "We wouldn't be talking with them until tomorrow anyway, right? I mean, it's already getting late."

Iain nodded.

Ted shrugged. "Then why not let her get a good night's rest at home? We'll go back to Albuquerque tomorrow and make the report."

Iain tilted his head back and forth in thought. "What if whoever this is will be watching her apartment?"

"And what if they're watching the hotel?"

Iain could see Ted's eyebrows go up as if challenging his logic. He realized they could be watching either place, both places, or neither place. He finally conceded the argument. "Okay, Ted. You win. I agree. Just because it's closer."

Once they reached Santa Fe city limits, Kaitlyn began to stir, but she still did not wake completely. Iain kept trying to stimulate her by patting her cheeks lightly to help her awake.

Once near Kaitlyn's house, Ted went through a car wash and then stopped at a drive-thru for some Chinese food.

By the time Ted pulled into the high-rise where Kaitlyn lived, she was becoming more coherent. As Ted parked, she lifted her head and tried to look around.

"Where . . . where am I?"

Iain took her hand. "You're home, Kaitlyn. Home."

"Home?" She developed a confused look. "How?"

Ted opened the car door. "Here. Let's get you inside and then we'll talk all about it."

Iain grabbed the food and drinks as Ted steadied Kaitlyn. She became more alert and steadier as they walked. The outside air seemed to help her revive.

Once in the apartment elevator, she put her hand to her head. "Everything is such a blur in my mind." She looked at

Iain. "Are you all right?" Her eyes suddenly went wide. "Your head. They knocked you out."

Iain smiled. "I'm fine. I'm more concerned about you."

"Better . . . now. Thanks."

The elevator doors opened, and Ted guided Kaitlyn into her apartment and to the living room sofa.

"Here," Ted said. "Have a seat and rest." He took the food bags from Iain. "I'll take these to the kitchen and serve them on plates for us."

Iain sat next to her and took her hand. "I was so worried about you."

"And I, you. I didn't know what they had done to you."

"Oh, they just knocked me out and tied me up." Seeing her eyes widen, Iain patted her shoulder. "No major harm done. I recovered quickly. But what about you? Why did they take you, and why did they want to kill you?"

Ted came back into the room with Kung Pao chicken and a side of fried wantons on plates for everyone. "Yeah, that's what I want to know. That seems . . . extreme."

Kaitlyn took a plate and set it in her lap. She ate one of the fried wantons. "It's a little complicated."

Ted sat in a chair next to them. "Complicated? Diabolical is more like it."

Kaitlyn nodded. "Yes, both. More than you can know."

Iain and Ted looked at each other, both confused, and turned back to Kaitlyn.

"Well, start from the beginning," Iain said.

She ate a piece of her chicken and sat back with a sigh. "As you were showing the scans, I thought we likely had blood samples which could give a quick read on what was going on to cause these patients' scans to look the way they did."

"Yeah," Ted said. "I thought the same."

Kaitlyn smiled. "We always did think alike." She paused and cocked her head. "Wait. . . . Walt let you have a blood sample? He told me I had to wait until the informed consent was prepared and signed."

Ted nodded. "Same for me. But when he wasn't in the room, I looked at the nanobot concentrations to determine if they were from two different dosing administrations. I didn't try to look for anything else as I didn't want to invalidate our study. The protocol allowed for verification of nanobot replication and verifying the concentration administered."

"I know I shouldn't have," Kaitlyn said, "but I took a blood sample." She gave a small shrug. "I just felt this was too important to wait for the proper paperwork." Her eyes suddenly went wide as she felt her chest; her voice grew panicked. "The blood sample! It's gone!"

Iain grabbed her hand. "Relax, Kaitlyn. It's okay. Ted took it."

Her eyes shot to Ted. "How did you know where to look when they didn't?"

Ted shrugged. "Well, I assumed that was where it had to be knowing they likely looked everywhere else."

Iain gave a curious look to both of them. "So . . . where was it?"

Ted's cheeks blushed slightly. Iain thought that strange and looked at Kaitlyn with eyebrows raised.

She pressed her lips together and said, "In my bra."

Iain's mouth fell open as he looked back at Ted.

Ted held up his hands. "Hey, it was your idea. I just did what was necessary."

Kaitlyn waved her hands. "Guys, never mind that now. But why? Why did you take the blood sample?"

Iain's attention turned to Ted. "Tracking! Ted, you need to track the blood sample."

Ted sprang from his seat. "Oh yeah! My computer's in the car. I'll be right back." He ran from the room and out the door.

Kaitlyn turned to face Iain. "What's going on?"

"Ted put your blood sample in the man's backpack so we can trace its whereabouts and know where he went. That's how we found you. Ted used the nanobots' GPS signal to locate where they took you."

"Wow!" Kaitlyn said, sitting more upright. "I would not have thought of that."

"I have to admit," Iain said, "Ted is one smart cookie."

"Always has been," Kaitlyn added. "He's not only smart, but quick on comprehension. If it wasn't for him, we would be way behind in our development of this technology."

Ted paused in thought. "Tomorrow, after you've had a chance to rest, we'll go tell Dr. Gomez what we've found and then go to the authorities."

Kaitlyn grabbed Iain's forearm. "No!" she said emphatically. "We can't do that!"

Iain furrowed his brow. "Why? He has a right to know that someone is tampering with his research."

"Iain, Dr. Gomez is the one trying to kill me!"

CHAPTER 19

EVIL PLAN DISCOVERED

Kaitlyn, Iain, and Ted sat in silence as Ted worked to narrow down where the vial of blood was now located.

While typing away, Ted glanced at Kaitlyn. "It's not that I don't believe you, but it's hard to wrap my brain around Dr. Gomez being involved in all of this."

"Well, I was just as surprised," Kaitlyn said. "It's all so surreal."

"How did it all happen?" Iain asked. He really wanted—needed—to understand. "Can you walk us through what happened?"

"Well, after Walt told me that I couldn't have the blood sample, as I said, I considered taking a vial anyway, but waited. Later, Walt said Dr. Gomez wanted to talk to me. So I went to his office, but he wasn't there."

"What did you do then?" Iain asked.

"I debated whether to wait for him or just come back later. That's when I saw it."

Ted looked up from his computer. "Saw what?"

"A vial of nanobots."

Iain sat up straighter. "*What?* In his office?"

Kaitlyn nodded. "Yes, and that's what made me so curious. I couldn't understand why he would have one, as they all must be accounted for by the pharmacy. Yet when I picked up the vial, I realized it wasn't one of ours."

Iain looked at her more intently. "Then what did you do?"

"That's when I decided I would take a blood sample and verify if Dr. Gomez was doing something with the nanobot administration or not. But when I put the vial back down, I noticed a memo sticking out of a folder on which the vial sat. It had a University of New Mexico logo partially showing." She shrugged. "I know I shouldn't have pried, but I didn't know Dr. Gomez worked with the university, so I was curious. I mean, if he had a conflict of interest regarding the trial, I wanted to know."

"Is he an adjunct professor or something?" Iain asked.

Kaitlyn nodded. "Yes. But with the College of Population Health."

Iain cocked his head. "That's strange."

"Well, not entirely," Ted said as he continued to type. He looked up at Iain. "The college is associated with the School of Medicine."

"That wasn't the strange part," Kaitlyn said. "It was the content of the memo. It was written to some population institute in Europe and hinted at population shrinkage due to the current over-population of our world."

Both Ted and Iain looked at her in disbelief. Ted shook his head. "I've worked with some of their faculty. That is not what they are about."

Kaitlyn held up her hands. "Oh, I'm not implying that at all. It's just that this is what Dr. Gomez is about, and he seems to be directing funds and grants to this particular institute."

She shook her head. "I just can't remember the exact name of the institution. It was written to a Dr. Haneberg, or something like that."

"I still don't understand how that is tied to our trial," Iain said.

Kaitlyn's eyes grew larger. "Oh, I haven't gotten to the worst part."

Iain looked shocked in returning her look. "Like what?"

"Dr. Gomez stated he would use a trial he was working on to see if certain nanobots would bind to a genetic mutation for Tay-Sachs disease and would check its success with bioluminescence using luciferase."

Iain sat up straighter. "Tay-Sachs! That's what I found those with exaggerated bioluminescence scans had in common in their medical history." He furrowed his brow. "But why?"

"Yeah," Ted interjected. "And why that mutation? Seems rather odd."

Kaitlyn's eyebrows went up. "Not if one is targeting Jews, especially Ashkenazi Jews."

"For what purpose?" Iain asked. "That just seems . . . bizarre."

Kaitlyn nodded. "That was as far as I got as I saw Dr. Gomez coming to his office. I tried to leave everything the way I found it—but evidently I didn't."

Iain sat back, rubbing his chin. "Yet, while incriminating, it doesn't seem like it would be worth killing someone over."

"Unless," Ted added, "there was something more in the folder and he didn't know how much more Bev had read."

"I did take pictures of the entire memo but haven't had a chance to read the remainder," Kaitlyn said. "But you're right. It must be pretty incriminating for him to take such drastic measures to be sure I couldn't tell anyone."

"Can we read it now?" Ted asked.

"They took my phone. I had it set to back up automatically. It just depends on whether the backup automatically saved before they wiped my phone."

Iain handed his phone to Kaitlyn. "Can you retrieve it using my phone?"

"Should be able to," Kaitlyn said as she took his phone and punched in information to locate the file. "Let me find out."

After a few minutes, Ted announced, "I've pinpointed the blood sample! Assuming they are still with it, they are in Albuquerque." He looked up. "At the University of New Mexico."

"And I have the document," Kaitlyn said, giving a brief smile. She was quiet for a few minutes as she read. Iain could see her getting more and more engrossed in her reading. Her hand would go to her mouth occasionally, and she would shake her head.

After several minutes, Iain couldn't wait. "Kaitlyn, what does it say?"

She looked up at him, eyes wide. "This is way bigger than I ever imagined."

Ted leaned in. "Well, out with it, girl. Don't leave us in suspense."

"Let me read part of this to you," she said. "It's . . . it's just too surreal.

"Dr. Haneberg, your idea, I feel, is only the first step in the necessary reduction in world population to make and keep our planet sustainable. If the tagging of the Tay-Sachs muta-tion in those of Jewish heritage is successful, as I believe it will be, then the project will be ready to target CMH as you

have desired. I then feel we can implement a more global approach."

Iain's eyes went wide. "CMH? What is that supposed to mean?" He looked from Kaitlyn to Ted. Both shook their heads.

"Well, let me see what I can find out here," Ted said as he went back to his computer.

"One doesn't have to know what CMH means to know what Dr. Gomez wants to do is not good," Iain said.

Kaitlyn nodded. "I fear this is a prelude to something more sinister than just tagging genes."

"Ah," Ted said. "Here it is. Cohen Modal Haplotype."

Iain laughed. "I don't see that as being more helpful."

Ted looked up and smiled. "It says here it's the standard genetic signature on the Y chromosome for the Jewish priestly lineage."

Iain scrunched his brow. "Really? These people are going to all this trouble to identify . . . Jewish priests?"

Kaitlyn shook her head. "I think it goes beyond identification. What Dr. Gomez said was to reduce global population. This Dr. Haneberg must want to eliminate them."

"Priests? But why?" Iain asked. "For what purpose? What does eliminating Jewish rabbis solve for global reduction?"

Ted looked up from his computer. "Not rabbis, Iain. Priests."

Iain scrunched his face. "Is there a difference?"

"Apparently. Listen to this," Ted said. "There are Orthodox Jews in Jerusalem who have been preparing for a new temple they plan to build one day. The high priest for the temple will be a direct descendant from Aaron, the first high priest after the Jewish exodus from Egypt."

Kaitlyn sat more upright. "That's remarkable."

"It is?" Iain felt like he had missed the connection that apparently Kaitlyn had put together. "Mind cluing me in?"

"They will know who can serve as priests for their temple because they will have this Cohen Modal Haplotype," Kaitlyn said.

Iain still felt not completely there in his understanding. "So, if those with this haplotype were to be killed off, there would be no priests for this temple the Orthodox Jews want to build? Is that it?"

"Seems to be," Kaitlyn said as she sat back into the sofa. "So they want to kill off these specific Jews and prevent a functioning temple."

"How does their absence prevent a temple from functioning?" Iain asked.

"No sacrifices," Kaitlyn said.

Ted shook his head. "But Jews don't do sacrifices. I've been to a Jewish synagogue service. It's not that radically different from church services I've attended."

Iain nodded. "Yeah, exactly. This doesn't make any sense."

Kaitlyn leaned forward and looked from one to the other. "But it does. My brother-in-law is a pastor in Phoenix. He was talking about this very topic last Christmas when I was visiting. He said to fulfill prophecy, the Jewish Messiah will return and set up a kingdom with a temple that will function like the temple prior to 70 A.D. when the Romans destroyed the Jewish temple in Jerusalem."

"Do you believe that?" Iain asked. "That seems . . . out there."

"I do," Kaitlyn said. "I thought you went to church."

"Oh, I do . . . sometimes," Iain said. "I believe what the Bible says, but I've never heard of what you just said. I've heard about a coming kingdom of peace, but . . . sacrifices?" He furrowed his brow. "I don't see the significance of that."

"Well," Ted interjected, "I don't want to get into a theological debate. The point is that this Dr. Haneberg believes it. And believes it so much he wants to be nefarious about it and kill them off using my—our—technology, no less."

"This is way beyond just me reporting my kidnapping," Kaitlyn said. "I think we have to report to a higher authority."

"Higher?" Iain asked. "You mean, like the feds?"

"Probably."

"You make a point," Ted said. "This could impact our entire nation. Israel for sure. And maybe the entire world."

Kaitlyn sat back and put her hand to her forehead. "This is all so overwhelming. I've got to get some rest before I can think about any of this." She looked from Ted to Iain. "Meet back here in the morning and we'll discuss it further?"

Both nodded.

She gave a weak smile. "Good. I'm turning in." She gave each of them a kiss on their cheeks—and Iain a quick kiss on the lips.

"Good night," Iain said. "We'll let ourselves out."

As they got to the door, Ted stopped and shook his head.

"What's wrong?" Iain asked.

"I can't just leave her here alone."

Iain nodded. "Yeah, I was feeling guilty about that as well. We don't know if we were followed or not."

Ted went back into the living area. "Bev . . . "

Kaitlyn came out of the bedroom. "What is it, Ted?"

"We can't just leave you here. I'm going to sleep on the sofa."

"But I'll be fine."

Ted walked up to her and put a hand on each of her shoulders. "You go to bed, and I'll sleep out here."

Kaitlyn cocked her head. "Ted—"

Ted put his finger to her lips. "You can waste time arguing, or you can get some sleep."

She stared at him for a few seconds but then chuckled, shaking her head. "Fine. I'll see you in the morning."

Kaitlyn headed back to her bedroom.

"Maybe I should stay as well," Iain said.

"No need," Ted said. "One of us should be enough. Plus . . . " He got a smirk on his face. "I want her to get some sleep. I don't want to chaperone."

Iain pushed on Ted's shoulder. "You're a riot. Good night, Ted."

Ted chuckled as Iain turned and left the apartment.

CHAPTER 20

TARGET IDENTIFIED

The next morning, Iain was back at Kaitlyn's apartment with a small box of donuts in hand.

Kaitlyn answered the doorbell with a bright smile and gave Iain a quick kiss. "Ah, just the thing to end our meal."

"End?" Iain laughed. "Isn't coffee and a donut a meal?"

He heard Ted in the other room as he entered. "Not when you have omelets."

Iain looked at Kaitlyn. "Well, someone felt industrious this morning."

"I woke up and couldn't go back to sleep." She shrugged. "Too much on my mind, I guess. Come in." She handed Iain a plate and followed him to the table where Ted was already sitting.

As Iain placed the box of donuts on the table, Ted looked over and pressed one with his finger. "Ah, lemon filling," he said with a happy tone. "May I?"

Iain laughed. "Help yourself."

Ted took a big bite as the filling oozed out and he used his tongue to ensure every bit hit his mouth. "I've been thinking," he said between gulps.

"Oh," Iain said. "About how to have better table manners?"

Ted's smile went to a look of irritation. "Uh, no. About calling the feds."

"Oh, really?" Iain took a bite of his omelet. "Kaitlyn, this is really excellent." He turned back to Ted. "And what conclusion did you come to?"

"I think Bev's right. This is a much larger issue than our local police can handle."

Iain nodded. "So, when do you propose we call?"

Ted wiped his mouth with a napkin. "I vote now. We don't want the trail to get cold."

"Okay," Kaitlyn said as she gathered her and Ted's plates and took them to the kitchen as Iain continued eating his omelet. "I tend to agree. The faster we deal with this the better."

At that moment the doorbell rang.

"That's odd," Kaitlyn said. "I'm not expecting anyone." She scurried to her door, looked through the eyehole, then opened it.

"Can I help you?" Iain could hear Kaitlyn ask.

He heard muffled voices. Nothing was clear, but Iain could have sworn he heard a female voice say, "FBI."

Ted pointed to his computer where he had pulled up a contact for a field agent of the New Mexico FBI office. Iain grabbed Ted's forearm, and Ted gave Iain a quizzical look.

"I think the FBI is here," Iain said.

"What?" Ted looked at Iain like he had three heads. "We haven't even called them yet."

Iain tapped Ted's arm. "Come on. Let's see who's at the door."

As he and Ted turned the corner, Kaitlyn was talking with two individuals—a man and a woman—each dressed in business attire but looking like they could be from a fashion magazine. The man had a rugged yet youthful face with a pinstriped beard and mustache. His hair was dark but the ends were dyed a dirty blond color. The woman, with beautiful, flawless skin, looked brunette although she too had colored highlights; they were of red, blue, and yellow hues. *Different*, thought Iain, *but quite stylish*, especially if they were FBI agents as he thought he had heard.

Kaitlyn turned to Iain and Ted as they entered the room. "These are the two friends I was talking about." She gestured toward them. "Dr. Iain Thornwhite, and Ted Jordan."

Both nodded.

Kaitlyn turned back to the two in her doorway. "These are Special Agents Horne and Atway."

The woman stuck out her hand. "I'm Amanda Horne. This is Sam Atway."

The man gave a quick salute-type gesture as he smiled.

"Forgive our intrusion," Amanda said, "but we thought it best to talk with you in light of what happened yesterday."

"Yesterday?" Iain asked, trying to sound as if he had no idea what she was talking about.

Amanda displayed a smile which clearly said: *You know exactly what I'm talking about.* "May we come in?" she asked. "I think we really need to have a talk."

Kaitlyn gestured for them to enter. "Why don't we sit at the table. Coffee?"

"Oh, that would be great," Amanda said.

Sam nodded in agreement.

As they sat, Ted pushed the donut box their way. "Care for one?"

Amanda smiled and shook her head. Sam's eyes went wide as he took a double chocolate. "This one is my favorite," he said. "Thanks."

Kaitlyn brought two mugs of coffee to the table and set down cream and sugar. "Help yourself."

Amanda poured some cream and began to stir. "You probably want to know why we're here when you haven't called us," she began.

Iain nodded.

"We were just about to call you," Ted said, looking at Amanda as if enchanted with her.

"Yes," Kaitlyn said. "Some . . . interesting . . . things have been happening."

"Like a hospital being demolished?"

Kaitlyn sat up straighter. "You know about that?"

Sam pushed the last bite of donut in his mouth; the consumption hadn't taken long. "Oh, you'd be surprised at all we know."

"Like what?" Ted asked.

Amanda gave another one of her all-knowing smiles. "We've been very intrigued with your nanobot research, Mr. Jordan. And it seems that others with not-so-altruistic beliefs as yours have become interested as well."

"You've been watching . . . *me*?" Ted asked as if he was almost happy about this.

"Oh, for some time now," Amanda said.

Ted looked almost giddy as Iain gave him a stare and shook his head slightly.

Iain looked back at Amanda. "Then why haven't you intervened before now?"

"Evidence," Sam said.

Amanda nodded. "We've had suspicions about Dr. Gomez, but no hard evidence. We know he often corresponds with Dr. Haneberg, but nothing so far has led to anything we could act on."

"Well, I hope you consider kidnapping evidence," Kaitlyn said. "He tried to have me killed, you know."

Iain turned directly toward the two and squinted. "And I don't recall you trying to help rescue her. Were you just going to let her die if we were unsuccessful?"

Sam held up his hands. "Whoa! Let's not start out on the wrong foot here. We were not following Dr. Sheridan; we were following Mr. Jordan."

"Yes," Amanda said. "We didn't know Dr. Sheridan was in danger until we saw you bringing her out."

Iain's eyebrows went up. "So you're here to apologize?"

Amanda gave a forced smile. "Not exactly. We're here to ask your help in catching Dr. Haneberg. We've known for some time he has plans to kill off part of Earth's population, but we had neither proof nor timing when such a plan would happen."

"Proof?" Kaitlyn said with determination in her voice. "I'll show you proof." She looked at Iain. "Let me see your phone again."

Iain handed Kaitlyn his phone. He knew she wanted to display the document she had found last night. But he soon noticed a look of panic on her face. "Kaitlyn, what's wrong?"

"It's gone!" She gave Iain a frightened look. "The document is gone!"

Amanda looked between Kaitlyn and Iain. "What document is this?"

"It clearly showed how Dr. Gomez and Dr. Haneberg are working together. Currently, to take out some Jewish priests, it seems. It sounded as if Dr. Gomez has additional plans that are, well, evil."

Sam wrinkled his brow. "Jewish priests? That seems rather odd."

"That's what I said," Ted added, "but Bev had an insight about it."

Kaitlyn looked taken back. "Oh, I, uh, just remembered something my brother-in-law said about an end-time prophecy."

Now Amanda developed a confused look. "Wait." She pointed at Ted. "You called her . . . "—Amanda pointed at Kaitlyn—"Bev. But you . . . "—now she pointed to Iain—"called her Kaitlyn."

Ted smiled. "Oh, it's just a nickname I have for her. We go way back."

Amanda looked from one to the other. "I see." She paused and then went on with another thought. "Anyway, as we were discussing, Dr. Haneberg is known to be some type of end-time prophecy—"

"Nut case," Sam interjected.

"Maybe 'enthusiast' is a better word," Amanda added. "Not everyone who believes in what the Bible says is a 'nut case,' as you put it." She cocked her head. "Yet, for Dr. Haneberg, that term may well describe him more accurately."

"Well, my brother-in-law said that in the future, Israel will build a temple and sacrifices will be offered again," Kaitlyn said. "Therefore, priests will be needed."

Sam cocked his head. "So if these priests are taken out, then that prophecy can't come true?"

Kaitlyn shrugged. "Good a theory as any, I guess. Maybe that's what Dr. Haneberg believes."

Amanda looked at Ted. "And your nanobots could do that?"

Ted shook his head. "Not directly. The nanobots can be used to target specific genes or mutations. Yet they could be used indirectly to accomplish that."

"What do you mean?" Sam asked. "Like point the way for something deadly to do its job?"

Ted nodded. "Correct. If you wanted to use a biological weapon, my nanobots could detect who had that particular marker."

Amanda's eyebrows went up. "Oh, so even though everyone is exposed to, say, a particular virus, only those with a particular identified genetic marker would be affected."

"Yes," Ted said. "That is how they can be indirectly used to achieve something like that."

"That's quite clever," Sam said. "In a scary way, for sure. But very clever."

"Okay," Amanda said. "We know some things about how someone could attempt such a feat. The real question is: how do we prevent it?"

CHAPTER 21

Ace up the sleeve

Amanda and Ted seemed to develop a chemistry together quite rapidly. The two of them began to talk about his nanobots, how they were made, and what they could do. He told her about Rocco and Roxie and the incident with Roxie. Whether she was acting to get more detailed information out of Ted or not, Iain couldn't tell. But it was clear Ted was head over heels for her even though he had just met her. For whatever reason, he seemed to feel that Amanda's having followed his every move was more than just her job but more of a personal interest.

Iain found himself hoping Ted wouldn't get too hurt when he fell from his cloud nine.

Sam took up Kaitlyn's and Iain's time while Amanda talked with Ted. He seemed to want to know every detail that each could remember from the last few days.

"Do you think others at the university are involved with Dr. Gomez?" Sam asked. "I'm trying to understand if he is a lone agent in all of this, or if he has accomplices."

"Well, he definitely has accomplices," Kaitlyn said. "I just don't know if they are connected with the university. I'm pretty sure the two that had me at the hospital were not with the university—or at least not at a professor level."

"What makes you feel that way?" Sam asked.

Kaitlyn shrugged. "The way they acted and talked. They seemed much more blue collar than white collar. They struck me as perhaps mercenary, as they were concerned about getting paid and not that interested in the rationale for why they were doing what Dr. Gomez wanted."

Sam nodded and jotted a few notes in his notebook. He glanced back at Kaitlyn. "Sorry, I don't mean to be rude with the writing. I just need to make some notes so I don't forget all the important details so I can debrief Amanda later."

"So, what's our next steps?" Iain asked. "Do you have witness protection or something like that for Kaitlyn?"

"Oh, I don't want anything like that," Kaitlyn said.

"But Dr. Gomez can't know you're still alive," Iain said. "Otherwise, he will just try and have you killed again."

Sam held up his hands. "Timeout here. Here is what I suggest. It's risky but will likely be the most successful."

Both looked at Sam with curiosity.

"While Dr. Gomez may be the bigger threat in the long run, Dr. Haneberg is the more immediate threat, and we need to flush him out. Confronting Dr. Gomez may be the better option to do that."

Iain scrunched his brow. "What exactly are you thinking?" He wasn't liking the sound of this.

"I would like for Dr. Sheridan to confront Dr. Gomez, and—"

Iain interrupted. "But—"

Sam raised his hand to stop him. "Hold on. Please listen. We will, of course, be there to back her up and help protect as needed. If Dr. Gomez realizes his plan failed, he will most likely contact Dr. Haneberg." .

"That's risky," Iain said, shaking his head.

"No, I want to do it," Kaitlyn immediately said.

Iain cocked his head. "Kaitlyn . . . "

"Iain, we can't let their plan go forward. Think of all the innocent lives that will perish."

"I'm thinking of *your* life," Iain replied.

Kaitlyn gave him a warm smile. "And I appreciate that, but this is too important to ignore."

"Well, I'm coming with you," Iain said.

Sam looked at Iain. "Well, to help you there, I think we'll need all three of you since you're all already involved. That should shake him up a little."

Iain looked at Sam and realized he would not necessarily blend in with a crowd. "No offense, but won't you stand out in a crowd?" Iain asked the agent.

Sam shook his head. "It's not about blending in, but making people think you're not an agent. Looking like I do actually gives me an advantage. No one suspects me as a federal agent. I get more out of people that way." He grinned. "I get to flirt and get paid for it."

Iain laughed. "Was that their recruitment pitch?"

Sam shook his head. "No, but Amanda and I came up with our costumes, you might call them. And we enjoy dressing this way." He shrugged. "It's worked out well for us so far."

"Well, for what it's worth," Kaitlyn said, "if I had to pick an FBI agent from a crowd, you'd be the last one I'd suspect."

Sam grinned. He looked over at Amanda and Ted. "Amanda."

Iain thought the two of them looked more like they were on a date than in a business discussion. He wondered how much business was being discussed.

Amanda looked Sam's way with raised eyebrows.

"I think we have a consensus of decision here. What do you have?" Sam asked.

"You have decision there," she said, "we have 'diabolical' here."

Sam's eyebrows went up. "Oh?"

"It seems Dr. Gomez or Dr. Haneberg can develop a contagious virus with Mr. Jordan's nanobots incorporated, and they can take out anyone with a specified genetic marker. Apparently, what Dr. Haneberg is targeting is a specific gene mutation on the Y chromosome known as the Cohen Modal Haplotype to take out those individuals who are descendants of ancient Jewish priests."

Ted nodded. "My guess is they will use something like a coronavirus because it is a variety of virus that easily infects and is akin to the virus causing the common cold. Some are fairly innocuous, but once they are released, they spread rapidly. There's no easy way to shut it down once released."

"But there is a way," Kaitlyn said. "That was one of the pieces of information Dr. Gomez wanted from me."

All eyes turned to her. "Oh, I gave him a partial answer, but not a complete one." She looked back at Ted. "How long to make an antidote?"

Ted shrugged. "I'd have to know some specifics of the protein structure they will be using. I can then target the carrier and chaperonin proteins so they will not make their derived proteins viable."

Sam scrunched his brow. "Come again?"

"Oh," Ted continued. "Each protein is made to be linear, and it must be folded into a three-dimensional structure to become active. That is the purpose of the chaperonin. Although we can't prevent these proteins from being formed, if I can tell the chaperonin to ignore these specific proteins, they will be present but not active. Over time, the body will get rid of them."

Sam nodded. "Okay. Even more reason to get to Dr. Haneberg as quickly as we can."

"While all of that is true," Kaitlyn said, "we still need to know how long it will take to create these anti-signal nanobots."

Amanda looked at Ted. "Can you predict that?"

Ted rubbed the back of his neck. "Hard to predict with accuracy. I think I would need at least three weeks to come up with a prototype. I can program them to replicate." He looked up, coming out of his thoughts. "How many doses are we needing?"

Amanda shrugged. "That depends upon how quickly we can get to Dr. Haneberg."

"But if it's released," Iain added, "we could be talking millions of doses."

Ted's eyes went wide. "Then I can't do that on my own. I can build a prototype, but we'll need other companies to help mass produce this."

Sam got a pained look on his face as he turned to Amanda. "This means we have to talk to Goldberg."

Amanda threw her head back with an "ugh," then added, "That will be a painful conversation."

"Who's Goldberg?" Iain asked.

Amanda breathed out hard. "He's our boss. He has a lot of clout within the agency, but he's not big on believing technology is the solution to problems."

"Sounds like he's Jewish," Kaitlyn said.

Sam suddenly sat upright. "That may just be the pitch we need. If he knows his family may be in danger, perhaps he'll take a larger interest."

Amanda grimaced. "I don't know. He's hardball." She turned to Ted. "Didn't you say Dr. Haneberg was targeting only those with a specific Jewish heritage?"

Ted nodded. "Ashkenazi Jews."

"How prevalent are they in the United States?" Sam asked.

Ted shrugged. "Don't know. Give me a sec." He typed furiously on his computer.

"What are you thinking?" Kaitlyn asked.

"Well, the more prevalent they are here," Sam said, "the more likely his family would be affected, and he would have more of an interest in stopping their plot."

Ted chuckled. "Well, that's surprising." He grimaced. "And concerning."

All turned his way.

"What is it, Ted?" Kaitlyn asked.

He looked up at and around at each of them. "It seems about ninety to ninety-five percent of American Jews are of Ashkenazi descent."

Amanda grinned. "I think we may have just found the ace up our sleeve that we need."

CHAPTER 22

A STUDY OF LIES

Kaitlyn looked extremely nervous. She sat in the front seat of the car with her head in her hands.

Iain reached over and softly rubbed her upper back. He really empathized with her. "You don't have to do this, Kaitlyn. We'll find another way."

Kaitlyn shook her head. "No. No, I'll be all right. I just have to get my mind right." She looked up and smiled briefly. "I thought I was ready, but the reality of what I'm going to do just hit me."

"You just have to pretend you don't remember anything that happened," Ted said.

"Yeah, I know," Kaitlyn replied. "But I do. That's the problem." She shook her head. "I'm just afraid I'll say something that will give that away."

"Remember what Sam told you," Iain said, trying to be as reassuring as possible. "They will rush in if the need arises."

Kaitlyn nodded and took a deep breath. "Okay. I'm ready."

As they stepped from the car and walked toward the building, Iain saw Kaitlyn become more and more confident in her appearance—or she was quickly getting into an acting persona.

They had a short wait at the visitor desk until Walt came out to meet them. His eyes grew wide. "Dr. Sheridan! So glad you could be back with us."

Kaitlyn smiled and nodded. "Thank you, Walt."

"I trust all is well?"

Kaitlyn cocked her head.

"Oh, it's just that Dr. Thornwhite said you had some type of development come up. I trust it all resolved satisfactorily?"

Kaitlyn gave a dismissive gesture. "Oh yes, thanks. It's fine now."

"Good. Glad to hear it." Walt then turned to Iain and Ted and shook their hands. "Good to see you again, Dr. Thornwhite, Mr. Jordan."

Iain smiled. "Lead the way, Walt."

Once he led them to the conference room, Walt gestured to the table under the window. "Help yourself to some coffee. I think there are some nutrition bars there as well." He turned, then turned back. "I'll get Dr. Gomez."

As Walt left, Kaitlyn went to the table. "I definitely need coffee." Iain and Ted let her go first knowing she was still quite nervous.

Ted and Kaitlyn had just sat down when the door opened; Dr. Gomez entered with Walt behind him. Iain remained standing.

"Good morning," Dr. Gomez said with a smile, although Iain thought it looked forced. "I wasn't sure you were coming today."

"Oh?" Kaitlyn said. She seemed to take this as a challenge, and this seemed, to Iain, to cause her nerves to settle. Iain could see a definite confidence building within her. "And why is that?"

"Oh, uh, I just mean you didn't come with Dr. Thornwhite and Mr. Jordan the other day."

Kaitlyn produced a smile. Iain thought it looked genuine even though he knew it was forced. "Yes, something came up." She waved a hand. "But it's all resolved now."

It was Gomez's turn to display a forced smile. "Glad to hear it."

"Yes, I must have had a fever or something," Kaitlyn said. "For the life of me, I can't really remember what happened that day." She smiled again. "But I'm better now."

"Good. Good. That's wonderful," Gomez said, though he kept eyeing her warily.

As Gomez sat, Iain tapped his hand on the man's upper back, as in a friendly gesture, next to his coat collar and then stuck out his hand to Gomez to shake it. "Just want to thank you for Walt's assistance the other day. He was a big help." In this swift move, Iain had placed a small listening device Sam had given him under Gomez's collar.

Gomez looked from Iain to Walt and back. "Yes, he is an asset all the way around."

Walt beamed.

Gomez opened his hands slightly. "So, what would you like to accomplish today?"

"A report of your findings would be helpful," Kaitlyn replied.

Gomez turned to Walt. "Can you update them, Walt, while I go and check on the progress with our coordinator?"

"Certainly, Dr. Gomez. I'd be happy to."

As Gomez left, Walt sat. "And what do you wish to discuss first?"

"What about the scans?" Ted asked. "Have you learned why they were so different from the other patients?"

Walt looked down and then back up, and suddenly looked rather nervous. "About that." He looked at Iain. "Your praise for me, Dr. Thornwhite, may be a little premature."

"Oh?" Iain said as he took a seat next to Kaitlyn. "Why is that?"

"It's really all my fault, I'm afraid. You see, we have another sponsor also with nanobot technology—"

"What!?" Ted interjected, his tone indignant. "I know for a fact that there is no one with more sophisticated nanobot technology than ours."

Walt's eyes went wide. "Oh, of course not. I wasn't implying that at all." He gave a nervous smile. "Yet that doesn't prevent others from trying." He shifted nervously in his seat. "Other companies are jealous as to what you have been able to accomplish. Many are trying to duplicate it, but with little success."

Kaitlyn shook her head. "I'm not following."

Walt's gaze went her way. "This is a competitive market right now. We must go where the funding is, so we have other sponsors initiating trials with nanobot technology." He held up his hands. "Don't worry. We keep everyone's information and intellectual property completely confidential."

Kaitlyn gave him a hard stare. "Go on."

"Well, I inadvertently mixed up some of the vials of the other trial with yours."

Kaitlyn's eyebrows rose and she sat taller in her seat. Walt's hands waved erratically. "Don't worry. It was a one-way accident. Theirs was inadvertently included in your trial but not vice versa. I double-checked that."

"So is that why you didn't want me to take a blood sample the other day?" Kaitlyn asked.

Walt nodded and gave a rather sheepish grin to try to hide his nervousness. "That was the main reason. I just wanted time to try and correct." He gave a quick shrug. "At any rate, it doesn't nullify any of your results. We just need to filter out the bioluminescence of these other nanobots, and your data will still be accurate."

"So, what were these other nanobots targeting?" Ted asked.

Walt's eyes grew large. "Oh, I'm afraid I can't tell you that. You weren't supposed to know about them. So, unfortunately, all I can say is that I am deeply sorry, and we have put corrective action into place so no such accident will happen again."

Iain stood. Seeing Walt look at him with apprehension, Iain patted Walt's shoulder. "Just need to take a bio break."

Walt nodded, and his stance relaxed a little.

Once Iain reached the hallway, he headed to find Gomez. He felt sure Gomez would be contacting Dr. Haneberg. While Sam and Amanda would likely be listening in, he wanted to know what was going on himself as they had refused to give him an earpiece to listen; they claimed that would compromise him. That didn't sit well with Iain. These one-sided trust deals never felt right to him.

Most of the staff paid him little mind as they seemed to be occupied with their daily duties. Patients were in the clinic on this particular day, so everyone was busy with various tasks. As he approached Gomez's office, Iain saw that Gomez's admin wasn't around. The clinic apparently used her skills in ways beyond simply handling Gomez's affairs around the office.

Iain picked up a file from the admin's desk and acted as if he was perusing it as he stepped close to Gomez's office. Gomez's door was slightly open, and he was speaking louder than he likely should have been. Iain could tell he was upset.

"Don't you dare tell me this is all my fault! I did everything you said I should do."

There was a pause. Iain could hear Gomez tapping a pencil on his desk in irritation as the person he was talking to was responding.

"She says she knows nothing . . . How am I supposed to know? . . . Listen here, doctor— . . . We must move forward. We have no choice . . . I can leave this Saturday and be there Sunday afternoon . . . " After a pause, Gomez let out a strong breath through his nose and said, in a curt tone, "Don't place blame where it isn't due."

He heard Gomez forcefully hang up with a loud sigh. Iain quickly put the folder back on the desk and scurried down the hall to get back to the conference room.

As Iain reentered the room, Walt was standing and shaking Ted's hand. "Please contact me at any time, and I'll give you an update."

Walt turned to Iain. "Goodbye, Dr. Thornwhite. I apologize again. And I can assure you I will be double vigilant moving forward to ensure your study is successful."

"Thanks, Walt. I'll be checking up periodically."

"Oh, absolutely." He looked at the others. "Shall I escort you out?"

"No need," Iain said. "We want to recap, and then we'll leave."

Walt nodded. "I understand. Until next time."

Both Ted and Kaitlyn looked at Iain as if he was going to debrief them as soon as Walt had stepped from the room.

"Did Walt give anything away?"

Both shook their heads.

"Let's go ahead and get out of here. I'll tell you what I found out once we get to the car," Iain said.

Both nodded and followed him out. As they approached their car, Iain's phone chimed. Before he could even say "hello," the caller was speaking.

"That was very careless, Dr. Thornwhite. You could have jeopardized everything if Dr. Gomez had caught you eavesdropping."

"Thanks for your concern, Agent Horne. But you left me little choice."

"Dr. Thornwhite—"

Iain cut her off. "Listen, let's get one thing straight here. Yes, you are the experts here, but this is our lives on the line. So you either include us or you're own your own. I will not let my life, or the lives of my colleagues, be in your hands without us being part of the process."

"Let's not get testy."

"Well, if you feel you can handle this by yourself without our involvement, go right ahead."

There was silence. Iain assumed he had either made her angry enough to end their working relationship, or she was contemplating her options.

"It's an all-in-or-nothing proposition, Agent Horne. The decision is yours."

"Very well," she replied. "We need all three of you in Washington day after tomorrow."

"What?" Iain was taken back. "Just like that, we uproot ourselves?"

"I thought you said 'All in or nothing.'"

Iain paused. He looked at Kaitlyn and Ted, who were both giving him a curious look. He knew he was deciding for them even before discussing the proposition. "I did. Very well. We'll be there."

"We'll have reservations for you at the Hamilton and discuss all this with you over dinner. And Dr. Thornwhite . . . "

"Yes?"

"The name is Amanda."

With that, the call ended.

CHAPTER 23

PROGRESS IN D.C.

"**S**he really said to call her Amanda?"

"Yes, Ted," Iain said. "For the fifth time, she did."

Ted sat in a leather chair in the hotel lobby opposite Iain and Kaitlyn, in deep thought with a silly grin on his face. Iain looked at Kaitlyn and shook his head. He wasn't sure whether to be happy or sad for the guy.

She smiled and whispered, "Oh, let him have his fun. I haven't seen him like this in quite some time."

Iain cocked his head and whispered back, "I just hope he doesn't get destroyed in the process. I'm not sure if she really likes him, or if she is just using him to get what she needs out of him."

Kaitlyn's eyebrows rose. "Oh, there's something there. I'm not sure it's the same as he has for her, but there's definitely a spark."

As Iain watched a few passersby, he noticed two individuals heading straight for them. It took him a few seconds to realize it was Sam and Amanda. Sam's hair was solid brown without highlights, and he had no pinstriped beard or mustache. Amanda was totally brunette with just a hint of dark auburn highlights.

Iain stood as they approached. Kaitlyn and Ted were taken off guard and stood after a few seconds, and in a bit of confusion. When Ted turned, his eyes went wide. "Amanda!"

She gave a big smile. "Surprised?"

Ted nodded. "And then some. You look . . . fabulous."

Amanda and Sam shook hands with the three of them. Iain gestured for the two agents to sit with them.

"Well," Kaitlyn said, "it seems you two are chameleons."

Sam laughed. "We change our persona whenever we come to D.C. Our boss isn't as understanding as our colleagues back in New Mexico."

"Speaking of our boss," Amanda said, "I invited him tonight. I hope you don't mind."

"Wow," Iain said, eyes wide. "You waste no time."

Amanda shrugged. "I feel we are under a very tight window of opportunity. We need him on board with us proceeding with a plan quickly."

"Plus," Sam added, "we need him here to get this on the official expense report."

Iain chuckled and gave a slight bow. "Well then, by all means."

Sam grinned. "But seriously, we wanted him to meet Mr. Jordan, here. I mean, Ted."

Ted's eyes went wide. "Why me?"

Amanda patted his knee. "Because you are crucial to getting an antidote to this potential threat. We need Mr. Goldberg to approve your working with the lab here in D.C. to manufacture that antidote." She waved her hands. "I know that, technically, it isn't an antidote, but it accomplishes the same thing."

"Just remember," Sam added, "keep things very simple tonight and don't get too technical. We don't want him to get lost in the details. If he gets frustrated, he is likely to just tune things out and not approve. He'll automatically jump to the conclusion we are trying to pull one over him."

Ted got a worried look. "I'll try, but it *is* rather complicated, no matter how you slice it."

"You can do it, Ted," Kaitlyn said. "You helped the protocol committee understand."

Ted nodded. "Yes, but our protocol is not as complicated as this is."

"True, but the concept of how to explain is the same," Kaitlyn said.

Sam suddenly stood. The others looked to where he was looking, and they also stood. Iain saw a man, neatly dressed but a little overweight, and with a touch of gray just above his ears. The first thing in Iain's mind was that this was a man who understood good food.

Sam stuck out his hand. "Mr. Goldberg, it's great to see you again."

"Hi, Sam. Hi, Amanda." He shook their hands.

Amanda gave a charming smile. "Mr. Goldberg, these are the scientists we referred to. This is Dr. Kaitlyn Sheridan, the one who initially developed the nanobot concept. Mr. Ted Jordan, who is the designer and developer of the nanobots. And this is Dr. Iain Thornwhite, the one who is currently working on a clinical trial with the nanobots."

Goldberg greeted each with a handshake. "Nice to meet each of you." He held up his hands. "I certainly don't mean to be short, but my time tonight is limited. I actually have another meeting soon after this one. Mind if we go informal and use first names? You can call me George." He gestured toward the restaurant behind them. "Shall we?"

George talked briefly to the maître d' as the rest followed the hostess to their table. Amanda held back with Ted in a discussion of some kind. Iain wasn't sure if it was business or personal. He hoped it was business, as every last one of them needed this meeting to go well and without distractions.

They took their seats, and George soon joined them and took his. "Forgive my forwardness, but you only need to order an entrée. A variety of sides will be served family style, and you can choose from those."

Kaitlyn smiled. "Oh, I think that is wonderful, George. I find ordering such a chore. This solves my dilemma."

George smiled in return. "Glad you approve."

The waiter came with a limited menu of entrées only. They ordered in less than a minute, the waiter poured each some wine, and he left the table area.

George leaned forward and clasped his hands together. He did not waste time. "Amanda tells me we are close to a huge threat that could prove to be both domestic and international. Now, before I raise the alarm, I need to better understand the evidence."

Kaitlyn nodded. "Let me begin and set the groundwork. Iain can provide a few details I don't know, and then Ted can provide the solution to this potential crisis."

George smiled. "Efficient. I like it."

Kaitlyn provided the information about the nanobots and what made them unique from what other institutions were doing, their potential for the benefit of medicine and mankind, and the potential for harm they had discovered but had not considered previously since they had been so focused on their benefit potential.

Iain briefly explained the ongoing trial and what it was designed to do, what they had discovered when examining the initial data, Kaitlyn's kidnapping and rescue, what they had discovered about Dr. Gomez, and his connection with Dr. Haneberg.

About this time their entrées arrived along with the various sides. George started the dishing and passed each along to the others.

"Okay," he said. "All that is very interesting. But I'm not understanding the real international threat here." He waved his knife and fork slightly as he paused cutting into his steak. "I know Amanda and Sam have had Dr. Haneberg on their radar for quite some time, but so far he hasn't really carried through with any of his threats. He's been mostly hot air. What makes things so dire now?"

"I think I can answer that," Ted said as he swallowed, took a sip of wine, and then a large swallow of water. "I think he has been biding his time for the right technological advancement to come along. What we have, I think, is what he has been waiting for. He wants to target a specific group of Jews, and my technology will allow him to do that. This technology can be combined with an infectious innocuous virus and will only affect those he wishes to affect."

"Did you say affect or infect?" George asked.

"Affect," Ted said. "I'm afraid the virus will infect almost everyone. And I'm pretty sure they will use something fairly contagious, like a coronavirus."

George grimaced. "Yeah, that is not going to go over well, considering what the world has been through in recent years."

"That is very likely true," Ted said. "Yet the common cold is a coronavirus, and it is very infectious, but rarely lethal. That's why it's a great vector."

161

George took his last bite of steak and dabbed his lips with his napkin. "Okay, so bottom-line it for me."

"A contagious virus will be used as a vector to deliver a deadly toxicant of some kind," Kaitlyn said. "It will be delivered to almost everyone but will only be lethal to those with the CMH, or Cohen Modal Haplotype, that is present in male Ashkenazi Jews. Over ninety percent of American Jews are of this descent, and about half of those possess this haplotype. The three countries of highest Jewish populations are the United States, Israel, and Russia."

"Do you have children, George?" Iain asked.

George nodded with his lips tightly pursed. "Yes, I have a twelve-year-old son and a ten-year-old daughter."

"There are many families like yours, George," Iain said, quietly but with resolve. "We need to protect them by doing whatever we can to ensure they stay safe."

George nodded slowly. "I agree." He put his napkin on the table and stood. "Sorry to eat and run, but I have another meeting. I thank each of you for your information. I think I have heard enough to get things rolling on my end." He turned to Ted. "I do hope you can stay. I want to get our government started on this antidote, or whatever you want to call it, as soon as possible."

"Whatever I can do to help, I will do," Ted said. "But I also need some clue as to what this Dr. Haneberg will be using so I can know what to develop to counter its effects."

George turned to Amanda. "Get him set up with Dr. Korvosky as soon as possible."

Amanda nodded. "Yes, sir. I will."

"And Sam, see if you can coordinate with Iain and Kaitlyn here to determine what Ted needs to get this solution off the ground." He went around the table and shook hands once more. "Wish me luck at my next meeting. I have to negotiate funds for this."

Kaitlyn smiled. "Thank you again."

As George left, the others returned to their seats. Amanda raised her eyebrows. "Well, we're stuck until Sam and I hear back from George tomorrow to see if we have approval to move forward."

"So what's our next move?" Ted asked.

Amanda waved the waiter over. She looked at Ted and smiled. "Dessert, of course."

CHAPTER 24

LUXEMBOURG BOUND

Luxembourg. Iain sat back in his seat and thought about this small country. Never in his wildest dreams did he think he'd be traveling to such a historic country. It wasn't even on his list of vacation spots, but it did sound quaint—and deadly, he had to remind himself. After all, they were going there to confront Dr. Haneberg. He apparently owned a castle in the northern part of Luxembourg.

Iain munched on some peanuts as he waited for Kaitlyn to return from the restroom. Sitting in the airport lounge, he looked out the window at the gates below where others were boarding a flight. He glanced at his watch. That would be them in about an hour. He felt excited and anxious at the same time. Sam came from the food line and sat across from him. Kaitlyn returned shortly after.

"Okay, Sam," Iain began. "I think you need to fill us in on Dr. Haneberg's background and what you know about him."

Kaitlyn nodded. "Yes, we only know that he seems to be an evil scientist who works with Dr. Gomez."

Sam took a sip of his coffee and shook his head. "It's Gomez who works for *him*. Haneberg is a multibillionaire. He's almost untouchable. I think that's why we haven't been able to pin anything on him. He has a fleet of lawyers who seem able to get him out of any accusations laid against him."

"That explains how he can afford a castle, I guess," Iain said with a chuckle.

Sam grinned. "Partly. He's savvy, obtaining the castle through a marriage arrangement. That is, maybe, how he first came into money, but he has increased in wealth ever since." He cocked his head. "Some say through shrewd investments. Others say through money laundering and other shady methods."

"What do you say?" Kaitlyn asked.

"Don't know, but I do know he's as crooked as they come."

"You said earlier he was a 'nut case.' I believe those were your words," Iain said. "Mind explaining more about that?"

Sam gave a small shrug. "Not much to explain. He has an obsession about end-time prophecy theories. I think he feels he is the harbinger of Bible predictions and wants to unite the world—under him, of course."

Kaitlyn wrinkled her brow. "The Bible states there will be a world of peace under the Jewish Messiah." Her eyebrows went up. "He feels he is the Messiah to bring about world peace?"

Sam chuckled. "I don't know about any of that stuff. But I think he wants to be the world dictator, for sure. He feels he knows best what the world needs."

"And he feels Jews are not needed in his new world order?"

"Evidently," Sam said. He turned to Kaitlyn. "Or maybe he believes the Jewish Messiah you speak of can't come if there are no Jews, or at least no Jews to administer temple duties." He shrugged again. "Either way, he's a total nut case, as I said."

"And what do *you* believe about the end times?" Kaitlyn asked.

Sam turned up the corner of his mouth. "Not sure how to answer that. I'm pretty much agnostic, I think. But I do know I don't want someone the likes of Haneberg dictating my future."

"And what do you hope to accomplish with this trip?" Iain asked.

Sam tilted his head slightly. "It's simple—in theory anyway. Get a sample of whatever he plans to release on the world and give that to your colleague so he can develop the antidote, or whatever he calls it."

"And you think it's in Luxembourg?" Kaitlyn asked. "Wouldn't it be in a lab somewhere?"

Sam nodded. "Right on both counts. I think his lab is at his castle."

Kaitlyn's eyebrows raised. "Really? Why?"

Sam gave a quick shrug. "Stands to reason. His castle is somewhat isolated in the mountainous area of the country, so there's no way for someone to easily snoop around it. Being there gives him more control over its development."

"Probably so" Iain said. "But what I don't understand is why we are going with you. What is our role if you plan to be clandestine?"

Sam gave a slight smile. "Oh, you too are the distraction so I can be clandestine."

Iain's eyes grew wide. "We're *what*?"

Kaitlyn leaned forward. "What exactly do you want us to do?"

"As I said, pretty simple. You already know Dr. Gomez is visiting Dr. Haneberg, right?"

Iain nodded. "But Gomez doesn't know we know that."

Sam looked at his watch. "Oh, by now he likely has heard of a rumor that you are aware of it."

Iain's eyes grew wide and he shot up straighter. "What did you do?!"

Sam held up his hands in a calming manner. "Please. Calm down. It helps our cause and will play into our plan."

"*Our* plan?" Iain's tone now bordered on sarcastic. "I don't think there is any 'our' to it at all."

"It's a good plan, though," Sam said, giving a broad smile. "You keep Doctors Gomez and Haneberg occupied while I snoop and go undercover in the castle. I'll find where the biological weapon is stored and . . . *borrow* a few."

Now it was Kaitlyn's eyes that were growing wider by the second. "And then what?" She looked from Sam to Iain and back. "He's already tried to have me killed. So what's to prevent him from trying again this time?"

"I'll have a team of snipers with me." Sam touched Kaitlyn's arm. "They're on the way and planning their positions now. Don't worry. I'll ensure you're safe."

Kaitlyn shook her head. "Somehow, I don't feel very safe." She gave him a stern look. "Do you even care what happens to us?"

Sam's head jerked back slightly. "What? Of course! I had your back in Albuquerque at the clinic. I'll have it in Luxembourg as well."

Kaitlyn sat back and rubbed her forehead, cupping it with her thumb on one side and her index and middle fingers on the other. "Why is nothing ever easy?" she mumbled.

Sam looked at his watch. "Okay. It's almost time to board. You two will be sitting next to each other. I'll be in the back. Don't want it to look like we're traveling together." He smiled and then stood. "When you get there, you'll receive an invitation to the castle."

Kaitlyn looked worried again.

"I'll catch up with you at your hotel in Validan." Sam grabbed his bag and quickly headed off.

Iain stood and helped Kaitlyn to her feet. He wrapped his arm around her shoulders as she looked extremely shaken. He gave her a slight squeeze. "Don't worry. It'll be fine. Gomez knows he's under scrutiny, so he's likely to temper any threat."

Kaitlyn glanced up at him. "Do you really believe that, or are you just trying to make me feel better?"

Iain smiled slightly. "Both. But I really do believe it. I'm not sure of all that Sam has in mind, but I do think Gomez knows he has to temper his actions."

"I certainly hope so."

"Come on. Let's board our flight to Frankfurt. We'll get settled, and you can get some needed rest."

CHAPTER 25

VALIDAN

As Iain took a bite of his muffin, he saw Kaitlyn enter the hotel café. He made eye contact with her and she headed over. "Care for some breakfast?"

"Oh, I really need coffee." She still looked quite nervous.

As she sat, Iain waved the waiter over. He brought a pot of coffee with him and poured her a cup. "Breakfast, Fraulein?"

"Just some fruit and a muffin, please."

The waiter nodded and came back only a few minutes later with her order.

She looked at Iain and shook her head. "How did you manage to get up so early?" She took a sip of her coffee. "I'm still half asleep. I couldn't rest in the car ride from Frankfurt to here."

Iain grinned. "I've already had half a pot, I think."

Kaitlyn chuckled. "I think that's what I need as well." She took a couple bites of fruit and sat back in her chair with a sigh. Looking out the window, she said, this time with a tone of awe, "Just look at it, Iain. It's magnificent."

Iain followed her gaze. The castle was indeed beautiful. It sat high above the town as though it served as its guardian. Yet they knew what was inside this structure was likely pure evil. It reminded Iain of a Bible verse about something looking good on the outside but being filled with bad on the inside. He couldn't recall the exact words, or who said it. He was rusty on his reading of Scripture. *Why did that even come to mind?* he asked himself.

"From what I heard," Kaitlyn added, "it used to be for tourists only, but now it's open that way only at certain times of the year."

Iain raised an eyebrow. "It seems money can get you almost anything you want."

Kaitlyn looked at him for a few seconds. "Almost is the operative word. Some things are beyond money."

Iain's attention turned to her, and he smiled. "True, but apparently not castles."

A grin slowly drew across her face. "Apparently. But the town getting an annual stipend from Haneberg likely helped that arrangement come about."

"Oh, so it's not 'build it and they will come.' But 'pay it and they will let you come'?"

Kaitlyn chuckled as she took another large sip of coffee; it was almost a slurp. "So it seems." She turned more serious. "How are we to do this? Have you heard from Sam?"

"I think Sam will be incognito from here on out."

Kaitlyn scrunched her face. "Well, that doesn't lend much confidence. How are we to know he's watching out for us?"

"Because he said he would."

"You have that much faith in him?" Kaitlyn asked.

"Not sure we have a choice at this point."

"So, we just walk up to the castle and knock?"

Iain shook his head. "I think we wait for an invitation." He shrugged. "At least that's what Sam said."

"You think he knows we're here?"

"Haneberg likely knows everything that goes on in this small town."

Kaitlyn chewed and swallowed a few bites of her muffin as she seemed to be in thought. "So how long do you think we wait for such an invitation? What if he doesn't invite us?"

At that moment the waiter returned to their table and laid down a note. "Pardon me, sir. This note just came for you. The front desk stated you would want this right away."

Iain's eyes widened. "Oh, thank you."

The waiter bowed slightly and left.

Kaitlyn's mouth hung open. "You don't think . . . "

Iain shrugged. "Maybe." He opened the note and read it. He looked up at Kaitlyn. "I hope you don't have plans for dinner this evening. It seems we dine at the castle tonight."

Kaitlyn's eyes widened. "Well, I guess you were correct." She paused in thought for a few seconds. "Actually, it's kind of unnerving he knows we're here right after we arrive."

Iain stood and held out his hand. Kaitlyn looked up at him with confusion.

"We have until this evening. Let's look around and focus on the positive aspects of this trip. We'll focus on the negative later."

Iain took the next several hours to keep Kaitlyn's mind occupied. He wanted her to enjoy herself for as long as she could. They found the town quaint with its colorful cottages, shoppes, bistro-style cafés, and farm stands. There was even a small hiking trail that went up into the surrounding hills. Along the trail they found all types of wildflowers and other natural scenery that proved breathtakingly beautiful. All in all, it was a day of great adventure.

As Iain walked her back to their hotel, Kaitlyn developed a more somber demeanor.

"Are you okay?" he asked.

"Just wondering what this evening will hold."

"Maybe it will be another adventure."

Kaitlyn gave a small, almost sarcastic, chuckle. "Optimist until the end, I see."

As they entered the lobby, the desk clerk motioned for them. "Dr. Thornwhite, I have another message for you."

"You think it's from Sam?" Kaitlyn asked.

Iain took the note and shook his head. "Not Sam. From Haneberg."

"What now?"

"He'll have a car pick us up at six."

Kaitlyn took a deep breath. "So only two hours until D-Day."

Iain chuckled and gave her a side hug as he led her to the elevator. She seemed in deep thought all the way to her room. After she opened her door, she turned. "Can we meet in the lobby at five-forty-five? I want us to be on the same page before we journey into who knows what."

"Sure," Iain said as he gave her a quick kiss. "I'll be waiting."

CHAPTER 26

ḥANEBERG'S CASTLE

Iain stood when he saw Kaitlyn step from the elevator. He thought her stunning. She wore a maroon evening dress that seemed to flow with her movement, complemented her reddish colored hair, and made her auburn highlights stand out even more as the ringlets she had placed in her hair jostled from the cadence of her walk and captured the light. He couldn't get over her natural beauty. He felt as though he needed to change into a tux rather than the coat and tie he was wearing.

"Kaitlyn, you've never looked more beautiful."

She developed a coy smile. "Thanks. Wasn't sure what to wear to a castle."

He chuckled. "Well, you'll definitely make the place look elegant."

She gave a dismissive wave as she sat in one of the leather chairs. "Oh, stop."

"You wanted to talk before the car arrived?"

Kaitlyn nodded. "We came all this way because Sam asked us to. Yet I don't really understand why we are here. What are we to accomplish other than occupy Dr. Haneberg's time so Sam can steal a vial of nanobots?" She shook her head. "I'm not sure he really needs us here to perform that task."

Iain took her hand. "Kaitlyn, Sam asked me not to tell you this, but now I feel like I need to."

She cocked her head. "Tell me . . . what?"

"Dr. Haneberg was insistent you come here."

Kaitlyn suddenly looked quite alarmed. "He *insisted* I come? Why?"

Iain shook his head. "I don't really know. All I know is that Sam said you are key to whatever Dr. Haneberg and Dr. Gomez have planned."

Kaitlyn stared at him, frozen as if a statue, for several seconds. Her gaze slowly turned to the window and then up toward the castle. "I'm tied to this evil plot of theirs?"

"Don't worry. I'm not going to let anything happen to you."

She nodded, but Iain could tell his words weren't helping her feel any better.

"Dr. Thornwhite," the desk clerk said. "Your car is here."

"Thank you." Iain stood and held out his hand to Kaitlyn. She followed him to the car outside, and a driver opened the door for them.

Iain began to wonder if he should have said anything about the matter at all. Still, he knew she would be angry if she was to find out he knew this and hadn't told her. But telling her this right before they arrived at the castle may have been poor planning on his part. She seemed lost in thought rather than enjoying the magnificent view as the car traveled up the steep hill to the castle above all the natural beauty that surrounded it.

The castle looked even more majestic the closer the car got to the structure. Once there, the car pulled around a large water fountain that lay in the middle of the circular drive. With the sun setting, the water captured the reds and golds of the evening sun and made the water from each tier of the fountain appear to glisten.

Once out of the car, Kaitlyn began to come out of her funk and started to take in all the beauty of the castle and its surroundings. Iain could see the amazement in her eyes as she panned the magnificent structure.

"Oh my," she said. "It's like stepping into another era."

A doorman opened the door and greeted them, directing them into a large parlor. There were elegant portraits that looked centuries old flanking an oversized fireplace which had a fire in its center area. It seemed it was more for ambiance as the fire covered only the very center of the hearth's massive area.

A tall, thin man entered; he had graying hair at his temples and more pepper-colored hair elsewhere on his head. He looked extremely neatly dressed in a dark charcoal gray-colored suit with a deep purple tie which gave him the academic look Iain had envisioned. The man also looked more spry and toned than expected. He gave a bright smile.

"Welcome, Dr. Sheridan and Dr. Thornwhite. I'm Dr. Haneberg. I trust your stay has been satisfactory so far?"

Iain nodded. "Yes, the town is quite lovely."

"And quaint," Kaitlyn added.

Dr. Haneberg clasped his hands together. "Wonderful. I'm glad to hear it." He gestured in the direction in which he had entered. "Dinner is ready. Shall we?"

They followed him into an elegant and expansive dining room. While the room looked capable of holding a large number of individuals, it apparently had been decorated to accommodate only an intimate gathering of people.

"Please, have a seat. I get few people visiting anymore, so I've made the space more accommodating."

Iain pulled a chair out for Kaitlyn and then took a seat himself. He noticed there was an extra place setting. "Oh, is someone else joining us?" he asked.

"Dr. Gomez will be here very shortly." Haneberg looked at his watch. "Not like him to be late." He gestured toward their plates. "Please go ahead and begin your soup course. It's bouneschlupp, our national take on what you would call potato soup. I'm sure you'll enjoy it." He bowed slightly. "I'll be right back." He smiled as he straightened. "Hopefully, with Dr. Gomez."

When the man left, Iain looked at Kaitlyn. "Not what I expected. If I didn't know any better, I'd think he was a charming host."

"Except for the feeling of this place."

Iain scrunched his brow. "What do you mean?"

"You don't feel it? There is an oppressive feel to this place despite how grandiose it looks."

"Well, I haven't felt that exactly, but I do have my suspicions as to his sincerity." Iain removed the lids from their soups and inhaled the aroma. "It smells wonderful and looks interesting." He took a taste and his eyebrows rose. *Mmm.* Quite tasty."

"It is good," Kaitlyn said. "It's just hard to enjoy it under these circumstances."

Haneberg returned. "Found him!"

Gomez entered right behind him. "Forgive me. I lost track of time."

Iain started to rise, but Gomez replied, "No, no. Don't get up."

Gomez quickly took his place at the table, as did Haneberg.

As they all began enjoying the soup, Haneberg gave a broad, warm smile. "Let's be informal tonight. Call me Alexander." He looked from one to the other. "Is everyone okay with that?"

Iain and Kaitlyn nodded. "Yes," Gomez said. "And you can call me Juan."

Over the next several minutes, as the others ate their soup, Kaitlyn took only a few spoonfuls. Iain noticed her now looking extremely unsettled.

Apparently, Haneberg did as well. He looked her way and asked, "Kaitlyn, is the soup not to your liking?"

She shook her head. "No, it's quite good, actually."

"Then what's wrong?"

She put her soup spoon down, sighed, and gave Haneberg a terse look. "Oh, I don't know. Maybe having the person who tried to kill me at the same table with me acting like we're good friends now. Maybe that's why I'm looking like I do."

"Oh, I hoped we could put all that behind us and move forward in a better light," Haneberg said.

Kaitlyn opened her mouth to say something, but she was interrupted by a lady collecting the soup course and a man delivering the evening entrée.

Haneberg smiled as he gestured to the main dish. "This is somewhat unique to Luxembourg. Many eat it with their fingers, so feel free to do so." He chuckled. "After all, we are being informal, right? The dish is called Friture de la Moselle, and it contains different kinds of fried fish."

Kaitlyn fidgeted in her chair. Iain could tell she was extremely uncomfortable in this setting. Perhaps Sam had enough time to do whatever he needed to do. He had to think of a way to end this dinner early.

Haneberg looked at Kaitlyn and gave a warm smile. "My dear Kaitlyn, let me put your mind at ease. I let it be known

I was insistent you be here because I knew that was the only way to ensure Iain would be here." He glanced at Iain. "He would do anything to ensure you are safe. Right, Iain?"

Iain looked at Kaitlyn and then back to Haneberg. "What?"

"What do you need Iain for?" Kaitlyn asked.

Haneberg's smile turned into a huge grin. "See, I just confirmed for you what you were unable to admit to yourselves. You two are in love with each other." He chuckled. "Now you don't have to pretend that your feelings are a taboo subject. You can now embrace your feelings."

Kaitlyn looked from Iain to Haneberg. "You got us here so you could play matchmaker?" She scoffed, then shook her head. "That . . . that makes no sense."

Haneberg shrugged. "Love is an illogical force that makes the strong weak and the eloquent sound idiotic." He laughed. "Such a true statement, don't you think?"

Iain looked at Kaitlyn but didn't know what to say or think. He knew something more was at play here—but didn't know what.

"I do admit," Haneberg continued, "I have additional reasons for you to be here, but let us finish our dinner before we discuss that." He gestured to their plates. "Please. Eat and enjoy."

"Dr. Haneberg," Kaitlyn began.

Haneberg smiled. "Alexander, please."

Kaitlyn sighed. "*Alexander*, this is all highly irregular."

"Yes, yes. I know. But let's have this little moment of civility. Please."

Kaitlyn resumed eating her meal but was not enjoying any of it. Iain did the same, unsure what else to do. He hoped the faster they got through the dinner courses, the faster they could leave.

After a short time, the man and woman reentered, taking away their plates and leaving a small-sized tart for each.

"This is a plum tart," Haneberg said. "I won't bore you with the official name. I think you'll really like it, though."

Iain took a bite. It really was very tasty. If he had it under any other circumstances, he would thoroughly enjoy it. Kaitlyn took a few bites of hers but stopped eating. It seemed she was too upset to continue.

Haneberg and Gomez were thoroughly enjoying their dessert; they would occasionally pause and give a look of reverie. Haneberg looked at Kaitlyn. "Anything wrong?"

She shook her head. "No, it's extremely tasty. I just don't have an appetite tonight."

"Oh, I'm sorry to hear that."

"But that's okay," Gomez said. "At least Iain has eaten his."

Iain looked at Kaitlyn and shrugged. He had no idea why that was important. She had a concerned look on her face.

She looked at Gomez, who was now chuckling, and turned to Haneberg. "What is that supposed to mean?"

Haneberg smiled. "Iain is the means to test the pace of our plague."

Gomez chuckled. "Yes, our Luciferian Plague."

CHAPTER 27

THE MAKING OF THE PLAGUE

Iain glared at the two men. "What are you two talking about?"

Gomez smiled. "It's a play on words. Quite clever, don't you think? If you were scanned right now, the bioluminescence from the luciferase would be everywhere in your body, much like those scans of the Jewish men in our clinical trial. And any physician would have a devil of a time trying to figure out what's wrong with you." He chuckled. "Get it? Luciferian . . . luciferase . . . *Lucifer* . . . *devil*." Gomez's eyes seemed to grow darker with each successive word.

Iain shook his head. No, he didn't get it at all.

Haneberg clasped and unclasped his hands as if explaining a simple topic. "You see, we need to know how quickly our manufactured plague will take effect. You, Iain—oh, I do hope we can still be on an informal basis—are the perfect candidate. You understand the issue and can report your progress in scientific terms, which will be so very helpful to us."

Kaitlyn looked from Haneberg to Gomez, horror on her face. "You are both insane."

Haneberg calmly looked at Kaitlyn. "Well, you must take some of the responsibility. After all, he's in this predicament because you love him."

Kaitlyn looked in horror once more. "What? You're killing him because I love him?"

Haneberg cocked his head as if in thought. "Not exactly."

Gomez jumped in. "We needed to test our control of transmission as well as the plague itself. Because you love each other, you two were the perfect candidates."

Iain looked at Kaitlyn. It was obvious she was as clueless about what these two were saying as he was. He looked at Gomez. "Want to rewind and tell us how you came up with all of this?"

Gomez's eyebrows went up. "Oh, sorry. I thought it was obvious." He shrugged. "I have been looking for years for a way to target specific individuals so we can depopulate our planet in a very controlled manner." He grinned. "After all, we want to keep the good gene pool and eliminate the bad. Right?" Gomez said this so casually. Iain could feel himself almost shudder.

Iain shook his head.

"Oh, come now, Iain. Did you really think you could bring the world nanobots like what Kaitlyn came up with and not have consequences?" Gomez tilted his head back and forth slightly. "Well, I'm sure 'consequences' is what you would call it. We call it opportunity."

Haneberg nodded. "When Juan, here, contacted me about your nanobot discovery, I realized this would allow us to initiate our plans almost immediately." He gave a slight bow. "For that, we are most thankful."

"Yeah? Well, you have a terrible way of showing gratitude," Iain said.

"Again, our apologies," Haneberg said with another slight bow. "However, we have to take opportunities as they are presented."

"And trying to kill me is one of those opportunities?" Kaitlyn said as she glared at the two.

Gomez put his hand to his chin. "Yes, I admit that may not have been too well-thought-through in the beginning, but it did turn out quite well in the end."

Kaitlyn shook her head with anger. "Again, you act like I know what you're talking about." She forced a smile. "Sorry, I don't think in crazy."

"Aw, now, Kaitlyn. Let's not get nasty. We're having such a polite conversation," Gomez replied, looking genuinely hurt.

Kaitlyn rolled her eyes but didn't say anything more.

"I admit," Gomez continued, "there was a risk in your demise. Yet I knew Iain would come to your rescue." He smiled. "After all, that's what one does when they love someone." He glanced at Iain. "Right, Iain?"

"What's your point!?" Iain asked, now fuming. He had almost had enough of these two. They were clearly delusional. Maybe insane. Maybe both.

Gomez ignored Iain and looked at Kaitlyn. "The rag placed over your nose and mouth contained a virus. One that we devised could be transmitted only when two people are extremely close to each other."

Haneberg grinned. "Yes, like with a kiss. Something you would likely do with only one other person."

"But I haven't had any symptoms of sickness," Kaitlyn said as she glanced at Iain.

He shook his head. "Neither have I."

Gomez gave a dismissive wave. "Oh, this virus was not to produce symptoms but to deliver nanobots. The same ones I used in our clinical trial."

Iain tried to understand the importance of this. "But that was for identifying gene mutations for Tay-Sachs." He shook his head. "I don't have that."

Gomez nodded. "You are correct. Or . . . were correct. You *didn't* have it—until now."

Iain squinted. "What is that supposed to mean?"

"You did enjoy your plum tart, did you not?" Haneberg asked.

"Yeah. So?"

Haneberg leaned forward slightly. "Did you happen to notice that the plums in your tart were redder than those in ours or Kaitlyn's?"

Iain shook his head slowly.

"Well, your plums, laid out in such a beautiful geometric design on top of the tart, were coated with an enzyme that will trigger the nanobots which you received from Kaitlyn into inhibiting the breakdown of certain proteins just like those who have Tay-Sachs disease." He grinned. "While you don't have Tay-Sachs, your body will act as if it does." He sat up straighter. "Ingenious, no?"

"No! No, that's not ingenious," Kaitlyn yelled. "That's insanity. Pure insanity!"

Gomez looked irritated. "Kaitlyn, please. We're trying to have a civil conversation. There is no need for outbursts."

Kaitlyn was now breathing hard. She looked at Iain, her eyes glistening with moisture.

Gomez looked at Iain. "Even now, the nanobots are inhibiting the activation of beta-hexosaminidase in your body allowing the buildup of sphingolipid GM2 gangliosides in your brain. You'll soon start getting symptoms: nervous twitching, slurred speech, cognitive decline, behavioral problems, difficulty swallowing and breathing . . . and eventually death. We want to know how fast all of this will take." He shrugged. "I know naturally it can take years, but with this happening in all cells simultaneously and not progressively, we are hoping it will be much, much faster."

Kaitlyn threw her napkin on her plate and stood. "We are leaving! I will not sit here another minute and listen to your insanity!"

Iain stood as well. He had come to protect Kaitlyn, and now she was the one trying to defend him. He couldn't believe this was happening. So far, he felt fine. *Is it a ruse?* he wondered. Either way, Kaitlyn was right. Staying was pointless.

Haneberg had a look of surprise. "We haven't even had our after-dinner tea and coffee."

Gomez nodded. "Or the chance to have a stimulating discussion regarding our plans of how to make this virus airborne so we can better test our theory and its spread."

"Oh, I think we've been served well enough," Iain said. "Assuming what you say is actually true."

"And I think we've had enough *stimulating* discussion, thank you!" Kaitlyn added.

Haneberg stood, dabbing his lips with his napkin and dropping it on the table. "Oh, we were truthful in our statements. Don't misjudge how you feel right now with nothing going on inside you. Trust me, your body is betraying you even as we speak."

Gomez held up his index finger. "And . . . Kaitlyn?"

She turned, rage in her eyes, to face him.

"No need to take Iain to the hospital. There is *nothing* they can do for him."

She returned a stare so full of hate Iain thought it made her look like something other than herself.

"And don't feel too bad about what you have done," Gomez continued. "After all, love often brings heartache."

"What *I* did?" Kaitlyn's stance turned nearly statuesque. She took a few steps toward Gomez, fist raised. "Don't you dare try and pin your diabolical plot on me. I'll not take one ounce of your blame! You are a monster! A monster that needs to be incarcerated."

Gomez's eyes grew wide, and he took a few steps back. Iain felt great pride in Kaitlyn, suddenly admiring her even more than he already did.

Haneberg chuckled. "Such fire! No wonder Iain was attracted to you. But none of this can come back to us. Once the damage is done in Iain's body, the nanobots will self-destruct, leaving no telltale signs except for a body ravaged by neurodegenerative decline." He looked at Iain with a smile. "Congratulations, Iain. You'll go down in the history books as the great medical puzzlement of the century: all the debilitating signs of neurodegeneration but with no evidence of neurodegeneration. You'll be the subject of medical debate for decades!"

Kaitlyn turned with a jerk and grabbed Iain's arm. "Let's get out of this insane asylum."

The doorman hurried to open the door for them. Iain glanced at the man, who seemed to have a touch of fear in his eyes. He wondered if this man could perhaps provide evidence to convict these two of their crimes. Yet, he wondered, would this man be too frightened to do so? Knowing these two, they likely had something over the head of anyone in their employ.

The car was waiting for them as they left the castle. The driver jumped out and opened the door for them. He drove them back down the mountain to the hotel. Neither uttered a word the entire way. What was there to say? They both knew Iain was dying . . . and apparently there was nothing they could do to prevent it.

CHAPTER 28

HINT OF HOPE

Sam stood immediately when Iain opened the door to his room. Kaitlyn was standing behind Iain. "Sorry for letting myself in, but . . . " He stopped midsentence upon seeing the look on their faces. "What's wrong?" He gestured to them. "After all, you're the ones who got to enjoy an amazing meal."

Tears began to stream down Kaitlyn's cheeks. Iain helped her sit. He knew all her pent-up stress and emotions were quickly coming to the surface, and they had to be released. She put her head in her hands and wept—hard.

Sam stepped over and knelt next to her, placing his hand on her shoulder. "Kaitlyn, I'm sorry." He glanced up at Iain in bewilderment. "What happened? Did something happen?"

Iain dropped onto his bed with a plop. "That's an understatement."

Kaitlyn looked up; she was starting to regain some of her composure. Her tears had stopped, but she still sniffled occasionally. "Doctors Haneberg and Gomez have used Iain as their human guinea pig."

Sam looked from one to the other, shaking his head slightly. "I don't understand."

"They gave me the virus and nanobots to develop Tay-Sachs symptoms," Iain said. "Apparently, it ends in death, and they want to know how long that will take."

Sam's mouth fell open. "They *what*?" He stood and sat next to Iain with his hand on his shoulder. "How do you feel? What can I do?"

Iain shook his head. "Apparently, there is nothing anyone can do."

Sam rubbed his hand over his mouth. "There . . . has to be something." He looked hopeful. "I got what I needed. Would . . . that . . . help?"

Iain shook his head. "I don't see how."

"We need an antidote," Kaitlyn said, looking at Sam as if he should know the next step to take.

"Kaitlyn," Iain said in a soft tone. "It's like they said. There is nothing anyone can do. Tay-Sachs is not curable."

Kaitlyn shook her head. "But you don't have Tay-Sachs— you just have a manifestation of its symptoms."

Sam suddenly looked hopeful. "Ted! Let's get Ted on the phone. Perhaps what I have and what he can do can tie together."

"Worth a try," Kaitlyn said as she took out her phone and found Ted's contact.

In a matter of seconds, Ted answered. "Bev! Hi. How's Luxembourg? I was at first sad about not being able to be with you and Iain, but this lab is absolutely amazing—top-notch."

"Ted, we have a problem."

"Problem?" He chuckled. "What, Iain didn't propose like you wanted?"

Kaitlyn put her forehead in her hand and massaged her temples. "Ted, you can be such an imbecile sometimes. Honestly!"

"Oh, sorry. He's standing right there, I guess, right?"

With annoyance in her voice, Kaitlyn responded, "Ted, both Iain and Sam are here. I assume Amanda is with you?"

"Yeah. What's up?"

"Put you two on speaker, and I'll do the same."

"Amanda," Sam said, "we have a real problem."

"What happened? Were you not able to get what you needed?"

"No, that part went fine. Iain and Kaitlyn ran into a horrible problem we did not anticipate."

Ted jumped back into the conversation. "What happened, Bev?"

Kaitlyn's eyes got wet, but she was able to hold back tears. "Haneberg and Gomez were able to get nanobots into Iain that will mimic the symptoms of Tay-Sachs disease even though he doesn't have the gene for Tay-Sachs."

"How on earth did they manage that?"

"It's rather complicated," Iain said. "It seems they gave me nanobots that are inhibiting the activation of beta-hexosaminidase in my body allowing the buildup of toxic gangliosides in my nervous system."

"Oh, man!" Ted exclaimed. "That's not good. Not good at all."

"Tell me about it," Iain said. "The question is: what can you do about it?"

"Well, it sounds like the reverse of what we were thinking of doing. I mean, rather than inhibiting the activation of that enzyme, we need to activate it."

"Explain that," Sam said.

"Well, for those with the Tay-Sachs mutation, the nanobots would turn on the gene which inhibits the carrier protein specific for that enzyme to deliver it to the chaperonin, so it creates a deficiency in the production of the enzyme. I wanted that sample you've attained to confirm that is what's happening. If it is, then we need to activate that carrier protein. It seems in Iain's case the nanobots are inhibiting the chaperonin itself so the enzyme can't be converted into its active three-dimensional structure. His body is still producing the enzyme. It's just not in an active state for the body to use."

"Can I have that in English?" Sam said.

Ted laughed. "Sorry. I just mean Tay-Sachs disease leads to a deficiency in the needed enzyme. In Iain's case, the enzyme is formed but can't be activated."

Kaitlyn perked up just a little. "Does that mean you can correct this?"

"Possibly, but I need Iain here so I can test a few things. The fastest way would be to reprogram the nanobots, but they may be password-encrypted, and decoding them could take time we don't have. It may be faster to program new nanobots, but that also takes time. Let me start on this—and you get here as fast as you can."

Kaitlyn's eyes watered again, but this time she had a smile on her face. "Thanks, Ted. I knew you'd come through."

"Bev, I'm not promising," Ted said softly, soberly. "I'll do everything I can. You know that."

"Yeah, I know," she said in barely a whisper.

"Thanks buddy," Iain said. "Looks like you'll turn me into a robot before all this is over."

Ted chuckled. "That's an idea. I need someone to bring me coffee every morning."

"You do this, and you've got it."

"And Amanda," Sam said, jumping in, "tell Goldberg it looks like the first deployment of this bioweapon may be in New York. I'll explain all that when I get there, but there were some things in their lab that seem to suggest that. Let him know so they can prepare."

"Do you know where?"

Sam shook his head. "Not one hundred percent, but they had a picture and map of the interior of Penn Station, so my thought is they are going there. That's likely the best way to get it moving west across the country."

"Why not the airport?" Amanda asked.

"I think they want to test its spread before they go global. I say that just based on what they've said to this point. Once they know that, I'm sure Israel and Russia are next."

"Understood," Amanda said. "You need to get here on the next flight out if at all possible."

"Roger that," Sam said.

"See you soon, Bev and Iain," Ted added. "I'll get right to work."

Kaitlyn ended the call and looked at Iain with a hint of a smile. "At least we have hope."

Iain nodded. "Hope is what I need."

"Okay," Sam said with a hand on each of their shoulders. "Give me a few minutes to get us a flight out of here as early as possible tomorrow. It's too late for a flight to the U.S. tonight."

Kaitlyn nodded and turned to Iain. "How are you feeling?"

Iain shook his head back and forth slightly. "Okay for now. My mind does feel a little fuzzy. But that could just be due to being tho tired."

Kaitlyn's attention jerked his way.

"Did I just slur a word?" he asked.

She nodded, with a concerned look.

Sam tapped his phone to end his call. "Okay. Got it." He grimaced. "It means we have to leave around four in the morning for a seven-thirty flight."

Kaitlyn shrugged. "Whatever it takes, Sam."

"Okay, I'll have the car ready for us then. It means we should arrive back in D.C. around dinnertime. I'll alert Amanda."

Kaitlyn kissed Iain on his cheek. "Get some rest, and I'll meet you in the lobby. We should both shoot to get down there about three-forty-five." She thought about that time. "Yikes. That's really early. But it's what we have to do." She gave Iain a concerned look. "Should one of us stay with you? We don't know what side effects to expect or how quickly."

"I'll stay," Sam said.

Iain shook his head. "No need. Morning isn't that far from now. I don't think it will work that fast."

Kaitlyn did not look convinced.

Iain smiled. "I'll be fine. Don't worry."

"Well . . . okay. But be sure you have me on speed dial, just in case."

Sam patted Iain's back with a touch of reassurance. "Have a good night, buddy. We'll do everything we can to get this fixed."

Iain closed the door behind them and sighed. This trip had taken the most unexpected of turns. He hoped Ted could turn it back. There was hope, he reminded himself. He had to cling to that.

* * * * *

"What do you think, Mikael?" Raphael asked as he watched Iain collapse onto his bed and lay his forearm over his eyes.

"It seems Lucifer is being very calculating this time," Mikael said after giving a bit of thought. "And wanting to time his attack on our Lord's chosen people."

"Is it that, or is he just trying to get all those who could oppose him out of the way?"

Mikael cocked his head in thought. "That very well could be." He looked at Iain, now asleep, and turned back to Raphael. "Let's see how things go in the morning."

Raphael nodded and sat on the edge of Iain's bed.

CHAPTER 29

hope loses control

As Mikael entered the hotel lobby, he saw a demon hurry outside and fly off. He walked to the doorway and looked up toward the castle. A whole host of Lucifer's demons was circling the structure.

"I guess he was the watchdog to see what's going on with Iain," Raphael said.

"Apparently so. They now know the debilitating efforts are swift," Mikael replied. "Lucifer and those two insane doctors are probably gloating." Mikael turned back and saw Kaitlyn set her suitcase down and drop onto one of the plush chairs in the lobby.

* * * * *

Kaitlyn looked up at Sam as he walked over to where she was sitting. "Where's Iain?" Him not being down yet made her concerned. Perhaps one of them should have stayed with him.

Sam shrugged. "I assumed he would be with you."

She looked at her watch. "It's not like him to be late. He knew what time to be down here." After a few seconds, she added, "We should go check on him."

"He couldn't have gotten worse overnight, could he?"

Kaitlyn stood, suddenly even more anxious. "Let's go see."

On the ride up the elevator, Sam patted his thigh nervously. "I didn't leave a lot of time to get to our flight. I sure hope he's ready."

Kaitlyn nodded. "So do I."

Once at his door, Kaitlyn knocked. After a few seconds, Iain opened it. Though his shirt was half tucked in his pants, at least he was mostly dressed. She realized his clothes were those he had worn yesterday.

"Hey, guys. What's up?"

"What's *up*?" Sam said with disbelief. "You were supposed to be in the lobby so we can get to the airport!"

"Oh, was that today?"

Sam shook his head. "Yes, Iain! That's today. This morning! We're heading back to the States for you. Don't you remember?"

Iain put his hand to his head. "Oh, yeah. Yes, of course. Sorry."

"Sam, he can't help it. The symptoms are speeding up," Kaitlyn said as she tried to comfort Iain, who was now getting upset at himself.

"Why didn't I remember that?" Iain said, tapping his head with his fist.

"It's okay, Iain. It's okay," Kaitlyn said. "We have time."

Sam opened dresser drawers, pulled out Iain's clothes, and hurriedly threw them into Iain's suitcase. He threw a light jacket over Iain's rumpled shirt and quickly ran a hand through Iain's messy hair. Looking at his watch again, Sam gently pushed Iain toward the door. "Okay, let's get going. We can't afford any other delays."

On the ride down, Iain looked at Sam. "S-S-Sam, I'm rrre-ally s-s-sorry."

Sam gave a worried look toward Kaitlyn and then forced a smile at Iain, giving him a pat on his back. "It's okay, buddy. It's okay."

Iain stumbled as he stepped from the elevator. Sam grabbed Iain's arm just in time to prevent him from falling. "Easy there, buddy. Let me help you to the car."

The desk clerk came from behind the counter. "Here, sir. Let me assist." The man followed them out with their suit-cases. The driver put them in the trunk.

"Thank you so much," Kaitlyn said as she tried to give the clerk a tip. Instead, the clerk shook his head, smiled, and gave a dismissive wave.

Iain sat quietly for about half the trip. Kaitlyn noticed his hands tremor periodically. She and Sam exchanged glances every so often, but neither said anything to draw attention to it. Kaitlyn tried reading something on her phone but found she kept glancing over at Iain.

"I'm thirsty," Iain muttered.

"You're thirsty?" Kaitlyn asked. She had finally gotten absorbed in her reading.

"That's what I said, didn't I!?" Iain shouted, annoyed. "Do I have to keep repeating myself!"

"Whoa, buddy," Sam said. "Relax. We've got you covered. I have some water here."

Iain snatched the bottle from Sam's hand and went to open it. Iain's hands began to shake violently; water splashed all over the car's rear area. Iain got so upset he dashed the bottle to the floorboard.

Sam quickly retrieved the bottle before too much more water spilled. Kaitlyn tried to comfort Iain. "It's okay. It's okay," she kept repeating.

In a fit, Iain pushed her away. "Leave me alone! Just . . . leave me alone! Nothing's okay!"

Kaitlyn pulled her hands back, her eyes now wide in fright. In a moment, recognition seemed to hit Iain. He put his hands over his face and began to weep. "I'm sorry. I'm sorry. Oh, so sorry." His whole body went into convulsions.

In a second, Sam took action. He leapt into Iain's lap, wrapped his arms tightly around Iain's torso, and pushed his legs tight against Iain's to prevent them from flailing. "I got you, buddy," Sam said. "I got you."

In only a few seconds, Iain's convulsions ceased. Sam drew himself out of Iain's lap and repositioned himself in his seat. "You okay now, buddy?"

Iain nodded slowly. He looked at Sam and then Kaitlyn, who had tears running down her cheeks. Iain's eyes filled with tears. "I'm . . . tho . . . thorry."

"I know. I know," Kaitlyn said, pulling Iain's head onto her shoulder. "Just get some rest."

Iain snuggled into her shoulder and fell asleep in seconds.

Kaitlyn looked at Sam, tears still flowing. "How are we going to do this for a nine-hour flight?"

Sam shook his head. "I don't know. We'll look for something that will help him sleep most of the way."

The convulsions wore Iain out so much that he slept the rest of the car ride to the airport. Once there, Kaitlyn jostled his arm. "Iain. Iain, we're here."

Iain slowly woke but looked discombobulated. "Here? *Where?*"

Sam helped Iain out of the car, but Iain's coordination was not good. He leaned Iain against the car. "Kaitlyn, hold on to him and I'll retrieve a wheelchair."

The driver checked their bags at an outside baggage area while Kaitlyn waited for Sam to return. Sam returned not only with a wheelchair but also an airport employee to help escort them to their flight. The employee helped with preflight checks and even with getting the three of them onto the flight ahead of other passengers.

Sam had Iain sit next to the window and then took his seat in the middle between Iain and Kaitlyn. "I'm not trying to come between the two of you," he said to Kaitlyn with a smile. "But I want you to not have to worry about him this entire trip. I'll be sure he's taken care of."

Kaitlyn nodded. "Thank you, Sam. I'm so glad you're here with us."

Sam touched her hand. "No problem."

Once the plane took off, Sam insisted Kaitlyn have a cocktail to relax her nerves. He made sure Iain had one as well. He held the cup for Iain as his hands would turn spastic without warning. Kaitlyn still had a hard time resting. She woke up many times and looked over at Iain. He was usually asleep, and when not, Sam was taking care of his needs.

Once, she woke up as Sam was trying to feed Iain but having difficulty with the job. Iain kept choking on his food. Sam looked over at Kaitlyn and smiled. "Oh, good. You're awake." He handed her Iain's breakfast plate. "Mind cutting this up into tiny bits? I think he'll do better that way."

After Iain was fed, he was out once more.

Sam leaned back and sighed. "Poor guy. Even eating is tiring for him now."

Kaitlyn looked at her watch. Her eyes became misty. "Sam, we're only halfway to D.C. If he's this bad now, will he even make it?"

Sam turned to her quietly. "Now don't you dare go there. He's strong. He's having difficulty." He nodded his head. "A lot of difficulty. But he has a strong and determined will. He's going to make it." He gave her a stern look. "Okay?"

A few tears trickled down Kaitlyn's cheeks. This was harder than she had envisioned.

Sam took her hand. "Okay?"

She nodded. "Yeah. Okay."

He gave her hand a pat and smiled. "We'll all make it."

Kaitlyn laid her head back and closed her eyes. For some reason, that was the assurance she needed. Before she knew it, she was asleep again.

* * * * *

Mikael sat on the arm of the seat next to Kaitlyn as Raphael stood next to him.

"You think he'll make it?" Raphael asked.

Iain suddenly opened his eyes. "Of course I will. Why wouldn't I?"

Raphael turned to Mikael. "He can hear us?"

"Of course I can," Iain replied. "Blue looks good on you, by the way."

"What?" Sam asked, pulling the earphones for the movie he was watching away from his head. "Did you say something?"

Iain shook his head, then nodded his head toward the aisle. "Just talking to the angel standing there."

Mikael saw Sam look but, of course, could not see them. Sam looked at Kaitlyn who was sleeping, and then looked behind him.

Iain smiled and gave Sam's arm a pat. "Finish your movie. I'm fine."

Sam went back to his movie but glanced Iain's way periodically; it was clear what Iain said had been unnerving.

Iain turned back to Raphael. "You're going to D.C. with me?"

Raphael looked dumbfounded but nodded.

"We need your help, though, Iain," Mikael said. "I know you've believed in God for a long time, and at one time you committed your future to the Messiah. But you've been out of practice with your prayers, Iain. You need to pray. Prayer is what gives us strength. Lucifer has targeted you, so you need to empower *us*. Prayer does that."

Iain smiled. "I always wondered about that. It's comforting to know you're with me."

"Our Creator is with you too, Iain. You believed in him, so you can talk to him now. Your conversations with him are what empower us. Can you do that?"

"Sure."

"Always remember that, Iain. Prayer changes things."

Iain cocked his head. "Are you really real . . . or are you just in my head?"

Mikael chuckled. "A little of both, I guess."

"So I won't see you when I'm cured, will I?"

Mikael shook his head. "Probably not. But that won't mean we aren't real, Iain, just as our Creator—and yours—remains real. Don't forget that."

* * * * *

Kaitlyn woke when she felt the tires hit the runway. She sat up quickly and looked over at Iain. He was awake but staring straight ahead.

Leaning over, she whispered to Sam. "How is he?"

"Doing better physically, but he's been talking to angels, apparently."

Concern swelled within her as she displayed a worried look. "That bad?"

"Apparently schizophrenia can be one of the symptoms. I've been doing some reading on the possible symptoms. It seems he's been getting almost all of them." He forced a smile. "No more convulsions, though."

"I guess we do need to thank God for small miracles."

Sam nodded. "At least talking to the 'angels' has kept him calm."

Kaitlyn wiped a tear from her cheek. "Who would have thought schizophrenia would be counted as a blessing?" She shook her head. "I hope those monsters pay for what they have done and are planning on doing."

"Well, if I have anything to say about the matter, they will definitely pay."

CHAPTER 30

ARRIVAL

Customs proved to be as busy as ever. D.C. is, after all, as much of a tourist city as it is a political and highly populated one. Sam, Kaitlyn, and Iain waited in line for what seemed way too long.

Kaitlyn kept looking at Iain with concern. She got Sam's attention and lowered her voice. "Do you really think Iain can go through customs on his own? Shouldn't we have someone help escort him through?"

Sam glanced at Iain and then back. "He seems fine for the moment. He still thinks he's talking to angels, and that keeps him calm, so we should be good. Besides, asking for assistance will only lead to questions, which will cause delays, which eats into time we don't have."

"You're right," Kaitlyn said. She looked at Iain, who was smiling and nodding. He seemed to be carrying on a conversation with someone. "I just wish this line would go faster. We need to get to the lab as quickly as possible."

* * * * *

Iain glanced around as if in wonderment. "There are so many angels here."

Mikael looked around also—but in concern, not amazement. "Iain, these are bad angels. They want you to be delayed and not get to the lab where your friend Ted can help you."

Demons were on the periphery, each looking at them but hesitant to act until they had larger numbers, which would not be long now.

"Raphael, go summon Quentillious, Uriel, Azel, and their armies. I feel we will have a battle today. Go now! Return as quickly as possible."

Raphael nodded and disappeared.

"Wow," Iain said. "That was cool. I wish I could do that."

Mikael smiled but kept a wary eye on the demons continuing to appear. "Don't worry. You'll be able to do that one day."

"Can I try it now?"

Mikael shook his head. "Can't do it today. But one day, when you're in the dimension the Master has created for all those who follow him, you will. Today, Iain, you need to focus on the questions the customs agent will ask. Only answer the questions, and don't try and carry on a conversation."

Iain got a worried look. "What if I can't remember what he asks?"

"Don't worry. That's why I'm here. I'll help you remember." He pointed to the demons that were starting to get braver and move closer. "Those will try to make you forget, or make the customs agent not approve your reentry. But don't worry. I won't let you down. So don't panic—no matter what."

Iain nodded.

"Iain, this is important: you may see me fight, but don't be alarmed by that."

"You mean I get to see angels fight? Cool."

Mikael laughed. "Not really an enjoyment, but it is necessary."

A look of disappointment suddenly swept across Iain's face. "I won't get to remember this, will I?"

Mikael looked around again, the demons moving ever closer. It seemed the closer Iain got to the customs agent, the braver and closer the demons came. "Well, that's really up to the Master. Yet your brain will likely tell you this was all a hallucination . . . if you *do* remember."

"Are all hallucinations this way?"

"Not necessarily. Some are real, many are not."

"How do I know the difference?"

Mikael touched Iain's chest. "By allowing the Holy Spirit to guide you into all truth. Scripture is that truth."

"Whoa!" Iain said as he put his hands on his chest. "I just felt warmth pass all the way through me." He looked over at Kaitlyn, eyes wide. "I was just touched by an angel."

* * * * *

Sam put his hand on Iain's shoulder. "That's wonderful, Iain. We should all be so lucky."

Iain nodded as a huge grin swept his face.

Kaitlyn turned away, pursing her lips, and blinking to remove the excess moisture from her eyes. Sam put his hand on her upper back and rubbed softly. "Deep breath. It will be okay. Don't worry; we'll get him back. We will. I just know it."

Kaitlyn took a deep breath and let it out slowly.

"Did that help?"

Kaitlyn looked at Sam and smiled. "Surprisingly, it did."

Sam pointed forward with his head. "Okay, you're up."

Kaitlyn walked to the customs agent who had just finished with another arrival. She gave a quick glance back. Sam nodded. She focused on what she had to do.

Sam got Iain's attention. "Okay, Iain. I want you to walk to the next open customs agent. Okay?"

"Okay," Iain said.

"Just answer the questions they ask. Don't say anything else."

Iain nodded. "Don't worry, Sam. I have an angel to help me."

Sam patted his back. "Great. Just listen to your angel, but only *speak* to the customs agent. Okay, buddy?"

Iain smiled. "That's what the angel said."

"You have one smart angel there, Iain. Okay, you're up." He pointed to the open customs agent, and Iain stepped forward.

* * * * *

Iain saw all the angels coming toward him as he approached the customs agent's desk. What did Mikael call them? *Demons.* They didn't look like what he pictured as demons, but they did look evil. They exuded a sense of foreboding and ill will.

"Try to focus on the customs agent and not the fighting that will go on," Mikael said. "Can you do that?"

"I'll try."

"Good." Mikael drew his sword. "Because . . . here they come."

Iain handed his passport and declaration form to the agent, but then flinched as a demon almost touched him before Mikael fought the demon back.

The customs agent gave Iain a curious look. "Are you all right, sir?"

Iain smiled. "Yes, I'm fine."

As the agent looked over his passport and declaration form, Iain looked at what was happening around him. He was amazed at how Mikael could fight off so many demons at once.

The first couple of demons Mikael was able to defeat quickly and easily. They each went catatonic, their swords falling to the floor. Yet as he fought, others tried to reach the customs agent to influence him to detain Iain. As Mikael was fighting two more, Iain saw another demon manage to elude Mikael and get next to the customs agent.

The customs agent picked up his stamp but then hesitated. He looked at Iain, giving him a curious look, something like mistrust. "Did you say you had something to declare?"

Iain shook his head. His eyes grew wide as he saw Mikael rush over to push the demon back.

The customs agent blinked several times and looked at Iain's passport as if this was the first time he had seen it.

Iain gasped when he saw Mikael unfurl his large wings and swoop into the air in combat. He thought it one of the most impressive things he had ever seen. Mikael's huge wings propelled him one way and then another as he fought demon after demon in swift succession. Another demon flew to the customs agent, but Mikael swooped down and made the angel turn catatonic.

"Sir. Sir, I asked you a question."

Iain looked back at the agent. "I'm sorry. What was the question?"

"Do you have anything to declare?"

Iain shook his head. "No, nothing to declare."

The agent gave Iain a curious look, followed his gaze, and then shook his head as he picked up his stamp. Another demon flew in and stood right next to the man, causing him to once again hesitate.

At that moment other angels appeared, and the battle turned into a vast organization of chaos. Angels and demons fought—some on the ground, many in the air, and some even a combination of the two. Demons fell to the ground in large numbers. A few of the angels went catatonic, but far more demons did so than angels.

Iain was enthralled with the spectacle. He noticed everyone went about their normal routine totally oblivious to the battle raging around them.

Another angel swooped down and engaged the demon next to the customs agent. The agent blinked rapidly and shook his head as if trying to recover from a state of confusion. He looked at Iain and then the passport. This time he stamped it and handed it back to him. "Have a good day," he said.

Iain gave a warm smile. "You too." He went through the turnstile and met up with Kaitlyn. Turning, he saw the last demon fall to the floor. The remaining angels rallied around Mikael as if waiting for new orders.

Iain shook his head. "Amazing, truly amazing," he said only to himself.

* * * * *

Kaitlyn breathed a sigh of relief. They had made it through one of her biggest worries. She just wished that was the only worry on her mind. "Let's get going," she said.

Sam grabbed Iain's shoulder and gave a squeeze. "You did it, buddy. Good job. I knew you could."

"Oh, it was the angels. They were amazing."

Sam looked at Kaitlyn with eyebrows raised and then back at Iain. "They always are, aren't they?"

Iain nodded with a grin.

Sam patted Iain's back. "Okay. Let's get a cab and get you to the lab."

As Sam led Iain out the doors to where the taxis were lined up for receiving passengers, Kaitlyn noticed Iain look back one final time and smile. Evidently he was still seeing the angels which only he could see. In short order, all three were in a cab traveling toward the city.

Kaitlyn, between Iain and Sam, sat back and let out a long sigh.

Sam patted her arm. "It won't be long now. Hopefully Ted will have some answers when we arrive." He leaned forward to get a glimpse of Iain. "How's he doing?"

She looked over. "Seems to be sleeping again. I guess all that wore him out." She furrowed her brow. "Why do you think it took the agent so long to stamp his passport? It was barely three minutes for the two of us. He must have been with the customs agent for a good ten minutes or more."

Sam shook his head. "But did you notice, while Iain was looking around like he was observing . . . something, the agent picked up his stamp several times. And then he would set it down and ask Iain the same question repeatedly."

Kaitlyn nodded. "That made me so very nervous. It was the strangest thing."

Sam sat back in his seat. "Well, that's over now. We can finally focus on getting him well. And on this looming national threat."

CHAPTER 31

PLANNING ON DUAL FRONTS

Until their taxi reached the National Laboratory, Kaitlyn kept an eye on Iain. Every so often his limbs would undergo involuntary tremors. These didn't seem to wake him, but they did appear to make him sleep less soundly. She knew this likely contributed to his sudden outbursts as lack of quality sleep lowers one's irritation threshold . . . as well as simply leaving that person with the frustration of having a body that can no longer be controlled. Yet for Kaitlyn, these understandings did not stop the horror of experiencing Iain's outbursts as they were so uncharacteristic of who he truly was.

When the taxi arrived, Sam jumped out his side and ran around to help Iain from the vehicle. Iain got about halfway outside the taxi when his body went into involuntary tremors. They were so violent they made Sam appear spastic as well while he held onto Iain as tightly as possible.

Kaitlyn's eyes glistened and she tried not to cry. It broke her heart to see him this way. As the tremors subsided, Sam gently wiped away the tears that were trickling down Iain's cheeks. "Okay now, buddy?"

Iain nodded as he straightened and held onto the car door. He took in a deep breath and let it out quickly through his nose in frustration—likely at himself. Sam stood next to Iain and put one arm around his torso just under his arm as Iain put an arm around Sam's neck.

Kaitlyn followed the two into the facility and to the floor where Ted and Amanda would be working.

Ted was at a lab bench when they arrived. When he saw them he stood, waved, and rushed over. "Bev, Iain, Sam, so good to see you." He gave Kaitlyn a hug and kiss on her cheek. Sam shook Ted's hand with his free hand. Iain held out a shaky hand. Ted shook it and gave Iain a pat on his shoulder. "Good to see you, buddy."

"S-s-same here, T-T-Ted," he said as his body went into a small tremor once more.

Ted smiled but gave Kaitlyn a look with eyes wide as if silently saying he couldn't believe Iain's deterioration was so swift. "Why not come to my office?" he said to Iain. "You can sit, and it even has a cot as I've had to sleep here sometimes."

Sam helped Iain get to Ted's office on the other side of the large room and helped lower him into a seat. Ted quickly retrieved a couple other chairs from nearby offices so everyone could have a seat.

"So what do we know?" Kaitlyn asked almost as soon as Ted had lowered himself to his chair.

"Well, I was able to get blood and tissue samples from Walt sent here."

"The informed consent went through, then, I guess?" Kaitlyn asked.

Ted nodded. "And I was able to isolate some of the nano-bots that Dr. Gomez had administered to the study patients and was able to figure out the code that made them do their tissue targeting." He shrugged. "It saved me some time in the long run as I was able to utilize the code Gomez had already created."

"And whaaat have you f-f-found?" Iain asked.

"Well, I need some of your blood, buddy, so I can see what you have and compare it to what I know and see if I'm in the right ballpark at least."

Iain held out his arm. "All yours."

Ted laughed. "Well, I think I can leave some with you." He stood. "Let me get a collection kit and I'll be right back. The faster I get started, the faster I can get to our goal."

Kaitlyn followed Ted out and ran into Amanda coming down the corridor.

"Kaitlyn! You're here." Amanda lowered her voice. "How's Iain?"

Kaitlyn's eyes watered despite her best efforts. She shook her head. "Not good, I'm afraid. He has so many deteriorating symptoms already."

Amanda gave a sympathetic look. "I'm so sorry, Kaitlyn." She put her hand on Kaitlyn's upper arm. "We'll do all that we can for sure."

Kaitlyn nodded. "I know. Ted's getting started already."

"Good," Amanda said. "I just came from a meeting about the information you and Iain provided about the coming threat. We need to talk and plan. Maybe we can do that over dinner. But I know Iain's well-being takes precedence right now." She gave a warm smile. "Let me go give Iain a hello."

Kaitlyn smiled back weakly. "Yes, he'd like that, I think."

As Amanda left, Kaitlyn went to find Ted. He had already obtained the blood sample from Iain and had it under a microscope.

"So, what's the plan? How can I help?" she asked.

Ted gestured to the microscope; Kaitlyn had a look.

"These," Ted said, standing behind her, "are very similar in structure to those Gomez used in the Jewish patients in our study."

Kaitlyn looked up from the microscope. "Does that mean they may be responsive to codes you develop?"

Ted grimaced. "In theory, yes. But they are likely highly encrypted, so they won't likely respond."

Kaitlyn gave a tired sigh.

"But this means *how* they function is likely very similar, so that will help me as I prepare coding for how to respond to their deadly scheme."

"You mean for Iain, or for what's coming?"

"Here." Ted pulled a chair in front of a monitor. "Sit here and I'll show you. I put this mock-up together to better help me understand and to show our uppity-ups what we're doing." He grinned. "The higher up the chain we go, the more of a visual learner almost all of them appear to be."

Kaitlyn nodded. "Fewer and fewer scientists the farther up you go."

"Exactly. So they find this helpful." Ted shrugged. "When they believe me, that is."

"So show me."

Ted focused on the task at hand. "The way I see it, there are two ways to affect the production of this needed enzyme."

"Either the carrier protein or the chaperonin."

"Precisely," Ted said. "As you see here in this cartoon I created, the carrier protein transports the mRNA for making the beta-hexosaminidase protein into the cell. In Tay-Sachs, this carrier protein is deficient or defective, so you get little of the protein made, thereby allowing a buildup of these neurotoxic gangliosides because there is no longer an enzyme to break them down."

Ted waited for the other instructional cartoon to initiate.

"Or, if the carrier protein is fine and the enzyme protein is made, it has to be placed in the protein structure—the chaperonin—for it to fold the enzyme protein into its viable three-dimensional structure."

Kaitlyn nodded. "And if that is defective, then you still don't have a viable enzyme protein to break down the neurotoxic gangliosides."

Ted sat next to her. "I think the first scenario is what happens to patients with Tay-Sachs. The second scenario is what has happened to Iain."

Kaitlyn sat back. "Okay, that explains *what* has happened, but not *how* we correct the problem." Her eyes started to grow watery again. "Ted, we don't have a lot of time. It's been less than forty-eight hours and he's almost helpless already. It won't be long before it affects his breathing. Once that happens . . . " She couldn't say the words.

Ted put his hand on her shoulder. "Don't go there, Bev. I need you with me here and now to solve this. I have ideas, just not solutions—yet."

Kaitlyn jerked to an affirmative nod to acknowledge Ted. "Okay. You're right." She took a deep breath through her nose and let it out through her mouth. "What do you need?"

"Okay, here is what I have so far. I know that the nanobots used by Gomez in the patients are similar in structure to what he used on Iain. Yet the ones in the patients were just identifying those with the Tay-Sachs mutation in their genome. The ones given to Iain act similarly but also affect the chaperonin for the activation of beta-hexosaminidase. I can't turn them off because I can't access their code."

"I thought you were going to create new ones to counteract the ones administered."

"Yes, that was my plan," Ted said. "But if I don't know how they are affecting the chaperonin, I don't know how to reverse the effect."

Kaitlyn cupped her face with her palms. "Those monsters! How could physicians become so inhumane?"

Ted sighed deeply. "They feel their cause is not only just but a righteous one. That makes them feel a few sacrifices are acceptable."

Kaitlyn's gaze shot to Ted with a look of disbelief.

Ted held up his hands in a defensive stance. "I'm not justifying them—at all. Just explaining how their deranged thinking works to allow them to sleep at night."

Kaitlyn sighed. "Our world has turned into a scary place." She got a faraway look in her eyes. "And we've helped create it."

Ted put his hand on her upper arm. "No, Bev. We plan to make it a better place. Don't put yourself in the same category as these deranged lunatics. You are *not*. Your goal is to ease suffering—not create it."

"But are we creating more suffering than we are helping?"

Ted put his hands on her shoulders and locked his gaze with hers. "Kaitlyn Beverly Sheridan Crusher, you listen to me. You are one of the most brilliant minds I have ever met." He bobbed his head back and forth slightly. "Next to mine, of course."

Kaitlyn couldn't help but smile.

"So you stop this negative thinking and start thinking positively. Iain, and the world, are counting on you."

Kaitlyn nodded and gave a big in-and-out breath. "You're right." She gave a smirk and pushed on Ted's shoulder. "But stop sounding like my mother."

Ted laughed. "I do whatever it takes. Now back to the problem at hand."

A thought suddenly hit Kaitlyn. "So you can't reverse what these nanobots have done or are doing?"

"Right," Ted said. He smiled slightly. "But you've come up with something, haven't you?"

She smiled back. "What if you have your nanobots . . . *destroy* the nanobots already in Iain's body?"

Ted's posture froze as though he had gone into suspended animation. He was in deep thought in that position for several seconds. His gaze then returned to her. "Bev! That's brilliant! Simply brilliant!" He looked from her to the microscope and then back. "A war. We need to create a nanobot war!" He looked down for a few seconds and then back her way. "But how do we make nanobots created identically recognize one as being different from the other?"

Kaitlyn put her hand to her chin. Another thought hit her. "Frequency!"

Ted froze again. His hands went wide. "Frequency! Of course!" His arms then flew around her torso in a big hug. "I knew that brain of yours would come through."

Ted looked nearly giddy, and he literally bounced up and down on his stool. "I don't have to understand Dr. Gomez's nanobots at all—just their composition." His eyes went wide. "Bev, I can start on this immediately!"

"And if you get a few made, you can have them self-replicate."

Ted shook his index finger. "Yes. I can have them replicate and destroy until no alternate frequency is detected."

Kaitlyn nodded. "And then have them self-destruct."

Ted's enthusiasm waned just a bit. "Why is that? They'll be inert once they complete their task."

"But hackable," Kaitlyn said. "I know you'll have them encrypted, but I don't want to take any chances. Once they do their job and the sphingolipid GM2 gangliosides are broken down for his neurocognitive function to come back to normal, we need to have them self-destruct."

"Okay," Ted said. "That should be easy enough to make happen."

"And how long is this going to take?"

Ted shook his head. "I don't really know." He was in thought for a few seconds. "Normally, I'd give myself a month to have a prototype."

Kaitlyn's eyes went wide and her voice developed a hoarse whisper. "Ted, we don't have that kind of time! Iain won't last that long."

"I know that, Bev. Let me finish, please."

Kaitlyn nodded. "Yes. Yes, of course. Sorry. Go ahead."

"But if we all work around the clock, we can speed that up to, hopefully, a few days."

Kaitlyn grew quiet. "I just hope that's enough time."

"So do I, Bev. So do I."

CHAPTER 32

PROGRESS AT LAST

Kaitlyn overheard Ted speaking to Sam and Amanda. She felt a mixture of worry and confidence in them.

Both looked at each other and then at Ted, shaking their heads.

"Ted, we're not scientists," Amanda said. "We've never done anything like this before."

Sam nodded his agreement.

"You've both baked a cake before, right?"

Both nodded, though Sam added, "It came out burnt, though."

Ted laughed. "No problem, because you don't have to put this in the oven." He held up a laminated piece of paper. "Just follow whatever it says to do here. Then come get me. It's basically a buffered solution, so even easier than a cake." He looked from one to the other. "This will be a real time-saver for me. Bev and I need to prepare the nanobots. Having you make the milieu to place them in will really help us, and in the long run, help Iain."

"Thanks for the guilt trip, Ted," Sam said.

"Did it work?"

Amanda nodded.

"Good. Now get to work, and I'll check on you a little later. If you get stuck, just call me or Bev. We're just a couple of lab benches away, okay?"

Both nodded and began to read the instructions Ted had prepared for them.

As Ted came to where Kaitlyn was working, she flipped up the binocular glasses she was wearing. "How are they progressing?"

Ted gave a small wave. "They'll be fine. I think they just don't want to make a mistake, but I'm sure they'll do fine once they get into it." He pointed to her work. "How's it going here?"

"So far, so good. I've duplicated most of what Dr. Gomez had done on his nanobots, but I added a different luciferin to ours. That way we can know they are working as they'll produce blue bioluminescence rather than the yellow Gomez was using."

"Bev, that's brilliant," Ted said with a broad grin. He shook his head. "We always do so much better when we work together."

Kaitlyn smiled. She had missed being in the lab with Ted. They seemed to function on a similar wavelength, and they always energized each other's creative thought processes.

"So I need you to work on the frequency component that will trigger their reactivity against the other nanobots," Kaitlyn said. She pointed to the monitor which displayed the nanobot on which she was working. "When I looked at Iain's blood sample, those nanobots seem to bind with this structure here." She used the pointer to show a slight protrusion on the nanobots' outer membrane. "My guess is that when it binds, it throws off the correct confirmation the chaperonin needs to bind to the enzyme."

"So if we destroy the nanobot," Ted said, "the chaperonin will go back to the proper configuration."

"Correct. As long as we can ensure this structure does not remain."

"Okay, I'll work on how the nanobot will decompose that structure, and you work on how our nanobots will destroy the membrane of the other nanobots but keep that of ours intact until we tell them to self-destruct."

Kaitlyn nodded. "Then we can verify they are doing what they need to do with a sequence of scans of Iain's body. At first the yellow should decrease and the blue increase. Then the blue should fade away. That would let us know his body is free of all nanobots."

Ted smiled broadly. "It seems we have the plan in place. We just need to execute it."

Kaitlyn looked at her watch. "I'm going to take a short break and check on Iain. And get him something to eat."

"Okay," Ted said. "You know where to find me if needed."

Kaitlyn patted his arm and walked to Ted's office where they had left Iain—asleep at the time. It seemed he needed more and more sleep, or at least he slept more and more. As she peered into the office, Iain was still on the cot. His eyes were closed, but his limbs jerked spastically. She paused and put her forehead on the doorframe trying to hold back tears. Seeing him like this nearly crushed her. After a few seconds she straightened, wiped her cheeks, and forced a smile.

"Hi, Iain. Getting hungry?"

No response. She bent over and lightly shook his shoulder. He slowly woke, looking disoriented until he saw her. Then a smile slowly came across his face.

"Hi," he said as he tried to sit up.

She grabbed his shoulders and helped him pull upward. "Hungry?"

He nodded. "A little."

"What do you want? I'll go get it."

Iain rubbed his temple. "I think someone already asked me that."

Kaitlyn cocked her head. She was afraid Iain's schizophrenia had kicked in again. Then she heard a light rap on the doorframe. She turned, and one of the lab techs was there holding a tray.

"Hi, Dr. Sheridan. I'm Tina. I hope you don't mind. I came in earlier as he seemed rather restless. He was hungry, so I went to the cafeteria to get something for him. There's likely enough for two if you want to eat with him."

"That's so thoughtful," Kaitlyn said, standing and taking the tray. "Thank you."

Tina made a dismissive gesture. "Oh, no problem at all." She smiled and turned, then turned back. "I just wanted to say it is an honor to have you with us. I've learned so much from your publications."

"Well, thank you. I'm glad you found them helpful."

Tina pointed to her workstation. "I'm on the last lab bench in the corner if you need anything."

Kaitlyn nodded as Tina turned and left the office. Suddenly, another thought came to her. She stepped to the door. "Tina?"

Tina headed back toward the office. "Need something?"

"Do you know Amanda Horne and Sam Atway?" She pointed to the two of them toward the middle of the room working at one of the lab benches.

Tina nodded.

"You think you could help them out? Do you have some time?"

"Oh, sure," Tina said. "No problem. What do you need?"

"They've been tasked with the milieu for the nanobots, but they don't really understand the technicalities. I'm sure they're capable, but they would likely really appreciate the help."

Tina's eyes went wide. "Oh, the isosmotic buffer you published last year?"

Kaitlyn nodded.

"I've made that several times." She smiled. "I've found it useful for more than just nanobots. It's also very good for certain tissue samples as well." She put her hand on Kaitlyn's arm. "I'll go over right now and offer my help."

"Thanks a million, Tina."

"Uh, Dr. Sheridan, I know time is critical."

Likely seeing the uneasiness on Kaitlyn's face of her forthright statement, Tina added, her voice low, "I'm sorry. Rumors get around, I'm afraid. I'm just saying that because there are several of us who are willing to help, you know—if you want."

Kaitlyn's eyes went wide. "Really? But you all have other responsibilities."

"Oh, to get a chance to work with you and Mr. Jordan . . . that would be such an honor." She pointed toward the door with her head and lowered her voice. "And for such a worthwhile cause." She shrugged. "I think all it would take is for Agent Horne to speak to our director, Dr. Korvosky."

"Well, I'll certainly talk with Amanda."

Tina put her hand on Kaitlyn's arm. "But even if our director says no, which I don't think he will, several of us would still be willing to help, to work on our off time—even pulling all-nighters if needed."

Kaitlyn put her hand to her chest. "Oh, Tina, that would be so helpful." She knew that would help them achieve their goal so much faster. *Why didn't I think of involving others?* she wondered. "Thank you—sincerely."

Tina smiled. "Not a problem at all." She was ready to leave the office area again when she looked back at Kaitlyn once more. "Dr. Sheridan, may I ask another question?"

Kaitlyn raised her eyebrows as if to answer with a yes.

"We've heard Mr. Jordan call you Bev. But others call you Kaitlyn."

Kaitlyn chuckled. "Yes, Ted and I go way back. It's sort of a pet name he's given me." She waved her hand in a dismissive gesture. "Too much explanation to go into."

"Oh, you don't need to," Tina said. "We were just wondering." She smiled. "That's sweet, though."

Tina walked to where Sam and Amanda were working and Kaitlyn turned back to the office, feeling so much lighter in spirit. She sat next to Iain.

"Okay, let's see what Tina brought."

CHAPTER 33

WORKING TOGETHER FOR A CURE

The next thirty-six hours were filled with a whirlwind of activity. Kaitlyn couldn't have been more impressed with the quality of the people in this laboratory and the work they performed. While Dr. Korvosky, the department director, was sympathetic to their plight, he was insistent that scheduled work get done. Still, the four technicians who wanted to help Iain banded together to get their work done and still contributed everything they could to help. To keep from complete burnout, Ted insisted everyone take a six-hour break to rest and sleep.

Before they turned in for their needed rest, Ted, Kaitlyn, Amanda, and Sam met in the break room for a small debrief. Kaitlyn poured her umpteenth cup of coffee and sat with the others. "So, how do you feel everything is going?" she asked, looking around the room.

"Kaitlyn, having Tina help Sam and I with the buffer solutions was such a brilliant idea," Amanda said. "She also recruited her friend Janice to help out."

Sam nodded. "They showed us so many shortcuts for getting things done. We never would have discovered those on our own. Their help saved us at least half a day."

"Oh, easily," Amanda added.

Kaitlyn added, "Her bringing Janice on board allowed her to help me with the nanobot assembly. Her dexterity with microscopic tools is remarkable." She looked at Ted. "You think we can recruit her once all this is over?"

Ted laughed. "Not only her, but Colm as well. His computer skills rival mine, and his coding speed definitely goes beyond what I can do."

"And don't forget about Charles," Kaitlyn said. "He seems to know something about almost everything and seems able to repair almost anything." She shook her head. "We hit a gold mine with all four of them."

"For sure," Ted said. "You know, I think we may be able to wrap things up by noon tomorrow. Then it's just a matter of self-replication by the nanobots, a final check, and I think we'll be ready for administration."

Kaitlyn's eyes widened. "Really? We're almost there?"

Ted smiled. "I think so, but I have to give a caution. We won't really know until the final check is done."

"But it looks promising, though. Right?" Kaitlyn asked.

Ted chuckled. "Yes, Bev. But we need to temper our enthusiasm and work on the side of caution. We owe that to Iain."

All nodded.

"Speaking of caution," Amanda said. "I need to bring this up so we can be ready for the next step after this."

All eyes turned her way.

"Our administration is looking at what we are doing very carefully. If we're successful with Iain, I think they will listen to us with more earnest." She looked at Ted. "They've been impressed with your presentations but have really looked at them as theoretical—not necessarily practical."

Sam broke in. "But Goldberg is on our side, and knowing what has happened to Iain has him gravely concerned. He's trying to help his superiors understand the concern as well."

Ted shook his head. "But what's holding them back from seeing the same concern?"

Amanda shrugged. "They hear the word 'virus' and think we can produce a vaccine to solve the problem."

Kaitlyn and Ted sighed in frustration, nearly in unison.

"Okay," Ted said. "Set up a meeting and we'll try and explain that this goes so far beyond what we have experienced to date. The virus is only a vector here. Even if the virus is killed, it won't stop what Gomez and Haneberg are unleashing."

Amanda nodded. "I'll try. Also, I heard that the intel reads that Gomez and Haneberg will be coming to New York some-time next week."

Kaitlyn scrunched her brow. "Surely you don't think they're the ones who will do their own dirty work, do you? They're too smart to be caught with their hands in the cookie jar, so to speak."

Amanda shook her head. "No, I agree. Yet they want to be present to witness the genesis of their plague." She looked at Kaitlyn. "What did you say they called it?"

"Luciferian Plague."

"Right," Amanda said. "The plague of the devil. Seems to fit, doesn't it?"

"What do you mean?" Sam asked.

Amanda shrugged. "Well, I heard that Haneberg wants to get rid of Jewish priests to prevent their future temple from being functional. Isn't that what the devil is supposedly trying to do: prevent the end of days from occurring so he can rule the world instead?"

"You lost me," Sam said.

"I just mean, first of all, it's a devilish thing to do, and if end times prophecy is true, getting rid of Jews, God's supposedly chosen people, would be something he would want to do."

"Are you saying Haneberg is being used by the devil?" Sam asked.

"Well, I don't know if I really believe in such things," Amanda said. "But after seeing what they did to Iain, I can't believe any sane person would do something like that to anyone. I wouldn't count possession out, necessarily."

"These people are definitely insane and deranged," Sam said. "But I'm not sure if possessed by the devil is where I would go."

"Not sure I would have before now, either," Amanda said. "I'm just saying I'm not ruling anything out at this point." She tapped her knees with her palms. "Enough of this discussion. We all need to get a few hours of sleep so we can function in a coherent manner tomorrow."

"Right," Ted said. "Find a chair, desk, or floor somewhere, and we'll meet back here in . . . " He looked at his watch. " . . . five hours. We then have four hours to complete everything. Then it's showtime."

When Kaitlyn got back to Ted's office to check on Iain, she found Charles and Tina just outside Ted's office door sandwiching an ottoman between two square plush chairs to form a type of bed. Tina had a blanket under her arm.

"What's this?" Kaitlyn asked.

Tina grinned. "A bed for you." She placed the blanket in one of the chairs.

Kaitlyn looked from one to the other. "Where on earth did you find these?"

Charles laughed and shrugged. "There's a lounge on the first floor."

"Plus, no one is using them at this hour," Tina added. "We can put them back first thing tomorrow."

Kaitlyn gave Tina and Charles a hug. "You two are sweet. Thank you."

"Get some rest," Tina said. "We'll be back here for the final prep." She gestured to the office. "I just checked on him. He's sleeping. Fitfully, but sleeping."

Both waved as they left.

Kaitlyn looked in on Iain. Tina was right. As she watched him, he went into periodic spastic movements. These woke him somewhat but not fully. He then fell back into a deeper slumber. She went closer and turned his pillow over. The top side had a good deal of drool due to Iain not being able to swallow well. She stood over him for several minutes, her eyes misty. And yet no actual tears formed.

She wondered: *have I become too insensitive already, or am I just out of tears?*

CHAPTER 34

NANOBOTS FOR IAIN

Kaitlyn heard a *beep, beep, beep;* the sound seemed as though it was coming from far away. As she woke, she realized it was her phone. As she turned off the alarm, her brain forced her to realize the importance of today, and an adrenaline rush kicked in; she sat up quickly. Stretching, she looked around to see if anyone else was up. She saw Charles and Tina working with Ted. Apparently, others had not yet awakened. She quickly went to the restroom, washed her face, and put on just enough makeup to make her feel comfortable enough to be seen in public.

As she approached Ted, she saw Amanda and Sam approaching from the other side. Colm sat on the other side of Ted looking totally exhausted. She appreciated his dedication despite how he must be feeling.

"Well, we're finally here," Ted said. "I just want to thank all of you for your hard work." He turned to Colm and patted his upper back as he was practically laying on the bench top. "And especially to Colm here, who helped me start the replication subroutine about two hours ago. That means rather than having the final checks at noon, we can likely administer at noon."

Everyone gave light claps so they wouldn't disturb those working in the lab, even though there were few in at this early hour.

"Here's everyone's assignment so we can be ready by noon. Amanda . . . " He looked around and pointed at her and then Sam. "Both of you slowly warm the buffer solution you made, bringing it to body temperature."

They nodded.

"And Janice . . . " He turned, then pointed and smiled when he saw her. "Take periodic temperature readings of the buffer solution and ensure it doesn't go over 37 degrees Celsius. Then check its osmolarity to be sure it's compatible with human physiological processes and then pass it through a 0.22 micron filter to make it sterile."

"And I'll assist in other ways where and when I can," Janice added.

"Great," Ted said. "Now, Charles and Tina, I want you both to assist Bev in checking periodic samples of nanobots to be sure they are replicating correctly and with the correct replication rate."

Both nodded. Ted wagged an index finger at them. "And call me or Bev if anything looks out of the ordinary."

"You got it," Charles said.

"I'll be working with Colm to ensure the proper coding is done and is robust and safely encrypted." He looked at his watch again. "Everyone, meet back here at a quarter to noon and we'll start Iain's treatment."

Everyone stepped away to their stations.

Charles walked over to Kaitlyn. "Dr. Sheridan, Tina and I will be with you in just a few minutes. We're going to take your bed back to the lounge on the first floor."

Kaitlyn smiled. "Sure. And thank you for that."

"No problem," Charles said. "Shall I bring something back from the cafeteria for Dr. Thornwhite to eat?"

"Yes, please. That would be most helpful. We all can take turns feeding him and watching him while we get the finishing touches together."

Kaitlyn then got to work examining the nanobots. It was a tedious but necessary process. Very quickly, she became engrossed in her work. After several minutes she looked up as she felt Tina and Charles should be back from their furniture return and food run. She turned suddenly upon hearing someone yell her name.

"Dr. Sheridan! Dr. Sheridan! I don't think he's breathing!" It was Tina rushing her way.

Kaitlyn immediately ran to Ted's office. Charles was kneeling over Iain with his head on Iain's chest trying to listen for a heartbeat. He immediately moved away upon seeing Kaitlyn enter. She tried to remain calm so she could think and remember what she would need to do if, indeed, his heart had stopped. She knelt and felt for his carotid artery on the side of his neck. She was hopeful because his color still looked good. She had to reposition her fingers a couple of times, but eventually she did feel his pulse. She breathed a sigh of relief.

"It's very faint, but there is a pulse." She turned to Tina. "His breathing is so shallow that his chest is barely rising."

Tina put her hand to her chest. "I'm so glad. Sorry for causing such a scare."

Kaitlyn stood and laid a hand on Tina's shoulder. "No, you did the right thing." She looked at the others. "We are literally running out of time. We need to get this done as fast as possible or all our efforts will have been in vain."

Everyone nodded and left for their stations.

Kaitlyn caught up with Ted. "Ted, we need to start administration before noon. I'm not sure if his body can hold out until then. Since you've already started the replication process, can't they continue to do that in his body so those already viable can begin working?"

Ted put his hand to his chin and slowly nodded. "That may work. They've been replicating for about two hours." He paused in thought and then looked back at Kaitlyn. "Let's do this: you, Tina, and Charles check as many nanobots as possible over the next twenty minutes to look for any issues. We'll then administer half of them and give the other half at noon. That gives us additional options for any corrections if needed." He looked at his watch. "I'll check on you at ten o'clock."

Kaitlyn nodded and went to report the news to Tina and Charles. They each worked as rapidly and efficiently as possible. She was surprised how quickly the twenty minutes went by and didn't even realize ten o'clock had arrived . . . until she felt Ted tap her shoulder.

"What have you found?"

"Nothing," Kaitlyn said. "All nanobots look consistent with each other and all appear intact and functioning properly."

She looked at Tina and Charles; both nodded their agreement.

Ted smiled. "Then I think we're ready."

He motioned for Janice to head their way with the buffer. They prepared the administration solution in the fume hood by combining the nanobots with the buffer and placing them in a sterile syringe. They all walked to Ted's office and looked in while he knelt where Iain was lying. Ted tried to rouse him but couldn't. Iain looked as if he was dead. The only signs he was not were a periodic gurgling sound when he had trouble swallowing and an involuntary gasp that occurred when his breathing became so shallow his body forced him to suddenly inhale for more oxygen.

Kaitlyn prayed silently that they had prepared the nanobots in time for them to work—and that no irreparable neurological damage had occurred. In some ways she felt they had been working for a long time on this remedy, but the time elapsed from when Iain received the deadly nanobots to now had been less than one week. How were they going to cope with this type of problem on a national or international level? She really had no idea, and it bothered her greatly. But right now, Iain was all that mattered. It wasn't that the rest of the world did not matter, but the crisis right now was Iain, and he was the only person on which she could focus. Would the reversal of the symptoms be just as quick as their onset? She didn't know but truly hoped that would be the case.

Ted stood after he had given Iain the injection. "Well, it's just a matter of waiting. I'll administer the second dose of nanobots around noon."

Everyone dispersed but also stayed near the office so they could hear updates on Iain's progress on a regular basis . . .

At lunchtime, all watched as Ted gave the second dose. No one could see any change in Iain's condition since his first nanobot administration.

"Why is there no change yet, Mr. Jordan?" Tina asked.

"Well, there likely is change," Ted said. "But his body has had so much buildup of neurotoxic gangliosides that it will take time for us to see a visual change."

"Why don't you all go to lunch and then get some rest?" Kaitlyn added. "Then you can see him in the morning. Hopefully, we'll have something to report then."

All reluctantly nodded, and the four technicians left together.

"Physician, heal thyself," Amanda said, giving Kaitlyn a stern look before a grin formed.

Kaitlyn laughed. "And what is that supposed to mean?"

"You come with me to my hotel room, get a decent shower, a change of clothes, and a nap."

"Yes, go ahead, Bev," Ted said. "I'll be here and can call you if necessary."

Kaitlyn slowly nodded. "That does sound like a good offer."

"Great," Amanda said. "Don't worry. Iain is in good hands."

CHAPTER 35

IAIN'S COMEBACK

Early the next morning, everyone gathered outside Ted's office. Kaitlyn had so many emotions running through her: anxiousness, worry, expectation, doubt, fear, and even guilt. All looked anxious to find out if the dosed nanobots had been able to reverse Iain's neurodegeneration—any of it, or all of it.

"So how is he, Mr. Jordan?" Tina asked. "Is he better?"

Ted shrugged. "Don't know yet. He was pretty much unresponsive most of the afternoon yesterday. I couldn't even wake him to give him anything to eat. He's been sleeping all night—fitfully at first, but his muscle spasms seemed to subside as the night went on."

Ted turned to Kaitlyn. "I think you should be the one to wake him this morning." He patted her arm gently. "Of all our faces, I'm sure yours is the one he most wants to see."

Kaitlyn nodded with a smile and just a bit of a blush. She entered and slowly knelt next to Iain, sound asleep on the cot. *He looks so peaceful,* she thought. His breathing looked rhythmic and slow. There were no spastic muscle movements. *Will he still be the same Iain I know? Will there be any permanent*

241

personality changes, motor deficits, speech deficits? He had gone so far down the road of neurodegeneration that Kaitlyn was almost hesitant to find out. She wanted so desperately to have her Iain back. *My Iain?* she thought. Was that really what she meant? She realized it was true. Despite what she hated about Dr. Haneberg and what he had done, this had forced her to admit that she really did love this man. She just hoped she could get him back as he had been. She took a deep breath. This was it. She gently shook his shoulder.

"Iain? Iain? Can you hear me?"

Iain moved slowly as though coming out of a deep sleep and not wanting to come to reality. His eyes opened slowly. He then jerked upward, resting on his elbows. Confusion in his eyes slowly changed to recognition as he looked into Kaitlyn's eyes. A smile began to come across his face. "Kaitlyn."

Although she tried to smile, tears came to her eyes instead.

A concerned look came across Iain's face. He took his right hand and brushed the tears from her cheeks. "What's wrong?" he said softly.

She shook her head. "Nothing. Now." She put her hand to his cheek. "How do you feel?"

Iain looked in deep thought for a few seconds, then slowly nodded. "Pretty good." He smiled. "The fogginess is gone. I feel somewhat weak, but otherwise okay."

Kaitlyn smiled. "Good. I'm so glad. You had us worried."

"Yeah. Me too."

He sat up all the way and swiveled to put his feet on the office floor. It was then he noticed all the faces in the doorway looking at him. His eyebrows went up.

"Well, hello."

Everyone smiled and waved.

Iain waved back but gave a confused look to Kaitlyn.

She laughed. "Iain, this is everyone who helped you get better. You know, of course, Ted, Amanda, and Sam."

Iain replied, "Good to see each of you again."

"Welcome back, buddy," Ted said.

Amanda and Sam nodded, large grins on their faces.

"And these other four amazing individuals are technicians in this lab who helped us, and you, over these last few days. They are wonderful, and they took a great interest in your care and well-being."

Iain nodded to them. "Thanks. Thank you very much."

Kaitlyn pointed. "This is Tina, who helped us with the nanobots to fight your evil nanobots."

"So glad you're better," Tina said.

Iain smiled and nodded.

"And this is Charles, who helped Tina with the nanobots and several other things."

Charles waved hello and grinned.

"This is Janice, who helped Amanda and Sam with the buffer for the nanobots."

Janice gave a nod and Iain returned the same.

"Then we have Colm."

Colm gave a type of salute. Iain smiled.

"Colm is a programmer extraordinaire. He saved Ted so much time in getting the nanobots functional."

Iain put his hand to his chest. "My sincere thanks."

"No problem," Colm said. "Happy to be part of the team."

* * * * * *

Everyone looked at Iain for a few seconds—a few *long* seconds—which Iain felt was becoming painfully awkward. He glanced at Ted and shrugged.

Ted clasped his hands. "Okay, everyone. There's still a lot for us to do." He turned to Colm. "Perhaps you can take Iain to the fitness center so he can get a shower and change clothes." He turned to Iain. "Yes?"

Iain nodded. "Oh, a definite yes."

"Then, Bev," Ted said, "you can take him to breakfast while the rest of us get other things ready." He looked at Iain. "When you get back, I want to do a scan to see how the nanobots are functioning inside you."

"And later today," Amanda added, "we have to meet to discuss the next threat." She pointed toward Iain. "Including you, if you're up to it, of course."

Iain nodded. "Sure." He held up his hand. "Okay, someone help me up."

Colm stepped forward and pulled Iain up slowly but securely.

Iain wobbled a little. Colm grabbed his shoulders to steady him. "Easy there."

Iain took a couple of steps with Colm assisting and then began to walk more steadily with each step. He smiled. "I think I'm getting the hang of this thing called walking."

Colm grinned. "You're doing great, Dr. Thornwhite."

Ted patted Colm's shoulder as they passed. Iain saw Ted whisper something to Colm, but Iain kept walking to show that he didn't need the assistance he knew Ted told Colm he likely needed.

Colm nodded. "Understood." He quickly caught up with Iain. "Let me continue to help . . . for now . . . until you're sure you're stable." He grabbed Iain's suitcase just inside Ted's office door, where it had remained ever since Iain arrived.

Iain could feel his strength returning with each step. As he rode the elevator to the ground floor where the fitness center was located, memories began flooding back. He could remember almost everything that happened: his bursts of anger, his slurred speech, his stuttering, his fighting off Kaitlyn when she was only trying to be helpful. He did a mental groan. He had some making up to do. Then another memory came back: his talking to angels. He slipped into a mental pause. *Did I really talk to angels?* His memory felt real, but his mind was now telling him that was impossible. At some point he would have to contemplate that one. For now, he only wanted a shower—and some food. Definitely some food.

The shower felt heavenly. Iain realized he truly reeked. He laughed to himself. That was probably why Ted mentioned this as the first thing on his to-do list. Yet Iain was extremely thankful for the suggestion. It made him feel human again. After drying off and putting on fresh clothes, he stepped out to where Colm was waiting and putting his old clothes into a plastic bag.

Colm looked a little sheepish. "Sorry, Dr. Thornwhite. But I didn't want to put these in your suitcase with your other clothes."

Iain patted Colm on his upper back. "Wise decision, Colm. I almost want to burn them."

Colm laughed. "There are some washers here. You can do laundry later if you wish."

"Good to know. Now, what's next?"

"The cafeteria is on this floor. I'll take you there. I called Dr. Sheridan, and she will meet you there."

Iain nodded. After leaving the exercise facility, Colm led him down a small corridor that opened into a large room with all glass walls that housed a very modern-looking cafeteria with several food prep stations. As they looked around, Colm spotted Kaitlyn waving to them. He led Iain to the table where she was seated.

"Thanks, Colm," Kaitlyn said. "Want to join us for breakfast?"

Colm smiled but declined. "I'll get back to the lab." He patted the suitcase. "I'll take this back for you."

Iain shook Colm's hand. "Thanks a lot, son. I owe you."

Colm shook his head. "No. It was my pleasure. See you two later."

Iain turned back to Kaitlyn and sat. His eyes widened. "Wow! You've gotten me blueberry pancakes, eggs, and bacon?"

She shrugged. "Didn't know if you were up to standing in line, so I went ahead and made an executive decision."

He grinned as he poured syrup on his pancakes. "I like your decisions."

She laughed as she watched him eat.

He took a bite and then pointed to her plate with his knife. "Aren't you going to eat? Or am I just that amusing to watch?"

She took a bite of her eggs. "No. It's just good to see you able to eat on your own." Her tone became softer. "Iain, we came very near to losing you. Your neurological deterioration happened so fast." She shook her head and then looked into his eyes. "It was scary—very scary." Her eyes moistened but no tears came. "What those monsters did to you . . . It's . . . it's criminal."

Iain put his fork down and placed his hand on hers. "I know. I'm sorry you had to endure that." He paused. "And I'm sorry you had to endure my fits of rage and me pushing you away when you were only trying to help." He shook his head as his eyes also now grew watery. "Please forgive me."

"Oh, Iain. There is nothing to forgive. I knew it wasn't you." She watched his fingers rubbing over hers and then looked back into his eyes. "It was hard to endure, but not because you did it, because others made you do it. I know you would never do that intentionally."

They ate for a few minutes in silence, occasionally glancing at each other and smiling. Kaitlyn broke the silence between them.

"So, you remember everything that happened?"

"Pretty much," Iain said. "But it's sort of like remembering experiences in third person. Like I was viewing them rather than experiencing them." He shook his head with a chuckle. "I know that doesn't make a lot of sense, but I'm not sure how else to explain it."

Kaitlyn sat in thought for several seconds pushing a few leftover scrambled eggs around with her fork. She looked up. "You remember everything?" She paused. "What about talking with angels?"

Iain's gaze shot to hers. "You know about that?"

Kaitlyn nodded. "Sam and I chalked it up to symptoms of schizophrenia."

Iain shrugged. "Maybe. Yet . . . " He shook his head. "The memories feel as solid as the other memories." He paused. "But that's impossible, right?"

"I don't know. Remember when we were in the castle, and I said it felt evil there?"

Iain nodded. "And I didn't feel the same."

"Maybe God was reaching you when he knew you couldn't push him away." She shrugged. "I don't know how schizophrenia works or what makes one think they are talking to beings that aren't there. But do we know enough to know angels *aren't* real? Did the neurotoxic gangliosides put your mind in a place where you could actually listen to spiritual things by inhibiting you from tuning them out?"

Iain thought about that. *Could that be true?*

"What did the angels say?" Kaitlyn asked quietly.

Iain paused. He wondered if he should be completely truthful with her. He looked into her eyes. He loved this woman. She likely didn't fully know that, but he did. Therefore, it was important to be completely truthful. He didn't want to build a relationship on a lie. He knew that kind of relationship would not last.

"He said I should speak to my Creator. That it's prayer that empowers the angels."

Kaitlyn's eyes widened. "Wow! That's pretty profound."

That made Iain smile. He smirked. "So you're saying it must be true for me to come up with something so profound?"

She slapped his hand lightly and smiled. "No, that is not what I'm saying. It's just, I've never heard you speak so . . . spiritually before."

He laughed. "That's because I haven't."

"Was there anything else?"

He nodded. "You won't believe this, but when we were in the airport terminal waiting for the customs agent to let us reenter, there was a . . . battle between angels and demons occurring all around us. I mean, a *physical* battle."

Kaitlyn's eyes went wide. "What? *Really?* Why?"

"I . . . this is going to sound crazy . . . but I think the demons wanted me to get held up in customs so I would die."

Kaitlyn's hand went to his with a squeeze. "Oh, Iain. That's . . . that's diabolical. Do you really think that happened?" She paused and her gaze went to his, eyes now turning wide.

"What is it?"

"The customs agent," she said. "He took more than ten minutes to stamp your passport. Sam and I went through in only a few minutes. I saw your customs agent pick up and put down his passport stamp several times. I just could not understand why."

"You think this is tied to that?"

"It must be. Iain, the battle was over . . . *you*!"

CHAPTER 36

THREAT ASSESSMENT

"Okay, everyone," Amanda said as she stood at the head of the table in the small conference room. "In just a few minutes we'll be called before Sam's and my superiors. I want to be sure we're all ready." She turned to Iain. "How do you feel?"

Iain bobbed his head back and forth. He did feel pretty much back to his old self. "Okay. Pretty much back to normal." He gestured to Ted. "Want to tell the others how my scans looked?"

Ted nodded. "It seems the nanobots are working as Bev and I had predicted—and hoped they would. There's maybe forty percent of the bad nanobots left. The good nanobots seem to be efficiently attacking the bad ones. We can't know about all nanobots leaving Iain's body until the good ones dominate."

"And when will that be?" Amanda asked.

Ted raised his eyebrows and tilted his head back and forth slightly. "Oh, I'd say by the end of next week all of the bad ones should be eliminated and the good ones then start to self-destruct."

Amanda nodded. "That's good. That will be important for our superiors to know."

"Absolutely," Sam said. "That should help them understand that we have a chance at being successful, and they will want to employ your technology, Kaitlyn." He pointed toward Ted and smiled. "With Ted's expert help, of course."

A young woman dressed in a navy business suit with a splash of color around the collar of her blouse stuck her head in the doorway. "They're ready for you and your colleagues, Agent Horne."

Amanda nodded. "Okay, everyone, follow me."

They walked to the end of the corridor and entered a large conference room with windows facing the outside along one side of the room. The five of them sat against the wall on the opposite side of the windows, and this gave them an awe-inspiring view of the Washington Monument in the distance. It was a stunning view, Iain thought to himself.

As Iain scanned the room, there were about a dozen people at the table, both men and women, all looking quite nearly like clones of each other. The only difference was that a few were military and had various badges and emblems representing their tenure, service, and awards. Among all of them, only two looked like they might be scientists of some sort, but of what discipline Iain could not tell. The only person he recognized was George Goldberg, whom he had met only once before in the hotel restaurant.

Amanda and Sam remained up front as the others took their seats. Amanda opened her arms in a welcoming gesture and then clasped her hands. "Ladies and gentlemen—colleagues—we are here to discuss the impending threat that is upon us and the implications of its potential national—and maybe even international—consequences."

Sam stepped forward. "We'd like to introduce the following individuals to you who will be instrumental in helping us assess the nature and seriousness of this threat." He gestured toward the three others. "First is Dr. Kaitlyn Sheridan, who is the developer of the nanobot technology that has been utilized in a current clinical trial to target cancer tissue in vivo and deliver targeted chemotherapy to those tissues. This is the same technology that has been pirated and used in the nefarious ways we will be discussing today."

Kaitlyn smiled, stood halfway, then sat again. All eyes looked her way, but no one said anything or welcomed her.

"Next to her," Sam continued, "is Mr. Ted Jordan, who is Dr. Sheridan's colleague and an expert in nanobot technology design and programming. Mr. Jordan has been instrumental in bringing Dr. Sheridan's ideas to life and has been assisting in the ongoing clinical trial in a consulting role."

Ted gestured in the same way Kaitlyn had done.

"Last, but certainly not least, is Dr. Iain Thornwhite, whose employer helped initiate and champion the cancer trial with Dr. Sheridan's nanobot technology. Dr. Thornwhite was recently the recipient of the pirated nanobot technology, causing him to go into a neurotoxic state, lose almost all motor functions, and endure a weakening of his vital responses significantly. This was before Dr. Sheridan and Mr. Jordan were successful in using their nanobot technology to reverse the effects the nefarious use of the technology caused Dr. Thornwhite."

Iain stood halfway and gave a quick wave.

This time several around the table spoke to each other in whispers. Nothing was said loud enough for anyone else to hear.

"And I am happy to report that Dr. Thornwhite is on the road to a rapid and productive recovery."

Amanda unclasped her hands and spoke. "Rather than giving a formal presentation, we thought it would be more beneficial to be as informal as possible and address whatever questions you have so we can, hopefully, come to a rapid decision, today, about how we will move forward to address this impending threat."

A woman raised her hand but began speaking immediately, without waiting for anyone to acknowledge her. Iain assumed her to be a high-ranking military person as she looked highly decorated. "Dr. Thornwhite, the report I read said your symptoms came on suddenly and significantly—even faster than the regular . . . " She looked at her report. " . . . Tay-Sachs disease can do. Can you explain that?"

Iain sat up straighter and leaned forward. "Well, I can address some of it. I developed the symptoms of Tay-Sachs disease without actually having Tay-Sachs. You see, I wasn't deficient in the enzyme characteristic of those with Tay-Sachs, but my body could not utilize the enzyme even though generated. So when the nanobots that Dr. Sheridan and Mr. Jordan created were introduced into my system, they allowed the enzyme which was already present to work, allowing my recovery to be quicker than a person with actual Tay-Sachs could have recovered."

"I see," the woman said. "So, what this impending threat will produce will not match your experiences?"

"Not exactly," Iain replied. "They will develop the symptoms, but for a different reason."

"If I may," Ted said.

Iain gestured to Ted to pick up the narrative.

"Dr. Haneberg infected Dr. Thornwhite differently to observe the progression of the disease so they could gauge how effective their nanobots would be when they are released on their main target," Ted said. "And that target is Ashkenazi Jews."

Another man at the table spoke up. "And what exactly is this difference?"

"Well," Ted continued, "not to get too technical—"

"Yes, thank you," the man interjected.

Ted smiled and continued. "Everyone will be exposed to the vector virus that will be released, but only Ashkenazi Jews who have a specific marker on their Y-chromosome will develop Tay-Sachs. These individuals will develop true Tay-Sachs disease but more rapidly than those who naturally develop Tay-Sachs. This is because the nanobots will be targeting all cells, so symptoms will occur more suddenly, and not progressively, as is common in those who inherit the disease."

"Thank you, Mr. Jordan," the man said. "If I understand correctly, these individuals of Jewish descent will develop many of the same symptoms as did Dr. Thornwhite, and just as rapidly, but they will not be able to recover as quickly."

Ted nodded. "That sums it up well."

Another man responded; he looked confused. "But why can't they recover just as quickly? I'm not understanding."

"The mechanism is different between the two," Kaitlyn said.

Ted nodded and gestured to her to continue.

"You see, in Dr. Thornwhite's case, he had the needed enzyme," Kaitlyn said. "It was always present, so when the nanobots were turned off, so to speak, the enzyme did its work. In these individuals of Jewish descent, they will actually be deficient in the enzyme, so even with treatment, their bodies will first need to manufacture the enzyme before it can then be effective."

The man put his hand to his chin. "So not everyone may recover even if treatment is received rapidly."

Kaitlyn pursed her lips. "That is very likely, sir. That is why this threat is so grave."

"How many people are we talking about here?" A different man quickly interjected the question.

It took Iain a couple of seconds to find who asked the question. He finally realized it was one of the two scientists at the table.

Amanda jumped in. "From our research, over ninety percent of Jews in America are of Ashkenazi descent. If we assume that fifty percent of those are males, we are talking about affecting as many as three million Americans, sir—both adults and children."

The man's face paled. "That's really diabolical."

Amanda nodded. "Yes, sir. We certainly agree. If this goes international, we are looking at another five million, minimum, who may be affected."

Goldberg stood. "So, as you can see, the threat is very real and very imminent. I think we need to have the President up to speed on this as quickly as possible. He may need to inform the heads of other governments. If a travel ban is imposed, they will need to know why and may want to do something similar to try and contain this if it gets out of hand."

Another man spoke. He looked to be the most decorated person in the room. "Mr. Goldberg, I want you to accompany me when I speak to the President. I want you and your team to coordinate how to address this threat and be ready to present that tactical to the President: where, when, how, and prediction of success and containment."

The man looked around the room. "Anyone have any disagreements or further questions?"

No one spoke. "Okay," the man said. "You are dismissed but are expected to be on alert and have any and all resources available for immediate deployment at any hour of the day."

All stood, and a few began conversing. Iain found it strange, but not necessarily surprising, that the only one who came over to address them was Goldberg, who shook each of their hands.

He patted Iain's back. "Glad to see you're on the way to a full recovery."

"Thank you, sir."

Goldberg looked at each of them in succession. "I need each of you to be part of this team and work with Agents Horne and Atway."

All nodded.

Goldberg smiled, giving a nod of his own. "Good. Very good. We'll be in touch shortly."

He quickly turned and headed to talk with others who were leaving the room.

Amanda walked over. Sam was still talking with others.

"Iain, Kaitlyn, Ted, thanks for being here today. I think you were invaluable to the decision today and taking the next steps."

"And . . . what *is* the next step?" Iain asked.

"There is an all-day strategy session tomorrow, starting at eight in the morning. I need all of you there."

Each nodded.

"There is a ton of paperwork for you to sign, so I'm giving you an hour before the meeting starts."

Iain rolled his eyes. "Sounds like you work for the government or something."

Amanda laughed. "Doesn't it?"

"What are we doing, signing our lives away?" Ted asked with a chuckle.

Amanda's eyebrows went up. "That may be truer than you know."

CHAPTER 37

The PRESIDENT'S ATTENTION

Frustrated, Iain plopped into a seat outside yet another conference room. Amanda and Sam always brought him to whatever meeting they were having because they felt he would add crucial details to their explanations of what could occur once Americans were exposed to the nanobots Haneberg and Gomez planned to release.

Yet this was the fifth meeting in three days in which he sat and was never called.

Iain checked his messages and answered email questions related to the clinical trial that was continuing. The site in Albuquerque had dismissed Gomez and made the lead sub-investigator the new principal investigator. So far, it seemed that despite what Gomez had done, the trial was not in jeopardy, and the data were looking extremely promising.

The door to the conference room flew open. Amanda, Sam, and George stepped out together walking at a fast gait. Two others were with them. Iain recognized the man as the military leader who had asked questions at their initial meeting the other day and had stated he would meet with the President. He didn't recognize the woman with them. Amanda motioned for Iain to follow. Iain put his phone away quickly and jogged to catch up with them.

"What's going on?" Iain asked.

"We finally got approval to meet with President Vanderbilt," George said.

"And we need to meet today before Senator Blye blocks us or tells the President some ridiculous lie which can delay us further," the woman said.

"Well, thank you, Senator Crane for being on our side and getting this pushed through this quickly," George said. "And General Hand, thanks for getting us on the President's agenda so urgently."

General Hand spoke through his teeth in anger. "I had us on the President's docket the day after our initial meeting— until Blye blocked us, which forced us to meet with him first so he can get the credit for having us meet with the President."

"Plus," Senator Crane added, "I always suspected Blye as being anti-Semitic. I think this proves it—at least in my book." She shook her head. "How can someone block this for three days when so many lives are on the line?" She suddenly turned toward Iain. "By the way, it's good to meet you, Dr. Thornwhite."

Iain nodded. "Same here, Senator."

She smiled and added, "I'm sure the President will have questions for you. Thanks for your time."

Iain nodded again but had a hard time believing he was going to be meeting with the President of the United States. It just seemed surreal.

Once they stepped from the building, a limo was waiting for them. All climbed in.

General Hand looked at George. "You have the where and how worked out?"

"Yes, General. We think it will likely occur at Penn Station. The how is likely by distributing it through the air, like in a ventilation system. Haneberg did say he was going to make it airborne."

Crane shook her head. "I still don't understand why you think they would not do this at an airport. That would maximize their distribution, wouldn't it?"

"True," Amanda said. "But the psych profile of these two show them to be more about their ego than a quick win."

Crane looked at Iain. "Is that your assessment, Dr. Thornwhite? After all, you're the one who has been the closest to them so far."

"I think Agent Horne is correct," Iain said. "Although I consider them insane, they are approaching this scientifically. First, getting data on how quickly their virus will work."

"By using you," Crane said.

"Correct," Iain said. "Now they want to see how quickly it can spread. So they will release it on one side of the country. New York has a high Jewish population, so it makes sense they would start there. Then they will see how the virus will spread across the country, which feeds their scientific interest. Once they have those data they will then go worldwide to see if their predictions based on their gathered data are correct, and to calculate exactly where to deploy."

"Dear God!" Hand exclaimed. "They're treating something so diabolical as if they're conducting an experiment in a petri dish or something."

Iain nodded. "You are correct, General. Their ethical parameters have totally evaporated. I truly believe them to be insane."

"Or possessed," Crane said. Everyone turned her way. She held up her hands. "Oh, I know that also sounds insane, but look at the history of the world. You can't tell me Hitler wasn't possessed. I don't think any human can devise such things on their own."

"Well, Senator," Hand said, "I'm not sure I believe in such things, but I can't really argue against what you just said either."

The limo pulled up to the White House guard station. All were vetted, questioned, and searched after they reached their destination. An aide met them in an outer foyer area and led them through a few hallways to President Vanderbilt's Oval Office, where the President's administrative assistant had them wait until he was available.

In a matter of minutes, the door to the Oval Office opened and the President escorted three individuals out. "I thank each of you for bringing this to my attention. It is definitely something that my platform can endorse," the President said as he shook each of their hands. He turned to his administrative assistant. "Margaret, work with Congressman Xye here to get on my calendar next month."

"Yes, Mr. President," Margaret replied. She looked at the Congressman. "I'll call your admin and set it up."

Xye smiled and nodded. "Thank you again, Mr. President."

The President turned and looked at each of the others standing before him. "Senator. General. Come in. Come in. I see you've brought an entourage. I read your brief. This is gravely concerning."

As they entered, Margaret closed the door behind them.

"Thank you, Mr. President," Hand said. "We would have met earlier, except for Senator Blye."

Vanderbilt waved his hand in a dismissive gesture. "Blye is an idiot. Everyone knows that." He laughed. "Blye needed some political points." The President shrugged. "Can't really blame him for that, though."

"Well, I can," Crane said. "He's caused a huge delay in meeting this threat head-on."

Vanderbilt pointed his finger at her. "Well, some could argue this is not much different from that ploy you pulled last year about the infrastructure bill."

Crane put up her hands. "We'll just agree to disagree on that, sir."

Vanderbilt laughed. "Agreed." He motioned for everyone to sit. He leaned against his desk and faced them. "So, how bad is this threat?"

"Mr. President," Crane said, "it is imminent, can be lethal to millions of Americans, and it could spread globally quickly."

Vanderbilt folded his arms across his chest. "Dr. Thornwhite, I believe you've experienced this threat and have recovered. Explain what we can expect."

"Yes, Mr. President. I experienced symptoms within the first twenty-four hours of exposure and within forty-eight hours I could barely function. I had muscle weakness making it difficult to walk and talk, had difficulty swallowing, had periodic and uncontrollable muscle spasms, uncharacteristic and unpredictable mood swings, and was beginning to have difficulty breathing before the cure was given."

Vanderbilt looked at Iain intently. "So in less than a week you were on death's door, so to speak?"

Iain nodded. "Yes, Mr. President. That is true."

"And you've made a full recovery?"

"Yes, Mr. President."

"Glad to hear it."

"Thank you, Mr. President."

The President's attention quickly turned to General Hand. "So, General, what's the plan?"

"There is evidence that the release will occur at Penn Station in New York City," the general said. "We will case the station, plant snipers throughout, and take them out as soon as they are spotted—before they have a chance to release the plague."

Vanderbilt's eyes went wide. "*Plague? Are you serious?*"

"Mr. President," George replied. "Just because it is not naturally occurring doesn't mean it won't act like a natural plague. As you've just heard from Dr. Thornwhite, it will be swift and deadly if released. It will appear to spread just like a plague: silently and deadly. As you also just heard, male adults and male children could be dead within a week after exposure."

Vanderbilt rubbed his chin. "Okay, and what do we have in place for containment? Do we have an antidote?"

The others took quick looks at each other. No one seemed eager to answer this question.

"Well?" Vanderbilt said. "Either we do or we don't. Which is it?"

"Not yet," Hand said. "Dr. Thornwhite's colleagues are working on it."

Vanderbilt's attention turned to Iain. "A large contingent, I hope."

Iain gave a grimace. "Not exactly. The National Lab director had the people we had helping Dr. Sheridan and Mr. Jordan go back to their regular jobs after they helped secure my cure."

Vanderbilt's eyes grew wide. "Well, that's just lunacy." He turned and picked up his desk phone. "Margaret, get me . . . " He raised his eyebrows at Iain indicating he needed the director's name.

"Dr. Korvosky," Iain said.

"A Dr. Korvosky at the National Laboratory. And patch him through when you have him."

Vanderbilt hung up the phone and turned back to Iain. "No offense, Dr. Thornwhite, but getting this cure, antidote, or whatever you want to call it, is more important even than what was done for you."

"Oh, I agree, Mr. President," Iain said. "Millions of lives are at stake." He glanced at the others, then added, "Uh, Mr. President, what about flights out of our country?"

"Come again?" Vanderbilt said. He looked from Iain to Hand.

Hand cleared his throat. "Yes. Well, Mr. President, if we happen to not be successful, this plague will spread, and we will need to contain it as best we can. We feel that all flights out of the country should be held."

Vanderbilt's eyes went wide. "All?"

Hand shrugged. "That would be ideal."

"And," Crane said, "you will likely need to talk to Israel, Russia, France, and maybe others as they have large Ashkenazi Jewish populations. They may need to restrict travel into their countries for the same reason we need to restrict travel from ours."

Vanderbilt rubbed his hand across his mouth. "I was so focused on what we had to do as a nation that I wasn't really thinking about the international impact."

The phone on the president's desk beeped. He picked it up. "Dr. Korvosky? . . . Yes, this is President Vanderbilt. . . . I'm glad you said that . . . You have a Dr. Sheridan and a Mr. Jordan working with you? . . . Good. I want you to give them whatever resources they need and as many resources as they need to work on a cure or antidote for this potential threat we have looming over our heads. Can I count on you to do that, Dr.

Korvosky? . . . Good. I don't want to hear of any roadblocks to this request. . . . Fine. I knew I could count on you. . . . Thank you, Dr. Korvosky."

Vanderbuilt hung up and smiled. "Well, one problem solved. I wish this next one was as easy."

He paused in thought for a few seconds. He picked up his phone again. "Margaret, call a full Cabinet meeting first thing in the morning. . . . Yes . . . top priority. . . . And get the Vice President and Secretary of State to my office pronto . . . then get our Ambassador to Luxembourg and the Secretary of Transportation on the phone—in that order. . . . Yes, you'll have to postpone my next several meetings. . . . This is priority. Thanks, Margaret."

When he ended the call, Crane spoke up. "Mr. President, how does the ambassador fit into this?"

"Well, if we're going to spend our resources on this issue, I think Luxembourg or even all of Europe should as well. After all, this Haneberg lunatic is under their jurisdiction. I want to be sure they bear some responsibility. Maybe they also have some ideas as to how to contain this threat if it goes beyond our borders."

"I was thinking of putting together a task force," Crane said. "After all, we have to tactfully explain this to the American public."

Vanderbilt nodded. "Very good. Why not put Blye on it as well since he was so helpful in bringing this to my attention."

Crane laughed. "I can't say no to a wise decision."

Vanderbilt laughed with her. "Now who's making a ploy?"

"Just following the lead of my leader," she said.

"Okay. Okay. It's starting to get deep in here. Let me show you out. We all have a great deal we need to take care of."

CHAPTER 38

DEVASTATING NEWS

T hinking back to how all this got started, Iain was amazed at all he had gone through. If he had known then what he knew now, would he have decided to get so involved in the clinical trial and stay in Santa Fe? But looking over and watching Kaitlyn sleeping made him realize anything was worth it if he was with her.

After returning to the lab from the visit with the President, things had gone into high gear in a short period of time. When Ted and Kaitlyn realized they basically had carte blanche authority to get anything they felt was needed, Ted had created a small army of workers. He rehired Tina, Janice, Charles, and Colm and then had about five other individuals reporting to each of them. Progress was being made extremely quickly now.

Iain had a hotel room nearby, but he was hardly ever there except to shower, change, and maybe get a few hours of sleep. Ted and Kaitlyn took turns using the cot in Ted's office for quick naps to rejuvenate just enough to keep going. As Ted rarely used his desk, Iain used it to keep up to date on the clinical trial and other business needs his work required. This arrangement allowed him to stay on task and remain close to Kaitlyn, as well as for whatever needs Amanda and Sam had for him. He had multitasked before, but never with such fervor.

Amanda stuck her head in the office door. Seeing Kaitlyn sleeping, she whispered, "Can you come to the conference room we've commandeered for our work? Sam and I need to talk to you. It's labeled Project SAJE: Save Ashkenazi Jews Everywhere. Neat, huh?"

Iain nodded with a chuckle and followed her to the end of the corridor outside the lab. As he entered, Sam looked up from a map or blueprint of some kind he was mulling over; he gestured for Iain to sit. Amanda sat as well, folding part of Sam's paper over to make room for herself.

"What's up?" Iain asked. He looked at what Sam was studying. "Is that Penn Station?"

"Yep," Sam said. "We think the attack will occur within the next couple of days. We have intel that Haneberg and Gomez have left Luxembourg. Our guess is they are on their way to New York. We're heading there tomorrow and want you to come with us."

Iain nodded. "Okay. So what's the plan?"

Sam turned his computer around. "Our team has identified four people we think Haneberg has recruited."

Iain leaned in to look more closely at the faces. He wasn't sure what he expected. They looked like normal people. There was nothing distinguishing or unusual about them. He pointed to one at the bottom of Sam's screen. "When were these taken? This one looks like the background is New York."

"They were taken yesterday," Sam said. "The bottom two are already in New York. The top two are still en route. They flew out from Frankfurt early this morning."

Ted stuck his head in the door. "Sam, you wanted to see me?"

He nodded. "Kaitlyn is sleeping, so I wanted just a couple of minutes of your time."

Ted came to the table and sat. "Okay, but I have a meeting with my team in about fifteen minutes." He looked from one to the other. "What do you need?"

"One," Sam said. "Just wanted an update as to where you are."

Ted tilted his head back and forth slightly. "Getting there. We have so many variables to consider."

"What do you mean? We're heading to New York tomorrow, and some of Haneberg's team is already there. We think the attack will happen in just a couple of days."

Ted shrugged. "We can't ramp up production until we have a sample of what they are going to deliver."

"What?!" Sam seemed flabbergasted. "You never said that!"

Amanda touched Sam's arm. "Calm down, Sam. Let Ted explain."

Iain also felt confused. "Ted, I thought you were basing your work on the nanobots you recovered from me."

Ted nodded. "Yes, that is true. But we are making various assumptions. Since we have a larger team now, I'm making several version prototypes hoping that one of them will be the right one to counter whatever they've come up with. I think I know how their version of nanobots will work, but I'm not one hundred percent. We can't afford to have the labs we've contracted with ramp up speed with the wrong version of the nanobot."

What Ted was saying finally hit Iain; his eyes went wide. "So you're saying we won't have a remedy to administer until sometime *after* the attack?" Iain shook his head. "I never fully realized that."

"Neither did I," Sam said. He wiped his hand across his mouth and grabbed his chin. "This is a game changer for sure."

Ted looked from one to the other. "Sorry if I hadn't made that clear."

"So, how long will it be to have a remedy once you have a sample?" Amanda asked. She looked worried. "I know you know this, but Iain was on death's door in less than a week. Now, we may have hundreds of thousands who will need this remedy, cure, antidote. Will we have it in time?"

Ted sat for several seconds biting his upper lip and not responding. "I know this is not what you want to hear." He paused. "But I'm afraid we will have a number of deaths before we get ahead of the curve on this."

Amanda sucked in a breath. "How many?"

Ted shrugged. "I don't know. There are just way too many things to consider. We don't know how fast it will spread, how fast people will get to a hospital or clinic. I have Janice's team working with the Transportation Department to talk to labs, hospitals, and clinics all over the nation trying to get them up to speed." He shook his head. "The best we can do is ship continuously as each batch is made. Yet the initial batch will likely take a couple of weeks minimum."

Amanda shook her head. "This could really turn into a huge disaster."

"Look," Ted said. "I can have some available from our lab here for a few local cases, but the majority must come from the labs we have contracted with because they have the mass production capacity. We deliver them a prototype, and then they replicate it. Once we start, we can then work to get ahead of the curve."

Amanda nodded, but she looked solemn.

"Anything else?" Ted looked at his watch. "I need to meet with my team if not."

Amanda looked at Sam, who shook his head.

"No, you can go, Ted," Sam said. "Thanks."

As Ted stood, he patted Iain on the back. "Good luck to all of you." He turned to Amanda. "And get me a sample as soon as you can."

They each nodded and Ted left the room. All three looked at each other in shock. This was not the news they thought they were going to hear.

Iain thought back to his symptoms and how quickly they came upon him. Although his case was severe, and devastating, things were likely to be much worse for these people.

He looked at Amanda and shook his head. "Those at ground zero are likely in real trouble."

She nodded. "More than in trouble. Maybe even doomed."

CHAPTER 39

WORST-CASE SCENARIO

As Iain looked around the Penn Station waiting area, he felt this was the worst possible day an attack could happen. It had rained overnight, causing flooding, and some of the bathrooms were backed up. The cleaning crew now had huge fans operating throughout the station trying to get floors dry.

"It's almost as if those here planned our arrival, isn't it?" a voice from behind him said.

Iain whipped around in his seat.

It was Gomez. He had a huge grin on his face. "Hello, Iain. I see you've made a full recovery."

"Well, you're quite brazen, aren't you?" Iain replied. He had not expected either of these two mad scientists to be so daring. Yet he should have known Gomez would want to flaunt all of this. "I could have you arrested, you know," Iain said.

Gomez shrugged. "I suppose you *could*, but what do you have, really? You *think* it was me who had Kaitlyn kidnapped. You *think* it was me who basically poisoned you, I guess one could say. And you *think* it is me about to unleash a plague on your beloved United States. But is that what a court would see?

Where is your tangible evidence? It's all what *you* think happened, and flimsy circumstantial evidence." Gomez smiled— more like gloated. "An arrest would be an inconvenience. But that's all it would be."

"You won't get away with this," Iain said emphatically, though not confidently.

"With what? I'm just waiting for a train." Gomez gestured around the station. "Just like all of these other good people." He paused. "Although, some may be waiting for a hospital." He glanced at Iain. "You think?"

"I think you're a monster. Some physician *you* are."

Gomez laughed and then turned somber. "Those over-populating our precious Earth and overusing our limited resources are the real monsters. I will help our Mother Earth breathe again. It's actually . . . biblical."

"What?! You're insane."

"Well, the one you call the Messiah is the one who said through death comes life. He was a savior. So am I."

"That's one of the grossest misquotes and applications I ever heard," Iain replied, working hard to remain calm. "That is not what he was talking about. He was prophesying his own death and resurrection. There is such a thing as context, you know!"

Gomez shrugged. "*Your* interpretation. My interpretation is about to come to fruition." He stood. "Nice to see you again, Iain. Perhaps we'll meet in the future as well. Hospital, maybe?" He laughed and walked off.

"Man, that guy makes my blood boil." Iain put his hand to his ear. "Amanda, did you hear all of that?"

"I did," she said through her comms. "What a nutjob. Yet it means the attack is definitely today."

"Yeah, and it couldn't happen on a worse day. If any of the vials get thrown into any of these large fans, it will send the virus everywhere: far and wide and down the escalators to the trains below."

"Well, we'll just have to get to them before that happens," Amanda said. "Just so you know, there are giant fans down between the tracks as well. It seems flooding was everywhere."

"Can we have the trains shut down?" Iain asked.

"That may make them more desperate. No, it's now or never, I'm afraid."

"Just be sure your snipers don't miss."

"Dr. Thornwhite," a male voice said. "We can all hear you. And we agree. We rarely miss."

Iain cringed inside. He had forgotten everyone was on the channel and not just Amanda. "Glad to hear it," Iain said. He hoped that was both affirming and cautioning at the same time.

"I see one," another male voice announced on the comm. "Approaching from the Seventh Street entrance. He has a briefcase."

Iain turned in that direction and recognized the man as one of those Sam had shown him who was to arrive this morning from Frankfurt. The man walked at a fast gait around the opposite side of the seating area from where Iain sat heading toward one of the large fans. "I think he's going to use the fan for disbursement," Iain said.

"Roger," he heard in his comm. "The man went into Hudson News. I don't have a shot."

Iain could partially see him inside the store, now placing the case on a counter. "He's opening the briefcase!" People were walking between Iain and the shop, and this impeded his vision. "I think he took something out. I can't tell."

"I don't see him," the same man said. "Anybody see him?"

Iain kept trying to peer around those walking between him and the news shop. He saw a blur of movement and then the man ran from the shop at full speed with a large vial in his hand. "He has the vial!" Iain yelled. "He has the vial!"

The man ran toward the large fan. In an instant, Iain felt his body begin to move; he rushed to intercept the man.

"I have the shot," the man in his ear said.

"Take it!" This was Amanda's voice.

The shot was silent. It looked as if the man tripped, but he threw the vial toward the fan as he went down. Iain ran with all his might to grab the vial before it reached its destination. He almost had the vial in his grasp when a ball—which seemed to fly out of nowhere—hit the vial and propelled it into the fan. The large rotating blades burst the vial, spraying its blue liquid in all directions, with some landing on those nearby, causing them to panic and scream. Iain hit the floor hard and slid into the wall of the juice bar adjacent to the news shop; this caused several people to scatter. There were screams from others now recognizing the man had been shot as blood oozed from under his body. Lying there seeing everything in what felt like slow motion, Iain's hands went to his head, disbelief overwhelming him.

Their worst nightmare had just come true.

A little boy came by and picked up his ball. He looked at Iain, now sitting up, somewhat dazed from the event. "Sorry, mister," the boy said and ran back to his mother, who now scolded him.

As Iain stood, he saw another man with a satchel traveling up one of the escalators. His face looked familiar. When this man saw his comrade on the floor, he turned and headed back down the escalator. "Escalator number fourteen!" Iain said as he ran in that direction. He knew more trained individuals were likely on it, but he didn't see anyone around, so this compelled him to pursue the man.

When Iain reached the escalator, he saw the man with his arms raised, another vial in his hand. A gunman stood at the bottom of the escalator pointing his weapon at the man. Iain then noticed the large fan at the bottom of the escalator and realized this man was waiting for when he would be in full alignment with the fan. Iain ran—more like slid—down the middle portion between the up and down escalators to get to the man before he could toss the vial.

"Get the vial!" Iain yelled. "Get the vial!" But his shouting only seemed to confuse the gunman.

When the man with the vial neared the large fan, he tossed it up and over the other side of the escalator toward the fan. Iain jumped with all his might and stretched to grab the vial. He was successful and pulled his arms to his chest to avoid the fan, but his body then crashed into a waiting train. Iain let out a loud *umph* before he crumbled to the platform. But . . . *he had the vial!*

Iain's eyes went wide. His escapade had distracted the gunman, and the man on the escalator now had another vial in his hand, as though he was holding a javelin. Iain pointed, but before he could say anything, the man threw the vial into the fan. Again the vial exploded, and the blue liquid went in every direction. Ian heard a *crack!* The gunman had felled the guy, but his action was too late; the damage was done. Many people on the platform screamed and were suddenly wiping blue spray residue off their faces and arms. After he recovered from the shock, Iain yelled, "Each man has more than one vial. More than one vial!"

Iain went to where the felled man lay at the bottom of the escalator, retrieved his satchel, and looked inside. It contained two Styrofoam containers, now empty. Iain put the vial he retrieved into one of the containers, swung the satchel over his shoulder, and headed up the escalator.

When he reached the waiting area, he was in shock. Mass pandemonium was all around him. A man holding up one of the vials had a woman hostage, and he was threatening to break the vial on the floor if he wasn't allowed to leave the station. When her two young sons, one around twelve years old and the other about five, Iain guessed, realized the man had no weapon but only a vial, they rushed him. The younger kicked the man's shins repeatedly, causing him to let the woman go. The agent with the gun waved for the kids to get away from the man, but they kept attacking him. The mother tried to call to the boys, but they were not listening. The youngest of the boys gripped the end of the vial and the man held tightly to the other.

The mother yelled, "Let go, Julio! Let go! It's okay now."

The boy didn't listen. The older son did a karate chop on the man's wrist, and this caused the vial to break into the man's hand, the glass inflicting bloody gashes into the man's fingers. The man yelled in pain as the blue liquid poured to the floor. The older son then kicked the man in his chest, propelling him backward. Because they were near the top of the escalator, the man fell backward and down the stairs. His satchel came open and two more vials were thrown out and crashed—one on the stairs of the escalator and the other on the platform below—directly in front of one of the large fans. The blue spray seemed to go everywhere.

Iain put his hands to his head. A worst-case scenario could not have played out.

The oldest son looked down at the man as the up escalator now brought him back up to where everyone stood. "That's what you get for messing with our mom!"

The man laughed. "Thanks, kid. I couldn't have done it any better."

The child looked confused but went to his mom, who hugged both boys tightly.

Iain looked around for the fourth man but did not see him. He then heard Amanda's voice in his ear. "Bringing up the fourth guy. Escalator six."

Iain stepped quickly in that direction. When he arrived, she was handing him off to others for custody.

"Did you retrieve the vials?" Iain asked.

Amanda shook her head. "His satchel is empty. I have other agents looking, but we haven't found them yet. I found only four empty Styrofoam containers."

Iain knew that wasn't good, and that likely this wasn't over. "Amanda," Iain said, "the worst-case scenario has just happened."

Amanda nodded. "Yeah, I know. And even worse, we don't have a vial for Ted."

A small smile came to Iain's face. "Au contraire." He opened his satchel and showed her the vial.

"Come with me!" Amanda nearly shouted. "I need to get you in a car back to D.C. right away. We'll deal with the mess here. You just get back to D.C.—after you wash and change. Let's try and contain the intentional spread as much as humanly possible."

CHAPTER 40

IAIN'S PRAYER

Stepping from the bathroom, Iain saw Sam sitting in a chair next to the room's window reading something on his phone.

"Thanks for letting me use your room to shower and change clothes," Iain said. "I had checked out of mine this morning thinking I wouldn't need it since I was heading back to D.C. today."

Sam smiled. "No problem. It gave me a chance to talk to Ted. He's excited about you obtaining a sample."

Iain opened his suitcase and pulled out khakis and a pullover and began to dress. "Yeah. Although a painful memory."

Sam nodded. "The whole day has been painful in one way or another."

Iain sat on the bed to lace his shoes. "So what did Ted say?"

"Oh, yeah. Some good news, I think. He said the nanobots he injected you with would likely neutralize the ones this virus exposed you with."

Iain sat up. "Really? How so?"

Sam shrugged. "You'll have to ask him the details as I didn't really understand all his technical-eze. He just said the ones he gave you, since not completely gone yet, will stop their self-destruction because of the new threat now present in your system, replicate, and do to these new nanobots what they did to the ones Haneberg gave you earlier." Sam smiled. "So, you shouldn't be infectious." Sam stood and put his phone away. "So you're likely the only one who's currently invincible." He raised his eyebrows. "Ready to go, Superman?"

Iain picked up his suitcase and laughed. "Yeah, I think so. So, that makes you, what? Lois Lane?" He draped the satchel with the vial in it around his neck and shoulder.

"I think you're stretching your metaphors a little too far there, bud," Sam said, giving Iain a slight push out the door.

Both quickly headed to the elevators.

Once they reached street level, they shook hands and Iain got into the limo.

Sam leaned through the front passenger window to address the driver. "Carl, Dr. Thornwhite needs to get to the National Laboratory in downtown D.C. as quickly as possible." He smiled and pointed at the man. "Don't break any laws in the process, though."

The driver chuckled. "Aw, there you go taking all the fun out of the job."

Sam laughed with him. "See you soon." He looked back at Iain and gave a final wave.

The car pulled into traffic. Iain sat back in his seat with a sigh. He knew that, in normal conditions, this driving time was about four hours. He wasn't sure what to expect this time, though. It had already been quite a day.

"Don't worry, Dr. Thornwhite," the driver said. "I'll get you there as soon as possible. I was listening to the weather before you arrived. It seems we may be going through some thunderstorms, so that may slow us down a little, but not too much, I don't think."

Iain nodded. "Safety ranks higher than speed."

The driver gave a thumbs-up and left Iain to his thoughts. Iain looked out the window. He could see the sky looking almost black toward the East. As the limo headed across the George Washington Bridge into New Jersey, Iain began to feel a kind of foreboding—almost the same feeling as he had experienced on the flight to D.C. from Frankfurt. He had assumed that was because of his neurotoxic-induced schizophrenia. If that was the case then, what was causing that feeling now?

* * * * *

Mikael and Raphael sat on the hood of the limo as it traveled east. Mikael knew the dark gray clouds ahead were more than just a thunderstorm. Dark forces didn't want the vial Iain was carrying to reach its destination. Mikael and Raphael were here to help Iain succeed in his mission to get the vial to Ted.

"Don't worry, Mikael," Raphael said. "Quentillious, Uriel, Azel, and their contingents will get here soon."

Mikael looked over at Raphael. "Yes, I know they will. It's just we seem to be in the same conflicts all the time. Yet each one always feels more dire than the previous one."

Raphael nodded. "I think Lucifer knows his time is getting short, and he's becoming desperate." He cocked his head. "I have to say, though, this scheme is one of Lucifer's most diabolical yet. He's taken full advantage of this new technology Dr. Sheridan has developed."

"That he has, my friend."

Angels started appearing above them in rapid succession. Mikael looked at Raphael. "Ready for another battle?"

Raphael stood and unfurled his wings. "Let's do it."

Mikael nodded as he stood and unfurled his large, majestic wings, larger even than those of Raphael's, and his were massive. Mikael was always amazed at how his Creator had made him so that even though he had such grand wings when unfurled, he appeared to not have wings when they were comfortably folded behind him.

Both flew toward the gathering throng. Quentillious, Uriel, and Azel met the two as the other angels continued to appear.

"What are your instructions, my captain?" Quentillious asked.

"This battle will likely be more intense than the last," Mikael said. "Just prepare your angels for anything, any trick at all. Although they will fight, they may also influence cars and drivers to prevent this vial Iain is carrying from getting to its destination."

Quentillious, Uriel, and Azel nodded and flew off to their respective angel contingents. Mikael looked at Raphael. "Prepare, Raphael. The horde is here."

The horizon not only had dark storm clouds, the demonic horde added to the darkness. Mikael could see not only the regular types of demonic forces with which they typically had to contend, but even higher demons now present. Apparently, this battle was extremely important to Lucifer.

* * * * *

As Iain looked through the windshield, things appeared almost as if a dark gray curtain lay before them. The cars across the median coming out of the dark curtain had their wipers on high speed. The ambient sound suddenly transitioned from the noise of the tires on the highway to the deafening roar of rain pelting the car. It really was like going through a physical curtain: from day to night, no rain to a deluge, visibility to just seeing a few red dots from the taillights of the vehicle ahead. The vehicles themselves were no longer visible.

Carl slowed the limo, keeping the red lights in front of them at as constant a distance as possible. "Hold on," the driver said. "This is going to be a tricky ride."

Iain sat back in his seat, not wanting to look but at the same time afraid to not do so. He was certainly glad he wasn't driving, but that also meant he had no control over his situation. He hoped Carl was extremely experienced. The rain did not seem to want to let up. It was thick and constant—almost like being trapped under a waterfall.

All of this increased Iain's anxiety, but that was not the worst part. The sense of foreboding became more intense. The words of the angel came back to him:

You've been out of practice with your prayers. You need to pray. Prayer is what gives us strength. Lucifer has targeted you, so you need to empower us. Prayer does that.

But that was a hallucination, wasn't it? Could prayer really change such things? Was there a force really against him?

Carl slammed on the brakes; the limo skidded and swerved.

* * * * *

Out of the corner of his eye, Mikael saw the limo swerve. As he glanced down, several demons were around it and the car in front of it. Mikael put extra effort into the fight against his immediate foe and was able to make this dark angel turn catatonic.

285

Mikael flew down to the limo carrying Iain where a demon was struggling with the driver for control of the steering wheel to make the car spin out of control. As Mikael neared, the demon looked up wide-eyed and dashed off, afraid of having to deal with Mikael. Yet as the demon turned to flee, he ran headlong into Azel. The demon backed up, but Azel, in a flash so quick the demon had no time to respond, plunged his sword into the demon's side. The demon's eyes went wide and his body catatonic, his weapon falling to the asphalt below. Azel brushed him aside aand flew to Mikael, who felled another demon kneeling on the hood of the car in front of the limo with his arm phased through its hood to reach the engine below trying to make the car stall.

Quentillious and some of his angels pushed and guided the car to the side of the road, but not before the limo had to swerve. With the other demons now out of the way, Carl was able to recover his steering of the limo and keep it on the road, just missing the car being pushed off the roadway.

"Quentillious, you and your angels stay extremely close with the limo to prevent this kind of thing from happening again," Mikael said. "They have too many variables on their side with this weather."

Quentillious nodded. "Yes, my captain." He flew ahead and arranged his angels in a defensive manner around Iain's limo.

Mikael and Azel flew back into the fray above them.

* * * * *

"You okay, Dr. Thornwhite?" Carl asked, giving him a glance in his rearview mirror.

"Yes, I'm fine."

Iain knew he wasn't fine, but he couldn't really explain what he was going through. He really didn't understand it himself. Yet he closed his eyes and began to pray. It was an odd sensation—prayer was something he had not done in more than a decade. It wasn't that he had given up on his belief in God, but he had given up on any type of relationship with him. He guessed this was an attempt to restore that. He had to do something because the foreboding feeling was getting more and more oppressive.

* * * * *

Mikael stopped his ascent and turned, now looking back down at the limo.

Azel, looking back and seeing Mikael stop, turned and flew back to Mikael's side. "What's wrong, Mikael?"

Mikael closed his eyes and breathed in, a contented look on his face. "Don't you feel that, Azel?"

Azel was puzzled at first, but a smile soon came across his face. "Prayer."

Mikael opened his eyes and nodded. "Yes, Azel. Prayer. There is nothing like it. The energy of prayer fills me like nothing else. It is truly powerful."

Azel nodded as both headed back into battle.

Mikael felt such a renewed strength that he was able to defeat several of his foes in short order. Yet he noticed that the closer the limo got to its D.C. destination, there was an increase in the number of more powerful demons he had to encounter. He knew this was a strong battle strategy by Lucifer because the more tired he and his angels became, the stronger Lucifer's demons grew. . . . Yet Iain continued to pray, and the intensity he put into his prayer gave Mikael the renewed energy he needed to defeat Lucifer's battle tactic. Mikael knew Lucifer's pride always made him forget the most obvious things to plan against.

CHAPTER 41

THE FORGOTTEN NANOBOTS

Quietness greeted Iain as he entered the lab. He did a three-sixty as he made his way to Ted's office. *Where is everyone,* he wondered. The lab's wall clock told him it was late, but he had never seen the lab entirely empty.

"Hello!" he announced, hoping someone would hear—but only silence responded. The only faint noise was the various whirring sounds from lab equipment.

Once he reached Ted's office, Iain stood at the door and smiled. There was Ted, completely asleep, with his torso sprawled across his desk. Iain walked over and shook Ted's shoulder. "Hey, Ted," he said in something a little louder than a whisper.

Ted slowly stirred and opened his eyes. Once he recognized who had awakened him, he sat upright immediately. "Iain!"

"Hey, buddy. Getting a few winks, were you?"

Ted looked at his watch. "What happened? I was expecting you, like, two hours ago."

"The weather out there is atrocious. I was beginning to wonder if I'd get here alive."

"Did you bring it?" Ted asked, eyes now wide.

Iain opened his satchel. "But of course. That's what this trip is all about, isn't it?"

Ted received the vial as though it was a priceless treasure. *Well,* Iain thought to himself, *in some ways it is, as this is the thing that will allow a cure for this plague to be manufactured.*

"Ted, where is everyone? I've never seen the lab more vacant."

"Well, when you didn't arrive on time, I sent everyone to dinner or a quick nap, if possible. I knew we would be pulling an all-nighter once you arrived, so I wanted them as fresh as possible for this." He glanced at his watch. "They should be arriving in a matter of minutes."

Iain followed Ted to the lab bench where Ted began working on the sample. A couple of minutes later, the others entered almost simultaneously.

Kaitlyn made a beeline to where Iain and Ted stood. She gave Iain a lingering hug followed by a kiss. "Are you okay?"

He nodded and waved at the others, who waved back as they came over to see the sample he had brought.

Ted turned and placed his hand on Kaitlyn's upper arm. "Why don't the two of you go to my office and get caught up?" He nodded to the others. "We'll get things started here and then you can join us in a little bit."

As they walked to the office, Iain heard Ted give directions to the others. "Tina, you and Charles work on identifying the nanobots and comparing them to the samples we have of the others."

Ted gave other orders, but they turned into background noise as Iain focused on Kaitlyn. He had her sit in Ted's chair as he sat on the edge of the desk.

"Ted said things didn't go well," Kaitlyn said, "but that you had a sample. That's about all the detail we heard. What happened?"

Iain shook his head. "Think about all that could go wrong—and that's what happened."

"Oh, Iain. All those poor people."

He nodded. "As far as we know, there were ten vials. I was able to save one, five were broken and their contents released, and four are lost. They're still looking for those."

Kaitlyn put her hand over her mouth and shook her head, her eyes starting to water. "What have I done?"

Iain's gaze shot to her. "What have *you* done?" He grabbed her hand. "Kaitlyn, none of this is your fault. It's the fault of deranged people like Doctors Gomez and Haneberg."

Kaitlyn shook her head. "It's my technology, Iain. Without my technology, none of this would be possible."

"But none of the good would have come forth either. Better it come from you so that we can know how to put safeguards in place going forward." He pointed toward the door. "What you and Ted have put together out there is what is needed moving forward: to have people working in all areas to advance the good and limit the bad." He squeezed her hand. "You did that. That will be your legacy."

Kaitlyn was still holding back tears.

"This plague will be the legacy of Gomez and Haneberg—*not* yours."

"I hope that is true," Kaitlyn said, her voice barely audible.

He helped her to her feet and pulled her in, wrapping his arms around her. "It will be true. It absolutely will."

Tina appeared in the doorway. "Sorry to interrupt, but Mr. Jordan has some news." She paused. "Uh, just come as soon as you can."

Iain nodded. Tina gave a quick smile and left as Iain looked back at Kaitlyn. "You okay?"

She wiped tears from her cheeks. "Yeah, I think so. Let's go find out the news."

As they walked back to the lab bench, Ted was like a cop directing traffic as he gave instructions to specific individuals for various tasks. A big grin came across his face as he saw them approach.

"Bev, good news," Ted said. "Haneberg used the same basic structure of nanobots that he used on Iain." He tilted his head back and forth slightly. "Not exactly the same, but similar enough, I think, for us to get started quickly."

Kaitlyn's eyes widened. "That's good." She glanced at Iain and then at Ted. "That's great."

"So how long will it take to start mass producing the cure?" Iain asked.

Ted scratched his head. "Not entirely sure—at least a couple of days."

Iain shook his head. "Ted, you know the Tay-Sachs symptoms will arise even faster than they did on me."

Ted gave Iain a stern look. "Yes, Iain, I am painfully aware of that. Believe me, I'm working as fast as I can. I can't just magically make things happen. We must be sure what we mass produce will actually work, or it's all just a waste of everyone's time—and probably a huge scandal to boot."

Iain nodded. "Sorry, Ted. I know you're doing all you can. You've done so much already."

Kaitlyn put a hand on each of their shoulders. "We're all tired. Let's not let our emotions get the better of us."

Both nodded. Iain's phone beeped. He didn't recognize the number.

"Hello. Dr. Thornwhite."

"I need you at Union Station," a man's voice said. While sounding familiar, Iain couldn't place it.

"Who is this?"

"Iain, you hurt my feelings. After such a nice dinner we had in Luxembourg, you've forgotten me already?"

"Haneberg?"

Hearing that name, Kaitlyn whipped around from her conversation with Ted and looked at Iain, fright in her eyes.

"And here I thought we were on a first-name basis. Alexander, please."

"And why, *Alexander*, should I do anything for you?"

"Oh, Iain," Haneberg said in a tone used by someone who pities one not understanding. "It really isn't for me, but for your adoring Kaitlyn. You would do anything for her, right?"

Iain shook his head. "What are you talking about? You're not making any sense."

"I completely understand, Iain. Context. You need to understand the context." Haneberg's tone suddenly turned curt. "You come to Union Station immediately, or Kaitlyn dies." His tone then became pleasant again. "Is that a strong enough context for you?"

"Kaitlyn is right here with me. You have no control over her anymore."

Haneberg laughed. It was nearly a maniacal laugh. Iain felt he had just about enough of this deranged individual and wanted to simply end the call. Yet the tone of the cackling made him second-guess that decision.

"Everyone was so focused on you, weren't they?" Haneberg said. "After all, you were the one with the symptoms. No one even thought to take into account the source of your symptoms."

"What are you talking about? The source were the nanobots, and they've been destroyed."

Haneberg chuckled again, but it was a laugh like a person has when the one they're speaking to doesn't understand an inside joke.

"Yes, in *you*."

"Well, of course in—" A switch of understanding flicked on in Iain's brain. "Kaitlyn!"

"Ah, it is possible for the dense to be taught."

Kaitlyn looked at Iain with curiosity as she grabbed his arm and mouthed, "What's going on?"

"She's fine. Has been all this time."

"That's the interesting thing about nanobots, though. They can be programmed to work rapidly or slowly. Sometimes slow is more effective in the long run."

"What did you do?"

"Let me guess," Haneberg continued without addressing Iain's question. "Mr. Jordan found something in the nanobots he had not observed before, right? He wasn't at our intimate dinner, so I'll stay formal when I speak regarding him. Time was so pressing that Mr. Jordan focused on the immediate need to save you. Then, when he decided to just destroy the nanobots in your body, the unidentified organelle didn't really matter, did it?"

There was a pause, and then Haneberg continued. "Until now."

Iain wasn't sure if this deranged man was telling the truth or lying to get something he wanted. Could he take that chance, though?

"What did you do, and what do you want?" Iain asked.

"Oh, I think a blood test for Kaitlyn will be the telltale she will need to grasp the situation. And don't think Mr. Jordan's tactic of just destroying the nanobots will solve her issue this time. They've been slowly working since their delivery in Taos. It will take her body a long time to recover—if it even can."

"You'll pay for this," Iain said. He wasn't sure he could carry through with that threat, but it was heartfelt.

Haneberg chuckled. "Oh, don't threaten what you can't deliver, Iain. Now, the fastest way for her to recover is for me to give you the code to help the nanobots speed up the healing process. So, if Mr. Jordan destroys the nanobots, he actually decreases her risk of survival rather than helping it. After all, if the nanobots are gone, how can they help heal once they have the correct code?"

"And what do you want in return?"

"I want you to get me safely out of Union Station. There are agents on the train and others will be waiting for me on the platform. I want you to call them off."

"Is that all? No safe getaway out of the country?" Iain said sarcastically, though still wondering of his limited request.

"Oh, I already have arrangements. I just need this one tiny request fulfilled."

"And what makes you think I have that power?"

"Oh, I don't know, Iain. Maybe because two of the agents are good friends of yours and they like Kaitlyn and want her alive. They may not care about her as much as you, but it's your job to make them care. Or . . . " He gave a dramatic pause. "She will not be alive for anyone to care about."

"Okay. Okay," Iain said. "Where should I meet you?"

"Gate C for the Acela train. And you have forty-five minutes to get here."

There was a click and then silence.

"What's going on?" Kaitlyn asked. Her eyes scanned Iain's face. "I don't like the way you're looking at me. Is something wrong?"

Ted turned. "Wrong? What else has gone wrong?"

Iain displayed a painful expression. "Everything." He looked from Ted to Kaitlyn. "Sorry. I don't have much time to explain. I need to get to Union Station and meet Haneberg." He turned to Ted. "I need you to test Kaitlyn's blood. He's done something to the nanobots in her system, and they're doing something to her."

"What!?" Kaitlyn looked confused. "I feel fine. I—" She stopped midsentence seeing the look on Iain's and Ted's faces. "What's wrong?"

"Bev," Ted said, gently pointing to her face. "Your nose. It's . . . it's bleeding."

"Bleeding?" She put her finger to her upper lip and brought back blood on her finger. She looked at Iain, now with fear in her eyes. "What did he do?" She took his arm. "Iain, what did Haneberg do to me?"

Iain shook his head. "I don't know. He said a blood test would tell you."

She looked at Ted, who just stared at her. As if a light switch suddenly turned on in his head, he jerked an index finger upward. "Right. Yes. Blood sample." He dashed off to get a collection kit.

"Kaitlyn, I'm so sorry. I have to go, but put your phone on speaker and I'll use my earbuds. We can speak when you know the results, and I can finish telling you what he said."

She nodded but looked shaken. He hated to leave her but had no choice. He kissed her cheek. "I'll phone you in just a few minutes."

He dashed from the lab to the elevator, putting his earbuds in as he went. Once at street level, he hailed a taxi and had it head to Union Station as fast as possible.

He dialed Kaitlyn.

"Iain, Ted just took the blood sample. It will take a while to know the results. What exactly are we looking for?"

"I don't know. All he said was that the nanobots had been doing something slowly over time, and it would not be easily reversed."

"I'll just do what I did for you," Ted said. "If we kill off the nanobots, then they can't do any further damage."

"No, Ted," Iain said. "He said he has a code that will make the nanobots reverse the damage faster."

There was silence. "Ted?" Iain asked. "Ted, are you there?"

"Yeah. Sorry. I was thinking. So, if we do nothing, the nanobots continue harming Bev until we get the revised code. And if we destroy the nanobots, reversing naturally whatever is going on, that may be too slow."

"Right."

"That man is insane," Ted said.

"That's my assessment for sure. Ted, I'll get back with the code as fast as I can."

"Okay, Iain. In the meantime, I'm putting Colm on this to see if he can decipher the code. He's incredibly intuitive on how these nanobots function and how to process code."

"Good. Keep me posted. And I'll do the same."

"Be careful, Iain," Kaitlyn said.

"Will do. Love you."

"I love you too," Ted said. Then a pause. "Oh . . . you meant that for Bev."

Iain had to chuckle—just a bit. Leave it to Ted to turn a serious issue into something with at least a bit of levity in it.

Kaitlyn spoke softly. "I love you too."

The line went silent. Iain sat back in his seat and sighed. *Will normalcy ever return?* He looked at his watch. Time was evaporating.

He dialed again. It was time to let Amanda and Sam know what was going on.

CHAPTER 42

THE LAST VIAL

Despite the time of night, Union Station was teeming with people. Iain glanced at his watch. The cab had made good time after all, and he still had fifteen minutes before the Acela train would arrive. Pushing his way through the crowd of people, Iain came to Gate C and looked around for Sam and Amanda.

After turning a couple of three-sixties, he saw Sam and Amanda in the crowd coming from the direction of the Metro.

"Everything okay at the lab?" Sam asked as he walked up.

"With the sample, yes. Ted has everyone working on the prototype nanobot for the cure. Did you ever find the missing vials?"

"Yeah. But the news isn't good."

Iain looked from one to the other. "What . . . happened?"

"As you know, the Acela has only a few stops between New York and D.C., so we phoned ahead to have agents board in Philadelphia and Baltimore hoping we'd have a chance to recover both them and Haneberg, thinking his target with those vials was probably something here in D.C."

Iain nodded. "And?"

"He threw the vials onto platforms along the route."

Iain's eyes went wide as he gasped. "No! Where?"

"Newark, Trenton, and Wilmington. We think he still has the last one with him."

"Yeah, he told me he has it. Somehow, it's linked to the cure for Kaitlyn."

"About that," Sam said. "I don't think we can just let him get away."

Iain's eyes widened. "You can't be serious. Kaitlyn's life is not a pawn on a political chessboard."

Amanda put her hand on his upper arm. "Iain, we understand how you feel, and we feel the same."

Sam nodded.

"But," Amanda added, "we must have him pay for what he has unleashed on the world. Our highest leadership wants him." She shook her head. "We are not allowed to negotiate. I'm sorry."

"More than sorry," Sam said. "Heartbroken. But we have our orders, and we can't not follow them."

Iain ran his hand across his mouth. This was not the news he wanted to hear. There had to be a way to achieve both goals. He looked from one to the other. "Well, Haneberg doesn't have to know that, right?"

Amanda cocked her head. "What do you mean?"

"I mean, let's make him think he has a way out, then as soon as I have the code, you take him down."

"I think you're trusting him too much," Amanda said. "Who's to say he's not already doing the same to you?"

"What do you mean? You think he's already double-crossed me?"

"Well, think about it, Iain," Sam said. "He put nanobots in you without an antidote of any kind. What makes you think he would do the right thing for Kaitlyn?"

Iain stared at Sam. What Sam was saying just did not compute in his brain. He couldn't allow such a thought to be true. There had to be a salvation plan for Kaitlyn. He shook his head. "No. No, I won't accept that scenario."

Amanda gave him a sympathetic look. "Iain, that's what he's counting on. He fills you with false hope just so he can negotiate, get away, and then leave you high and dry."

"Here," Sam said as he gave an earpiece to Iain. "Put this in so we can communicate and know what you and Haneberg say."

Sam tapped Amanda's arm. "It's time." He turned to Iain. "Just keep him talking."

"But—" Iain started, but both Sam and Amanda had dashed away in different directions.

Iain turned in a huff, putting in the earpiece, and walked to the Gate C exit to wait for Haneberg. In only a few minutes, Iain saw him. Their gazes met for a brief second. Haneberg motioned with his head to the side of the station behind a group of passengers. Iain followed him that way.

"Well?" Haneberg asked. "Do you have safe passage for me?"

"I don't know," Iain said. "Do you have the code? I need evidence I can trust you."

Haneberg looked hurt. Iain was dumbfounded. Haneberg was the one inflicting massive pain on the world, and he had the audacity to appear hurt.

"Iain, I have never lied to you. You may not have liked or agreed with my messages, but I did not lie about any of it. And I'm not lying now."

Iain felt conflicted. He knew if he helped Haneberg and got caught, he and the vial would be in custody and Kaitlyn would not be helped. If he didn't help him, Kaitlyn would be in the same predicament.

Before he could decide, he heard a loud, "Freeze!"

Both he and Haneberg turned to see Sam holding a gun on them.

Haneberg shook his head. "Iain, I'm so disappointed in you. I thought you loved Kaitlyn more than this. I thought you two made a lovely couple. You both seemed to have a crush on each other in Luxembourg. It was . . . " A smile spread across his face. " . . . fun to watch."

Iain held up his hands. "Sam! Sam, wait. I don't think he's lying. He has the code. The vial is the key."

Sam shook his head. "We can't trust him, Iain. You can't trust a maniacal lunatic to tell you the truth."

Haneberg laughed. "Oh, Agent Atway. How little you know about maniacal lunatics. We're often more truthful than you know." He shrugged. "Perhaps dangerous, deranged, and dia-bolical, but often truthful." He turned to Iain. "It's all in your court, I'm afraid."

Iain looked from Haneberg to Sam and back. His mind was racing. He took a step, but then he heard Amanda behind him.

"Don't do it, Iain. Stay where you are."

Iain closed his eyes. He felt so confused. He wanted to help for the sake of Kaitlyn, but if he got shot, how could he help her? But if Haneberg got shot, how could he help her then? *Pray.* The thought seemed to appear out of nowhere in his mind, and he had to do a mental double-take. But that is what he did. Iain didn't close his eyes, but he prayed. *Dear Lord, I don't see a way out of this. I truly hope and trust it is your will for Kaitlyn to live. Please let me know what to do.*

Haneberg reached into his coat. Both Sam and Amanda stiffened in their stances.

Haneberg grinned. "Don't worry, I have no weapon." He shrugged. "No gun, anyway." He pulled out the large vial of liquid.

Iain's eyes widened. The liquid was red—not blue! There was definitely something different about this vial. As he looked at Sam and Amanda, they did not seem to register the difference.

Haneberg looked at Iain and smiled knowing Iain was aware there was a difference. Haneberg's attention turned back to the agents. "This strain is more virulent than the other one. People will die even faster here." He gestured. "Look around you. Do you want this number of people exposed? Their fate will be on your heads—not mine."

Haneberg began to back up toward the corridor between the gates and the shops on the opposite side. Sam and Amanda followed him, guns pointing.

"I warn you," Sam said. "If you take another step, I'll be forced to fire."

"Do you want to bear the burden of all the ensuing guilt, Agent Atway?"

"Oh, the guilt is all yours, I'm afraid."

Haneberg turned quickly to grab a woman as a hostage but wasn't aware of a small child who pulled away from his mother at that very moment. Haneberg tripped over the child and fell backward.

Iain seemed to observe all this in slow motion. Haneberg's eyes went wide. He tried to catch himself, but there was nothing or no one for him to grab onto as the woman had bent down to grab her child. Haneberg's hand holding the vial hit the railing surrounding the gate area, and this caused it to slip from his hands, hit a table, then a chair, and roll on the floor toward a shop on the opposite side of the corridor.

Iain ran for the vial. It was his only hope of saving Kaitlyn. Sam and Amanda were focused on Haneberg. Yet before he could get to the vial, another passerby kicked it with his foot. Iain looked up; the kick seemed deliberate. *Gomez!* He displayed a wicked grin and kept walking. Iain frantically looked for the vial again. He saw it roll and roll . . . under the wheel of a cleaning cart. Before Iain could grab it, the cart crushed the vial, its red contents leaking out and spreading slowly across the floor . . .

Without thinking, Iain grabbed several napkins from the cart and soaked up as much of the liquid as possible. Next he grabbed a plastic bag, stuffed the napkins with the vial remnants inside, quickly tied the bag, and ran down the corridor as fast as possible to find an exit. He heard yelling, followed by gunshots, then screams. He paused briefly and looked back; people were gathering where Dr. Haneberg had gone down earlier. Iain contemplated going back to be sure Sam and Amanda were okay, but then he looked at the plastic bag in his hand. *This takes precedence right now,* he thought. He ran for the exit and didn't stop or look back again.

Iain wasn't sure if anyone was after him or not, but he wasn't willing to take the time to find out. Getting to the lab as fast as possible was his only focus. He also felt badly he had left Sam and Amanda now that he knew Gomez had shown up. He was afraid Haneberg was no longer in custody. The gunshots he heard were likely from Gomez to create a distraction of some kind for Haneberg to escape. He'd have to confirm that with Sam later.

After running out of the building, Iain dashed down the street to find a cab somewhere else as the immediate cab line was way too long at the station. After running for several blocks, he hailed a taxi and shouted that he needed the National Laboratory right away. He sat back in the seat of the cab, pushed the plastic bag into his coat pocket, and reached for his phone. Ted had to get ready to examine the contents from this last vial.

CHAPTER 43

EVEN MORE DIABOLICAL

Everyone in the lab turned their attention to Iain as he burst into the lab and rushed to where Ted stood with Colm, Tina, and Charles. Iain pushed the plastic bag into Ted's hands.

Ted gave him a blank stare. "What's this?"

"The contents from the last vial."

Ted's eyes went wide. He quickly traveled to the fume hood, donned gloves, opened the bag, looked in, and gave a confused look. "Blood on napkins?"

Iain shook his head. "No, the contents of the vial were red. The contents spilled onto the floor, and this was all I could think to do."

"That was fast thinking," Tina said. "Ted, we can reconstitute this with Kaitlyn's buffer solution."

Ted looked at her and nodded. "Okay, you and Charles try and do that."

"Where's Kaitlyn?" Iain asked. "How's she doing?"

"I have her in my office on the cot."

Iain turned to head in that direction, but Ted grabbed his arm. "Just want to prepare you, Iain," he said quietly. "She is not doing very well at the moment."

"Did you find out what Haneberg did to her?"

Ted nodded. "Her platelet count is extremely low—dangerously low. The nosebleed was only the tip of the iceberg. It's only gotten worse. She has petechiae and bruises on her limbs."

Iain's eyes went wide. He didn't understand all that Ted said, but he knew it wasn't good. His throat constricted and he could barely force out his question. "She'll pull through, though, right?"

"Once I get the results from Tina and Charles, I can better answer that."

Iain nodded; he didn't know what else to say or ask. He quickly headed for Ted's office. When he reached the door, he stopped abruptly and gasped before he even realized he had. Thankfully, Kaitlyn was asleep, and this gave him time to recover from what he was seeing. He walked over and knelt beside her. There were little red spots on the back of her hands and up her arms as well as large purplish bruises. He gently shook her shoulder. "Kaitlyn."

She stirred and slowly opened her eyes, then smiled. "Hey."

"How are you?" Iain asked. He wasn't sure why he asked because it was obvious she wasn't fine.

Iain helped her sit up and placed a pillow behind her back. He tried to hold himself together. It was hard seeing her this way. Even her eyes were bloodshot.

She smiled weakly. "I'm really tired." She lifted her arms and sighed. "And I look atrocious."

Iain bent down and kissed her forehead. "Never. Plus, you'll get better soon, I'm sure."

"It feels like this happened suddenly. I seemed fine until today. Now look at me." Her eyes watered. "Iain, I'm really scared. I don't want to bleed to death."

Iain held her hand. "Now, now. We're not going to let that happen. Remember how bad I was? And I recovered."

She turned up the corner of her mouth. "Yeah. You really were pathetic."

Iain raised his eyebrows. "At least your sense of humor is intact." He gave her a serious look. "At least, that had better be your attempt at humor."

Kaitlyn gave a small chuckle.

Ted, Colm, and Tina appeared at the door, then came in. "I think we have something," Ted said.

Ted set his laptop on his desk and turned it to face Kaitlyn and Iain. "I want to show you something." He touched a key on the computer and the monitor displayed a cartoon of a nanobot. "This is a visual representation of the nanobots that you have, Bev." He looked at Iain. "Which are the same ones you had."

Iain nodded. "Okay. So, what do you want us to know?"

Tina pointed to a structure in the nanobot. "We never identified what this organelle—for lack of a better term—is or does."

"I never identified any coding that affected it," Colm added.

"And, as you know," Ted said, "since we just had the nano-bots killed off, we never concerned ourselves with knowing what it did."

Tina jumped back in. "But it seems to be the culprit affecting the platelets in Dr. Sheridan's body. The good thing is, it doesn't seem to affect their synthesis, but it is making them less sticky." She shrugged. "Sorry, I don't know the scientific term. In other words, it makes the platelets not allow clotting."

"These nanobots are far more complex than I originally realized," Ted said. "They are basically two nanobots in one. The good thing is, one function nullifies the other."

Iain shook his head. "Sorry, Ted. You're confusing me. I don't really follow."

"These nanobots have two functions: cause Tay-Sachs symptoms or inhibit platelets—but not both," Ted said.

Iain nodded slowly. "Okay. So because I received the trigger in the plum tart, I got the Tay-Sachs."

"Yes," Ted said. "And because Bev didn't, she got her platelets inhibited."

"And," Tina added, "yours was fast acting. Dr. Sheridan's is slow acting."

Kaitlyn gasped and her eyes went wide. "Ted! You know what this means, right?"

Ted nodded. "Unfortunately, the plague is more diabolical than we thought."

Iain looked from one to the other. "What? What am I missing?"

Kaitlyn grabbed his arm. "Iain, it means that everyone who is exposed to this virus will have symptoms: either Tay-Sachs or faulty platelets."

Iain's eyes went wide. "So a combination of what Haneberg wanted, getting rid of Ashkenazi Jews, and what Gomez wanted, a general depopulation. Gomez did tell me he was going to help Mother Earth breathe again. I just didn't realize he was talking about this."

"Ted, what do we do?" Kaitlyn asked.

"Well, first we get you on the road to recovery," Ted said. He turned to Colm. "Please share what you found."

"This new nanobot in the red vial seems almost identical to the first, but this second organelle nanobot is counter to the one in the blue vial. I think this is the code Dr. Haneberg was referring to."

"But how do you get access to its code?" Iain asked.

"It will take way too long, unfortunately, but I have a potential solution," Colm said, pointing to the monitor again. "We will take this secondary nanobot out of the first nanobot and replace it with the one from the second nanobot. We can then have them self-replicate as we did previously."

"And more importantly," Ted said, "once you are cured, Bev, the nanobots will self-destruct."

"Ted, you need to have two cures," Kaitlyn said.

He smiled and nodded. "That's already in our plan."

She turned to Iain. "Amanda and Sam need to know this."

Iain nodded. "Well, I'm not sure if they're happy with me right now."

"Well, there's truth to that." It was a male voice from the doorway.

All turned to see Sam and Amanda standing there.

Amanda gasped. "Kaitlyn! I had no idea. Are . . . are you okay?"

"She will be," Ted said.

Iain stood. "Sam, can I talk to you and Amanda? Things are way more complicated than anyone ever knew."

Amanda turned from talking with Kaitlyn. "*More* complicated? How is that even possible? Gomez is dead, Haneberg escaped, Kaitlyn is ill—you mean there's more?"

"Look at me," Kaitlyn said. "This will happen to everyone infected with the virus plague. It's not just a plague against Jews, but against everyone."

Ted nodded. "If we don't get this solved, and quickly, we will all be in the same stage as Bev is right now. I'm afraid Iain is the only person on earth right now immune to this plague."

Amanda looked from one to the other, a look of near horror on her face. "What!? Everyone?"

Sam rubbed the back of his neck. "This is worse, way more evil, than I think I can even comprehend!"

Iain looked at Sam with eyebrows raised. "Haneberg escaped, and Gomez is dead?"

Sam nodded. "Goldberg is not very happy. I can tell you that."

"Come on," Iain said to Sam as he started to accompany him from the room. "I'll fill you in as you fill me in. You need to let your boss and the President know about this new threat. With how this went down, likely the whole world needs to know."

CHAPTER 44

IAIN'S CHARGE

The meeting did not start well. Iain looked around at those in the Oval Office—the same players who had been here before. He couldn't believe they were arguing over something that had already happened and no one could change, trying to place blame on anyone but themselves or their departments. Iain had had enough.

"Does it matter!?" Iain blurted. He realized his words were louder than he had intended. "I'm sorry." He paused. "But it seems we are missing the whole point here."

Everyone looked at him, dumbfounded.

Iain sighed. "Look, the damage is done. That can't be changed. Could it have gone down better? Maybe. It always seems obvious after the fact that someone could have known something more or could have done something better. But the fact is, if that was the case, then that would have been the scenario we would have pursued. Now we have to deal with the hand we have been dealt. I know that's cliché, but the real question now is: what are we going to do about the international crisis we're facing? Trying to blame someone for where we are is counterproductive to deciding future actions."

"You're right, Dr. Thornwhite," President Vanderbilt said. "To keep to the cliché, we all have egg on our faces. That's a PR problem we will have to manage with the press and our citizens." He turned to Goldberg. "But just how did this Haneberg escape?"

Goldberg gestured to Sam, who sat up ramrod straight and cleared his throat.

"Well, Mr. President. It seems Gomez was unhappy with Haneberg for being willing to give away the reversal for what he had devised for population reduction. He fired his gun at Haneberg twice. The first bullet nicked Haneberg's shoulder but killed the guard holding him. The second shot missed Haneberg and hit the leg of a bystander. Another guard jumped into the action before we could stop him. His shot, toward Gomez, was fatal."

Amanda picked up the account, but sighed first. "Because Haneberg's restrainer was now dead, he got away in the chaos through the panicked crowd."

The President nodded but looked worried. "Yeah, a big PR problem." He paused for a second, then sat back in his chair. "But now we have an international crisis to deal with." He looked at General Hand. "We just got through telling the presidents of the other countries they only had to worry about Jews. They're not going to take this updated news well."

"Agreed, sir. But we only need tell them we found out about it ourselves just recently, and informing them is one of our top priorities."

"Not mention how this whole thing got botched, I take it."

Hand pursed his lips. "Preferably not, sir."

"Well, work with the press secretary as to how to phrase all this for the press. Give them enough, but without details." He shrugged. "I'm sure it will leak out fast enough. Social media will be sure of that."

Hand nodded. "Yes, Mr. President."

Vanderbilt turned to Senator Crane. "And by all means, Senator, please keep a lid on this—especially to Blye. If anyone asks, you were privy to only the most basic of information."

Crane nodded. "Absolutely, sir."

The President pointed to Iain, Sam, and Amanda. "You three, you can leave for now, but I want you to remain here in a room nearby. I will likely need you later."

The three looked at each other and then back to the President. They nodded.

Vanderbilt picked up his phone. "Margaret, I have three individuals who need to hang around for a while. Can you set them up in one of the offices?"

In only a couple of minutes, a side door opened and Margaret entered. Vanderbilt motioned for them to join her.

They followed Margaret down a small hallway to a spacious office which had a desk and small conference table. All the furniture looked to be made of walnut with a lustrous finish. She gestured for them to step into the room. "If you'll please wait here, I'll get you when the President needs you again." She smiled pleasantly. "I'll bring in a few refreshments for you while you wait."

As they sat, Iain looked at Sam and Amanda. "What do you think the President wants us to do?"

Both shrugged.

"They're not looking for a sacrificial scapegoat, are they?" Iain asked, feeling a little worried about such a scenario. He wasn't used to the political arena but could see such a thing happening.

"I don't think so," Amanda said. "George is pretty good about owning up to the responsibility of his team."

"Just what is Ted and Kaitlyn's plan for combating this plague?" Sam asked. "I'm sure the President will want to know that."

"I'm not sure I know everything," Iain said. "But I know Ted has contracted with several other companies that have a strong methodology for scale-up. I know Janice and her team have been working with the Secretary of Transportation as to how to get the cure distributed throughout the country."

"What about internationally?" Amanda asked.

Iain shook his head. "I don't think anything has been done yet. We were focused on the immediate threat, not thinking the threat would turn so global."

Amanda nodded. "I understand that. But now I'm sure other countries will want something done quickly."

Iain raised his eyebrows. "Well, I think we'll need to bring on other countries with the capability for scale-up. I'm sure Ted will be able to share how."

A man entered with a small cart containing a few pastries, coffee, sodas, and water. "I'll set these on the credenza and you can help yourself," the man said.

"Thank you," Iain said. "Those smell wonderful. I can't pass on having one."

The man chuckled, used silver tongs to set one on a plate, and passed it to Iain. "They are hard to resist."

As the man left, Iain got up and grabbed a soda; Amanda poured coffee.

Sam opened a bottle of water and looked at Iain. "And what about us? How long was it before Kaitlyn started having symptoms? A couple of weeks?"

Iain nodded. "Yeah, that's about right."

"But what about George?" Amanda asked. "He could start having symptoms as early as tomorrow, like you did, Iain. Of course, it depends upon how quickly the virus spreads, but being airborne, it'll likely spread quickly."

"I know Ted's team can develop a few cures, but they can't mass produce like these other facilities can. But I agree. We need some people to receive the protective nanobots as early as possible so we can defeat this." He looked from Amanda to Sam. "But who chooses? The supply produced in the lab will be very limited."

"Another question for the president," Amanda said.

After a few more minutes of conversation, Margaret reentered the room. "The President will see you now. Follow me."

They followed her back to the Oval Office. Only George was still there.

"Thank you, Margaret," the President said as she left the room. President Vanderbilt gestured for the four of them to sit.

"We have some logistics to work out," he said. "Now, I had already limited the travel of Ashkenazi Jews internationally, but I had not limited other travelers. So we already have many who have traveled out of the country. The consensus that we reached was we will not change our instructions at this time so as not to make things more confusing."

George added, "We need to limit the amount of panic, especially, as I understand it, that we have a couple of weeks before the second series of symptoms may exhibit in people."

"That's true," Iain said. "But we likely won't have the cure out to everyone before some start developing symptoms."

George nodded. "Understood, but we must direct our attention to one crisis at a time. I already have reports that New York City hospitals are becoming inundated with people with Tay-Sachs symptoms."

"What can the hospitals do?" Sam asked. "There is no treatment."

"Yes," George said, "but people don't know what else to do. We're getting reports already as far south as Atlanta and even here in D.C. It's only going to escalate, and move quickly, across the country."

"I've already talked to the Secretary of Transportation about distribution of the cure once they are produced," the President said. "So I think at least we have a strategy in place. I know the casualties will be high, but I think we can hold off mass pandemonium by announcing our strategy." He looked at each of them. "So how do we describe this cure? It all sounds so complicated. I'm not sure the general population will understand it. Do we call it a vaccine? People understand that term."

Iain shook his head. "Sir, I think we need to be as truthful as possible. If we're caught in a lie or misinformation, there will be resistance. I think the public is savvier than perhaps the government gives them credit. We shouldn't try and hide this."

"So what do you suggest?" Vanderbilt asked.

"I'll have Ted and his team come up with an explanation most will be able to understand," Iain said. "Perhaps we can say that some deranged individuals who do not appreciate all people being special, and having inalienable rights, have targeted some human physiological vulnerabilities. And that the cure, which has been developed, will put one's physiology back to its natural state."

The President nodded. "I kind of like that. Truthful but not . . . very detailed."

"Yes," George added, "but there will be . . . thom . . . who want more specifics."

Iain's gaze quickly shot to Amanda to see if she heard George's slur. She returned a concerned look.

Iain looked back at George. "We can point them to publications by Dr. Sheridan and Mr. Jordan and maybe have them do a few additional ones on the cure and how it works. That way, the geeks can know the details and the public will not feel they've been given misinformation."

Vanderbilt raised his eyes at George as if asking for his thoughts. George nodded.

"Okay, then. Let's do it."

"And sir," Iain said. "People—like Mr. Goldberg here—are already starting to have symptoms. Ted's team at the lab can develop a few shots for the cure but not that many. We need your office to provide a list of who you feel should get a shot as soon as possible prior to its mass production."

"Understood." The president turned to George. "I want your team to develop such a list and pass it by me. I'm already commanding you to include you and your family on the list. We need you one hundred percent to help coordinate this distribution."

"Thank you, sir," George said, appreciation in his eyes.

"Anything else?" Vanderbilt asked.

Everyone shook their heads.

"Okay, now for another task assignment." The President turned to Iain. "As I understand it, you're the only person on earth who is immune right now."

"Yes, sir, that is what I have been told."

"Then I need you to go to Israel."

Iain's eyes grew wide. "Sir?"

"Their prime minister just informed me that, amazingly, he was contacted by Haneberg. Apparently, he is heading to, or already in, Israel and is going to do something at the Temple Mount within the week. I need someone there who can help—and very possibly help their police apprehend Haneberg. You seem to be the only one right now who can do that."

Iain looked at each of them. He wanted to object, but he knew the President was almost certainly correct.

"Don't worry," Vanderbilt said. "I'll send you reinforcements as soon as they have received the cure. But from what you just said, it will be a few days before that is available even from the lab here in D.C."

"Yes, sir."

"I need you on a plane to Israel first thing tomorrow morning."

Iain started to object, but he was so stunned that no words formed. Instead, he just nodded. After all, what could he say? There really was no one else.

"Sorry to put you in such a spot, but you're the only person I can clear for such travel right now. I'll send help just as soon as possible."

"Yes, sir. Thank you for your confidence, Mr. President."

Vanderbilt laughed. "You're a fast learner in political-speak."

CHAPTER 45

ISRAEL

Sitting in the airport, Iain thought about the role that had been thrust upon him. Kaitlyn was not yet healed, and here he was leaving her. That irked him, but she had been insistent he go ahead with this mission. She was definitely in good hands with Ted, Tina, Charles, and others helping to get the cure up and working. Iain badly wanted to be present when she was getting better and be part of her healing. Yet he also understood the urgency of the President wanting him to fly now because, in a few days, flight crews and airport personnel might well be too sick to work. Flights would be canceled automatically because no one would be fit for duty. Iain's mind understood, but his heart was with Kaitlyn.

As he waited to board his flight, he looked at the monitors in the waiting area displaying news feeds. Things were not good, and folks were on the verge of panic. He was surprised at how quickly the spread was occurring. There were already reports of people ill in Boston, Chicago, Fort Lauderdale, Dallas, Denver, and Las Vegas. The emergency rooms in the larger cities were beginning to be inundated due to the large Jewish population in those areas.

Iain's phone beeped. It was his boss; Iain answered. "Bill, how are things?"

"Not good, Iain. I know you've tried to be on top of this, but those you mentioned to me who were Jews in your study are deathly ill or already dead: the three on the East Coast passed away last night. I just heard from investigators in Denver, Spokane, and Albuquerque. They started showing symptoms this morning."

Iain shook his head. He wanted to tell Bill things were only going to get worse before they got better, but he remembered what the President said about not giving out information before George thought it necessary. Besides, everyone would know in a few days. And still more, there was nothing he could do for Bill until Ted had the cure available. He told himself that just as soon as he knew it was available, he would contact Bill.

"I was afraid of that happening," Iain said. "I'm glad you called. The President has me leaving this morning for Israel. I'll be back just as soon as I can."

"The President!" Bill nearly shouted into the phone. "When did you become chummy with the President?"

"Bill, I'll explain it all when I get back. I can't go into details right now, but it's important. Otherwise, I wouldn't be doing this."

Bill sounded irritated but cautious. "If I find out this is some kind of hoax, all this extra travel is on your dime."

"Don't worry, Bill. This one is on the federal government."

Bill gave a small laugh. "You're just a modern-day Tom Sawyer, aren't you?"

"Not by choice, Bill. Believe me."

"Well, fill me in when you get back. I'll keep an eye out here on the trial for now. But you need to hurry back. I need you, Iain."

"Understood. Hey, my flight is boarding. I'll talk to you soon."

Iain ended the call, stood, and headed across a couple of aisles to board. "Flight seems sparse today," he said to the attendant as she did a final check of his credentials.

The woman looked up after examining his ticket. "Yes, sir. Only about a dozen people on board today." She smiled, then giggled. "I guess that means you can eat as much as you want."

Iain grinned. "My lucky day."

Once he reached his seat, he settled in for the thirteen-hour trip. He slept, ate, walked around the cabin, and even talked with some of the attendants since they had extra time on their hands due to so few passengers. His main goal was keeping himself busy because, when he stopped, his mind would automatically turn to Kaitlyn, and he would start to worry. He even tried watching a movie but couldn't stay focused on its plot. Pulling out his computer, he decided to try to answer work emails. Having Bill see he was still engaged in the trial would be helpful.

When the flight was only a few hours from landing in Tel Aviv, Iain began to have that familiar foreboding feeling. He was unsure why, but it became more oppressive the closer the plane got to Israeli airspace. He thought about the times he had this feeling before. Something bad had occurred or was about to occur. Could that be true this time as well? He went back to his seat, sat quietly, and prayed.

He prayed off and on until he felt the plane's wheels hit the runway. The foreboding feeling was not as strong, but he still felt it.

Once through customs, Iain saw a man with a placard displaying his name. Iain approached.

"I'm Dr. Iain Thornwhite."

The man smiled and took his suitcase. "Follow me, and I'll take you to the prime minister. Our trip will be a little more than an hour."

As the car traveled the roughly forty miles to Jerusalem, Iain saw the landscape change from mountains and lush valleys to a more rugged mountainous landscape with an arid climate. Once they reached Jerusalem, the car weaved through the various streets to reach its destination. An aide came to the street level and ushered Iain to the prime minister's office.

A man with dark hair, seemingly in his mid-forties and wearing a kippah, stood and extended his hand. "Welcome, Dr. Thornwhite. I'm Prime Minister Ezra Cohen. I trust your flight here went well?"

Iain shook his hand. "Yes, everything went fine. Feel free to call me Iain. If we're to work together, I feel that will make things easier."

The prime minister gestured for him to sit. "Please, get me up to speed. Tell me more about this Dr. Haneberg. And what is your role?"

"Well, Prime Minister, Dr. Haneberg is a scientist, a very wealthy scientist, I might add, who has pirated a technology utilizing nanobots that Dr. Kaitlyn Sheridan, of the U.S., developed. He has devised the nanobots to target male Jews with a specific gene that identifies them as being descendants of the original high priest, Aaron."

"You mean the Kohanim?"

Iain nodded but also held up his hands. "I don't know your belief in religious matters, but Haneberg is determined to wipe out those who have a priestly ancestry so a future temple cannot be operational."

Cohen ran his hand across his chin. "Well, I'm not sure I believe in all of that, but we have many orthodox believers who have been preparing for a future temple." He shook his head. "But my bigger concern is that this threat is coming when we'll have a large contingent of our people at the HaKotel for Pesach."

Iain cocked his head.

Cohen smiled. "You're probably more familiar with it as what is known as the Wailing Wall. We treat it as an outdoor synagogue. There will be many people there at Passover."

"And when is that?"

"In three days," the prime minister said. "How do you expect us to prepare for this threat? Is there a way to prevent it?"

Iain shifted in his seat. "I'm not entirely sure, sir. We were not very successful in my country in preventing the release of what some are calling the Luciferian Plague."

Cohen squinted. "They're calling it that because . . . "

"Two reasons. One is that its effects are observed in vivo with bioluminescence from an enzyme called luciferase. And . . . some say it is a devil of a plague."

Cohen gave a small smile, then looked somber. "It does sound evil, for sure." He opened his arms slightly. "So what can we do?"

Iain rubbed his chin. "Give Haneberg's photo to every last agent, police, or guard you will have surrounding the area; be ready both on ground and in the air." He paused. "I really have no idea what he will do. We in the U.S. government consider him a madman, so anything is likely fair game for him."

Cohen nodded. "I see. Sounds like you need someone with creative and uncommon ideas."

Iain chuckled. "Very true, sir."

Cohen pressed a button on his desk. "Have Dr. Friedman come in."

Iain heard the door open and a man, somewhat skinny and tall, entered. Cohen gestured to the man. "Dr. Iain Thornwhite, this is Dr. Naftali Friedman."

They shook hands. "Naf, please work with Iain to devise a plan for a potential attack with a bioweapon at the Temple Mount."

Freidman looked from Cohen to Iain and back. "Well, this sounds very serious."

"Indeed it is," Iain said.

Freidman turned to Cohen. "We likely need help from guards on the Temple Mount itself."

Cohen raised his eyebrows. "That could prove difficult."

Iain looked at both men. "Is there a problem?"

Cohen nodded. "We have limited access to the Temple Mount itself. I'm not sure the death of Jews would necessarily incur . . . the cooperation we need if it doesn't affect non-Jews as well."

"Oh, but it does, Mr. Prime Minister. This plague affects everyone." From his satchel he retrieved, then showed, a picture of Kaitlyn with her petechiae and bruises. "Not as quickly, but it will eventually affect all who are exposed."

Cohen's eyes went wide. "This should definitely be compelling."

He showed the picture to Friedman. "Very compelling," Friedman said as he handed the picture back to Iain. "I'll contact my counterpart there. I'm sure he will be willing to cooperate knowing these facts." He gestured to the door. "Come; let's get to work. We have little time to waste."

* * * * *

Mikael stood at the entrance of the building as Iain and Friedman walked by and stepped into a nearby car. He looked up. Demons were everywhere. Something big was going to happen here, no question. He appreciated the prayers Iain had provided on his way to Israel. The strength they provided would most likely be needed once more.

"Come for the show?" It was a voice from behind Mikael.

He turned—but didn't need to. That voice could come from only one being.

"Lucifer. So this is where you've been all this time?"

"Oh, I get around. Busy, busy, busy, you know."

"Yes, no doubt," Mikael said.

"It's almost here."

Mikael cocked his head. "What's almost here?"

"My reign."

A smile swept across Mikael's face. "I hardly think so. This is just another mess you've created that we will clean up."

Hatred filled Lucifer's gaze. "Don't you dare treat me like a child. My hour has come. You'll see."

"This is not your hour, Lucifer. This will be a failed attempt, as were all the others. The Almighty has not yet given his permission for you to be successful in your goal."

"*Humph*. As though I need his permission for anything I do. I'm not his lackey, like you."

"And yet," Mikael said in a condescending manner—he knew he shouldn't have, but he couldn't resist—"you report to him whenever he commands you."

Lucifer stuck out his chest. "Whenever he requests my presence, you mean. I attend out of curiosity—nothing more."

Mikael laughed. "Sure, Lucifer. That must be it."

Lucifer took a step closer. Mikael didn't budge. "You just stay out of my way this time, or you won't be so condescending once I'm through with you," the dark angel said.

As Lucifer disappeared, Raphael appeared. "Was that Lucifer I just saw talking with you?"

Mikael nodded. "He came to warn me to stay out of his business."

Raphael chuckled. "Doesn't he know by now that he *is* our business?"

Mikael looked up again. "One thing is for certain. Something big is going down here. I haven't seen this many demons in one place since we fought them in ancient Babylon."

Raphael followed Mikael's gaze. "Looks like we need several contingents of angels this time."

Mikael nodded. "Let's report to Ruach. Then I'll gather the army."

They looked up one last time, then disappeared.

CHAPTER 46

PREPARATION FOR PASSOVER

Naf smiled at Iain's joke that he could now put "plan for terrorist threats" on his resumé. After two days of nonstop meetings, preparations, and explaining why Iain was in Israel, they were seated at an outside bistro for coffee and a falafel.

"You know, I've never had a falafel before," Iain said. "It's quite good."

Naf grinned. "Going to put that on your resumé also?"

Iain smiled and shrugged. "Why not? It's at least a little more believable."

Iain's phone beeped. His smile faded quickly when he saw the number.

Naf cocked his head. He whispered, "What's wrong?"

Iain put his finger to his lips as he put his phone on speaker so Naf could hear the conversation.

"I didn't expect a call from you, Dr. Haneberg."

Naf's eyes went wide, but he didn't say anything.

"Well, I'm pleased you kept my number. That means a lot, Iain."

"Never know when you need an opinion from a deranged lunatic."

Haneberg laughed. "Well, I see they've sent the lone immune to save the world for them."

"Something like that, I guess. After all, you and Gomez left very few who could."

"Yes, it's a shame Juan can't be here to witness his triumph. I warned him to trust me, but alas, he did not."

"Is that the same 'trust me' speech you gave me?"

"Well now, Iain, desperation does force us to do things we regret."

"Oh, so you regret lying to me?"

"Let's just say it was necessary. My mission had not yet been accomplished. I had to fulfill my Passover."

That statement made Naf turn red with anger. Iain put his hand on Naf's shoulder and repeated his index finger motion to his lips. Naf began to visibly calm.

"That seems a little arrogant, even for you, Alexander."

"Oh, you used my first name. I'm pleased we are still on a first-name basis. That's good. But I don't do arrogance. It's confidence, really. Just stating a fact without pomposity."

Naf rolled his eyes. Iain hoped he would stay quiet, but he wanted the Israeli doctor to hear the type of person they were dealing with.

"So, does that mean you'll be joining us?" Iain asked, trying to get more information out of Haneberg.

"Oh, I may drop in for a short visit, but can't stay long, I'm afraid. We really must schedule some time when we can have another dinner together."

"No longer fond of plums, though," Iain said.

Haneberg cackled in laughter. "Oh, I guess not. I hope I haven't turned you off from them forever. They are quite tasty."

"Why are you doing this, Alexander? What do you have against Jews?"

"Oh, just trying to correct a wrong. Lucifer has spoken, and I obey. You see, this world belongs to him now. Jews, unfortunately, are not *his* chosen people."

"So you worship Lucifer?"

"Let's just say we are aligned. It's unfortunate we are on opposite sides, Iain. I rather like you. Well, I must go now. It was a pleasure, as always."

The call ended.

Naf shook his head. "That man is a total lunatic."

Iain nodded. "I agree. I wanted you to hear him to understand that we are not dealing with someone stable, not someone who thinks rationally. He is totally unpredictable."

"Calling our holiday *his* Passover. I wanted to reach through the phone and strangle him!"

Iain laughed. "Oh really? I couldn't tell."

Naf looked at him with a blank stare, then smiled.

Iain shook his head. "But I think he was giving us a clue—and not making a statement about the holiday itself."

"What do you mean?" Naf asked. "Explain."

"My experience with this guy is that he is first and foremost arrogant, despite what he says. So he tends to flaunt rather than be subtle. So, let's think about this . . . why is Passover called Passover?"

Naf cocked his head. "Because the death angel passed over those who applied blood to the doorposts of their homes."

Iain nodded. "I think Haneberg is saying *he* is going to pass over the Temple Mount."

Naf stared at Iain for a few seconds; recognition then seemed to come to him. "He's going to be in a helicopter or plane?"

"Or something," Iain said.

"A helicopter or plane would have the military on high alert as soon as it's spotted," Naf said. "Surely he's smart enough to know he wouldn't be successful with such an attempt."

Iain put his hand to his chin. "What about a hot air balloon?"

Naf raised his eyebrows. "Would be considered less of a threat, and would likely be vetted before any action would be taken."

"Well, let's keep our eyes peeled tomorrow. What time is the blessing given?"

"Should be in the morning, around nine-thirty." Naf's eyes raised. "You think that is when he will make his move?"

"That's my expectation with this guy."

Naf nodded. "Okay. I will alert the prime minister as well as our and Jordan's militaries. Both will be patrolling the area on high alert."

Naf stood and Iain followed. "Have a good night, Iain. I'll see you bright and early. Meet me across from the Wailing Wall at the Temple Mount. We'll observe from the top of the buildings and be out of the throng of people, but still able to watch everything closely."

They shook hands and went separate ways.

Iain walked back to his hotel. It was a pleasant night, and the streets were already more crowded than when he first arrived.

He still couldn't shake the foreboding feeling he had ever since arriving.

* * * * *

Mikael stood with Raphael, Uriel, Azel, and Quentillious on top of the building housing the bistro café and watched Iain head down the sidewalk. As he looked around, there were numerous demons also watching Iain. They seemed cautious, likely due to the presence of the angels watching over Iain.

"Their numbers are growing," Raphael said. "I think this is going to be a pivotal battle tomorrow."

Mikael nodded. "Quentillious, I want your contingent of angels to keep a special eye on Iain. There are way too many demons with their attention on him."

Quentillious bowed slightly. "Yes, my captain. I will see to it."

"Uriel and Azel, have your angels guard the Temple Mount. I'm not exactly sure what will happen tomorrow, but Lucifer is here, so this, evidently, is where he is targeting his efforts."

Both nodded and flew with their angel contingents to the Temple Mount to wait for morning. Quentillious flew and followed close by Iain. As Iain entered his hotel, Quentillious and his angels perched on its roof to guard him through the night.

Mikael and Raphael flew to the building across from the Wailing Wall to wait out the night and observe until whatever was going to happen would occur. There were some visitors at the sacred wall even at this time of night. It all looked so peaceful as he looked down. But as Mikael looked up, he realized . . . peaceful it was not. Hundreds of demons were gathering, and their number was continuing to grow.

CHAPTER 47

ALWAYS NEXT TIME

Dread filled Iain. As he watched the crowds below in front of the Wailing Wall, a hot air balloon began to rise over the Dome of the Rock. He yelled at Naf to begin to prepare. Another balloon appeared, and then another and another. Within minutes there must have been dozens of the balloons approaching from all directions.

Before anyone could get into place and retaliate, hundreds of vials of blue liquid fell and burst all around them. Those in the crowd below began to change and turned into freakish zombies, their flesh rotting in seconds, making them look ghoulish, and they began attacking each other. Frightened at what he saw, Iain turned to Naf to help him escape, but Naf now . . . had the same zombie-like appearance.

Iain recoiled in horror, but Naf grabbed him and pulled him close, trying to bite into his neck. Iain pushed Naf's face away with his hands, the rotting flesh tearing away from his grasp and producing an almost unbearable odor, and yet Naf's strength had increased drastically; Iain was losing the battle as Naf's face grew closer and closer. He now felt Naf's hot breath on his neck and his warm, thick saliva drip down his neck and into his shirt collar. He tried to hold Naf off, but couldn't. Iain screamed . . .

Iain bolted upright in bed, breathing hard. He couldn't recall ever having such a nightmare. He looked at the time on his watch: slightly past five o'clock in the morning. He fell back on his pillow, now wide awake. There was no way he would get any more sleep after that dream. Throwing back the covers, he went to his window and looked out. He saw a man walking a dog and then a man and woman jog by. Otherwise, everything seemed quiet.

He got up, showered, shaved, and dressed. Before leaving, he grabbed a protein bar from his bag. He left the room and began slowly walking toward the Temple Mount. The closer he got, the more people he saw; all were traveling to the Temple Mount. Clearly, they wanted to be sure they would be as close as possible to the Wailing Wall before the expected crowds arrived.

Iain went to where Naf had said they should meet and watched others begin to congregate in the space between where he stood and the Wailing Wall. He was surprised at the diversity of people who were gathering. Several were young and laughing and joking with each other. He found their laughter infectious. He wasn't sure what they were laughing about, but he found himself smiling when he looked their way. One was laughing so hard he was turning beet red, and this made his companions laugh even harder at him, which caused him to laugh still more. The young man had to walk away for a few minutes to be able to catch his breath. Seeing the young enjoy life like this gave Iain a brief bit of morning encouragement. It made him temporarily forget the foreboding feeling that persisted with him ever since being in Israel.

As the sun began to rise, Iain saw Naf approach. Naf stopped short upon seeing him. "Iain! I wasn't expecting you this early."

Iain shook his head. "Couldn't sleep, so I just came here."

"Well, come on up."

Iain followed Naf up some stairs to reach the top area so they could look over the Wailing Wall below. Where they stood, they were almost at the same height as the Temple Mount itself. Iain noticed guards there looking over the edge at the gathering crowd below.

Naf opened a bag and handed a cup of coffee to Iain as he laughed. "Being here early ensures you get hot—not cold—coffee."

"Oh, thanks," Iain said. He took a sip. "That certainly hits the spot."

Naf handed him some type of pastry.

"Well, you're just a regular café this morning, aren't you?" Iain said, smiling.

Naf grinned. "Just prepared."

That made Iain laugh. "You got me there."

As they finished their pastries, Naf pointed to two cylinders on their side and two on the Temple Mount. "Those are lasers. Next to those are guns which will deploy nets to stretch from here to the Temple Mount to protect the people below, if necessary. The lasers will define the area the nets will cover."

Iain raised his eyebrows.

Naf laughed. "You did say vials of blue liquid will be dropped, right?"

Iain nodded but cocked his head, still not understanding.

"Hopefully, if that occurs, the nets will prevent the vials from hitting the ground and breaking. We also have rifles that shoot a gelatinous matrix which will encase the falling vial, and this will deploy a parachute. Those should prevent the vials outside the defined net area from bursting and allow them to fall to the earth without breaking."

Iain's eyes widened. "Naf, you are a genius. That's brilliant."

Naf grinned. "Hopefully that will be enough." He spent the next few minutes communicating with various soldiers via his comm to ensure they were engaged and in position.

The crowd grew larger as the morning went on. Soon the crowd within the Wailing Wall area was so dense it looked like there was no space at all between individuals. By the time nine-thirty arrived, the crowd was all the way back to the building on which Iain and Naf stood and even poured down side streets and into corridors. People sat on nearby half-walls and stairs all attempting to get a better view.

As the Kohanim entered, even though the crowd was congested, the people made way for them to walk through the masses and reach the stairs that had been constructed for them to stand on. The height of the stairs would allow them to bless the people properly.

Iain turned his head. He thought he heard something different from the normal ambient noise of the crowd. Then he saw someone—something—coming over a building.

A man with a jetpack!

* * * * *

Mikael stood on a nearby building eyeing the crowd and watching the demons who now stood all around the Temple Mount.

"What are they waiting for?" Raphael asked.

Mikael shook his head. "I don't know, but be on your guard." He noticed that Quentillious and his angels had surrounded Iain and Naf.

Raphael pointed when he heard the noise coming over the far building. "Look!"

Most of the demons swarmed and attacked while others distracted the guards and soldiers so they had no time to focus on any one thing.

Mikael lifted his sword and spread his majestic wings to their full extent. He rose swiftly with one mighty swish of his wings. "Angels, prepare!" he yelled. He saw Uriel and Azel with their angels fly in from opposite sides. Quentillious had half of his contingent follow them and directed the others stay to protect Iain and Naf.

Mikael lifted his sword and flew into the fray.

* * * * *

Naf spoke into his comm. "Who is that with the jetpack?"

"Don't know, sir," came the reply.

"Get him down—but be careful of the crowd!" Naf said.

"Roger," came the reply.

Iain didn't hear the shot, but he saw spray come out of the jetpack on the man's back and then watched the man begin to lose altitude.

"Capture him and secure him!" Naf said.

Iain saw several guards rush in the man's direction.

Two more men with jetpacks appeared, each approaching from opposite directions. Another flew over Iain's head and created a disturbance among the crowd. A few of the women screamed, but everyone remained in place. The Kohanim managed to maintain a sense of calmness in the crowd as they quoted Scripture and had the crowd sing a hymn of some kind.

One of the guards next to Naf shot and made a second man lose altitude, causing him to barely clear the Wailing Wall. The man skidded across the ground on top of the Temple Mount. More guards rushed the man.

"What are these men doing?" Naf asked.

Iain shook his head. "No idea. This is not making any sense."

Suddenly, the foreboding feeling overwhelmed Iain. He responded in the only way he could think to do so: he dropped to his knees.

Naf bent down. "Iain, are you all right? Are you hurt?"

Iain shook his head. "No. Just let me pray, Naf."

Naf gave him a strange look, then patted his shoulder. "Perhaps that is what we need, my friend."

* * * * *

Mikael briefly watched his angels. They were taking out demon after demon; he could see dozens of them go catatonic with their swords falling to the ground. But there looked to be just as many more demons coming to replace those who were falling.

The wave of prayer hit Mikael. He took a deep breath and felt new strength begin to rejuvenate him. He looked down and saw Iain on his knees. "Pray, my warrior. Pray."

As Mikael looked around, he saw each of his angel-warriors gain a renewed sense of strength. He smiled. That was just what they needed. He looked up and saw something approach, but it was obscured by the number of demons surrounding it. As he flew higher, more and more demons attacked him. Because of his regained strength, he was able to get past their defenses much faster than would have been the case a few minutes earlier. He saw there was some type of balloon structure approaching surrounded by numerous demons. Lucifer was in the basket with the human!

Mikael looked down and then back up. The demons were preventing the humans below from seeing the balloon by creating the many distractions with the men in jetpacks. This real threat before them was not being realized. Mikael flew back down to Quentillious.

Quentillious looked eager to fight but was staying in position because of Mikael's orders to guard Iain. "What are your orders, my captain?" he asked.

Mikael pointed. "Lucifer is coming and having his demons hide the threat from the humans. Do you see it?"

Quentillious nodded. "Vaguely, but yes." He looked at Mikael. "What shall we do?"

Mikael looked at the number of angels Quentillious had in reserve. "Leave three angels here; you and the rest of your contingent go and attack the demons around Lucifer. We need to get these humans to notice that balloon! That is the real threat they need to worry about."

Quentillious, eager to engage, smiled. "Yes, my captain. We will do as you say." He turned to his angels, pointed out three to stay, and he and the others flew straight up, stopping only long enough to deflect any demon who got in their way.

Mikael flew to Raphael. "Follow me."

Raphael nodded, bested the demon he was fighting, and flew directly behind Mikael.

The swarm of demons surrounding the hot air balloon was formidable. Lucifer had saved his strongest for this task. It took Mikael, Raphael, Quentillious, and his angels quite some time to defeat enough of the demons to make the balloon partially visible.

Lucifer peered over the edge of the balloon and laughed. "You won't get through, Mikael. I have made a perfect plan this time. As I stated, my time has come."

Mikael had no time to reply to Lucifer's rantings. He had to concentrate on each demon he fought by studying each of their swings and thrusts to see where their weaknesses lay. Some took longer to figure out than others, but a weakness, even though subtle, was eventually found and exploited. As more and more of the demons were turned catatonic, Lucifer's boasting became less and less.

Looking below, Mikael noticed the number of demons had decreased during the battle. He smiled as he knew they would soon be unable to create the level of distraction needed for the humans to fail to notice the imminent threat above them.

* * * * *

"Where did all these flying men come from?" Naf asked as he gave another order for a guard to fell one.

Iain shook his head. "They don't seem to have any vials of blue liquid laced with the virus to throw at the crowd, so what are they doing? Maybe . . . they're just a distraction." With that thought, he began to look around, ignoring the jetpack men to see if there was something else he was missing. Then he saw it. *A hot air balloon!* Just what he had proposed to Naf yesterday as a possible scenario. *Why did they not see it earlier?* It was now almost directly overhead.

Iain grabbed Naf's arm as he pointed. "Look!"

Naf's attention jerked Iain's way and then upward to where he pointed. His eyes widened. After looking into his binoculars, he yelled into his comm. "Deploy the net! Deploy the net!"

He handed the binoculars to Iain. Iain gasped seeing something blue falling from the sky. There looked to be dozens of them. Hearing a large swish, he saw nets fly from the top of the Wailing Wall to the buildings on the side where he and Naf stood. Four lasers at the corners pointed straight into the sky.

Naf spoke quickly into his comm. "Snipers, target all vials over you not within the laser square! Float them down and gather."

Iain observed all this through his binoculars. These guns shot something looking like beanbags but containing the soft gelatinous mass to absorb the force of the shock as they encased each vial. After impact, each mini parachute deployed, and the entire mass floated down on the breeze. The vials inside the laser square landed safely within the nets that had been deployed just moments earlier.

"Have the snipers target the balloon, Naf!" Iain said.

As Naf gave the command, Iain saw the giant balloon begin to deflate, and this drove it and its contents farther from the Temple Mount. He then saw a figure falling, heading directly for the net. He knew the man's weight would crush the vials!

Iain grabbed Naf's arm. "Target that man!"

Naf wasted no time in his command. Two snipers shot the beanbag-type weapon, each hitting and encasing one of the man's feet and deploying the small parachutes. The man floated upside down and landed on the Temple Mount. He was surrounded by soldiers before he even touched down. They roughly pulled him to the ground and put him in custody.

Once the man was secured, Iain could tell it was Haneberg. Evidently, the balloon being hit had dislodged him, causing him to fall from the basket.

Iain slapped Naf's upper back and laughed. "You did it, Naf! You saved the day!"

Naf grinned. The crowd below cheered, clapped, and whistled.

"You certainly gave them a Passover they will remember for a lifetime," Iain said, patting Naf on the back once more. "You are something else, Naf. Truly. Something else indeed."

* * * * *

Mikael, Azel, Uriel, and Quentillious defeated the remaining demons surrounding Lucifer and then surrounded him with their swords. As Mikael looked below, the other remaining demons either disappeared or quickly flew off. With Lucifer captured, they knew the battle was lost.

"As I stated," Mikael said to the chief dark angel, "today is *not* your day." He looked down at Haneberg being led away, his arms behind his back in cuffs. "And apparently not for your human buddy, either."

Lucifer shrugged. "It was close, though. The slightest error would have tilted the victory to my side." Looking down at Haneberg, he chuckled. "Humans are so ironic, aren't they?"

Mikael cocked his head.

"Oh, don't act so naïve," Lucifer said. "Greed and extortion are what get them incarcerated, and greed and extortion are what get them out of jail." He held up an index finger. "Good lawyers know that. Great lawyers know how to leverage that." A grin spread across his face. "And this man has great lawyers . . . and he has me." He nodded as if to himself. "He could still be useful."

"Do you never yield defeat?" Raphael asked, shaking his head.

Lucifer's face developed a stern look. "No! Never!" He looked at Mikael and spoke with a haughty tone. "My defeat is not complete. The humans still must deploy the cure. All will not survive."

"But the Kohanim will continue, and the future temple will be built," Mikael said.

"Most, but not all, will live, yes. Yet whether the temple will still happen has not been decided. Only the future will tell that. I concede this fight, but not the entire battle. There is always next time."

"What is it with you, Lucifer?" Raphael asked. "It's always 'the next time' with you."

"Each time I fight, there are small victories and increased technology. Soon, both will tilt to my favor, and you will be on the losing side."

"Time will tell," Raphael said. "And time is *not* on your side."

"So you say," Lucifer said.

He disappeared.

Mikael looked down at the crowd of people and then at his fellow angels. "In the past, our Lord created the ultimate victory for these humans at a Passover. It is fitting that we gave our Master another victory on this day."

CHAPTER 48

GOING HOME

The next morning Iain was back in the prime minister's office with Naf and Cohen. Iain felt comfortable enough with the prime minister at this point to call him Ezra.

"We all thank you, Iain, for helping us contain this plague within our borders and preserving our heritage," the prime minister said.

Iain gave a slight bow. "You're most welcome, Ezra, but most of the praise goes to Naf. He executed a defensive strategy brilliantly." Iain shook his head. "It would not have been such a successful outcome without him."

Naf was humble and simply replied, "I'm just glad our country is now safe."

"Safer, anyway," Iain said. "There will likely still be outbreaks before the cure can be administered to everyone."

"Yes," Ezra said. "I just heard reports that Tay-Sachs symptoms have been reported by some in Tel Aviv. An announcement is going out later today to address this and provide the people hope."

"Hope?" Iain asked. He had not heard from Ted yet, and he did not know where the team stood in D.C. with finalizing a cure.

Ezra nodded. "I just got off the phone with President Vanderbilt before my meeting with the both of you. Nanobot prototypes have been made. One of your scientists will be speaking to several of ours later today, and a sample is being flown here even as we speak. These prototypes will be used for us to mass produce so we can administer to our people." Suddenly, however, he had a solemn look. "Deaths are inevitable, unfortunately, but most will be saved, and we have you and your team to thank for that."

"Without you being here," Naf said, "our death toll would have been so much greater. You gave us all a Passover we will commemorate for years to come."

Iain stood. "I am just happy things are in a better place than they could have been. We will have sorrow, but not ultimate despair."

Naf nodded. "Very true, my friend."

"Now, if you both can excuse me, I have a flight to catch. It seems this is the last flight out to the States until the cure is implemented." Iain looked at Ezra. "I suspect I have you to thank for that."

Ezra shrugged. "My position gives me a few perks."

Iain laughed. "Well, I'm certainly glad."

They shook hands and Iain left for the airport.

Just outside Tel Aviv, Iain's phone beeped. It was Ted.

"Ted! It's great to hear from you. How is everything there?"

"Well," Ted said. "There's good and bad. The bad news is that the death toll is going to be significant both from Tay-Sachs symptoms as well as many people . . . bleeding to death."

There was a pause. Ted's voice grew softer. "Such a horrible way to die."

"And Kaitlyn?" Iain asked, fear in his voice.

"She's . . . better. I must admit, I had my doubts. It took us way longer to get suitable nanobots that were viable to reverse this awful plague. We were all getting sick, so that slowed us down considerably. I can tell you, Luciferian Plague is certainly an appropriate name for this."

"Everyone there is all right, though?"

"Yeah. We've all received the cure and are now getting better." There was another pause. Ted's voice came back, barely audible. "Iain, if Bev hadn't been on the President's list for first cures from those produced by the lab, I'm not sure she would have lasted long enough for the cure to be given."

"But she will be okay, right?" Iain asked, desperation in his voice.

"I think so. I mean, I've seen a subtle improvement, but it will take some time to tell. I'm hopeful it will be like you: nothing, and then vast improvement very quickly. By the time you get here, she should be much better."

Iain closed his eyes and took a long breath. Relief flooded through him. *Thank you, God.*

Ted went on. "We've given prototypes and instructions to the various labs contracted for mass production. Janice's team is setting up distribution plans even as we speak. It will likely be another week for the first samples to roll out, I'm afraid."

"Ted, can I ask a favor?"

"Sure. What is it?"

"Can you let my boss, Bill Harmon, know the nearest facility for receiving the cure? I promised myself I'd let him know as soon as possible."

"Okay, just text me his information."

"Will do. I heard there is a teleconference with Israel this afternoon. I assume that will be you?"

"Yes," Ted said. "Although it will be late morning here in the States. The President is working out meetings with other countries, and we'll do the same for them. I'm training my other colleagues here to handle many of those."

"Makes sense." Iain's car pulled to the ticketing area at the Tel Aviv airport. "I need to catch my flight. I'll see you in about fourteen hours."

Iain hung up, grabbed his bag, and hurried into the airport. This was one flight he did not want to miss.

CHAPTER 49

NEW OPPORTUNITIES

happiness filled Iain when he felt the wheels of the plane hit the runway. He was home. That brought such a feeling of relief.

As he stepped from the plane and headed for customs, he remembered the last time he had done this. He was pretty much out of it at the time. *Or was I,* he wondered. Standing in line at customs was where he had seen the angelic battle between good and evil. The memory brought back scary, but awe-inspiring, images to his mind. This was when the angel told him to pray because prayer changes things. He thought back to his time in Israel. Was that why things went better this time, because he prayed for the outcome? He wasn't sure, but he knew there certainly had been a spiritual battle in Israel just as much as a physical one. Maybe even larger than what occurred in the physical.

There was no holdup with the customs agent this time. Iain only had to answer the typical couple of questions and he was through. Because travel was so light at this time, there was barely a line for a taxi and not much traffic on the road. He arrived at the National Laboratory much faster than he would have thought possible.

He rushed to the floor that housed Ted's office; he assumed that was where Kaitlyn would be. As he entered, Tina and Charles were busy with something. Both looked up and gave him a wave.

"Welcome back, Dr. Thornwhite," Tina said.

He gave a small wave but made a beeline to Ted's office. Ted was sitting at his desk as he entered, and Kaitlyn was lying on the cot. He couldn't keep his eyes from watering. He had missed her so much.

"How is she, Ted?"

Ted came around and patted Iain on his upper back. "Better, my friend. So much better."

Iain glanced down and noticed bruises on Ted's arms. His eyes grew big. "Ted, your arms! Are you okay?"

Ted smiled. "I'm fine. We're all fine here." He held up his arm. "A little battle-worn, but doing fine. We should be back to normal in no time." He glanced at Kaitlyn. "Bev will be too, but her recovery may take a little longer than ours." He gently pushed Iain toward Kaitlyn. "Go ahead. She was asking about you earlier."

Ted walked out of his office, leaving Iain alone with Kaitlyn. He appreciated that. He went over and knelt next to her. "Kaitlyn." He gently shook her shoulder. "Hey, Kaitlyn."

She stirred and slowly awoke. Then she jerked upward, resting on her elbows. "Iain! You're here!"

Iain smiled broadly. "Indeed I am. How are you?"

She sat more upright and put her arms around his neck. "Better now that you're here."

Her eyes darted over his face as he leaned in. His lips touched hers and she leaned into him, reciprocating in a full way. After a long while he broke the kiss, pushed her hair behind her ear, and cupped her cheek with his palm. "I have missed you so much." His eyes looked over her face and arms. There was still some light bruising, but the petechiae had vanished and her eyes were no longer bloodshot. "Are you sure you're better?"

She nodded. "Yes, Iain. Much, much better." She paused. "Still a little weak, but I'm getting my strength back." She smiled. "Better each day." She scooted back on the cot, putting her pillow behind her, leaning against the wall. "So, tell me how things went."

Iain smiled brightly. "It all went extremely well. All the vials Haneberg wanted to use were captured without a single one breaking."

Kaitlyn gave Iain an enamored look and a smile.

"Oh, and you would have loved Naf—Naftali Friedman. He is such a brilliant scientist, and now a good friend. He devised a type of weapon that could trap the vials in midair and keep them from breaking."

"So the two of you saved the day, huh?"

Iain smiled. "Not just us." He paused.

Kaitlyn cocked her head and said, in a hushed voice, "What is it?"

"Kaitlyn, I also felt that we were in the midst of a great spiritual battle. I got this overwhelming sense of foreboding, so I just had to pray. That's when things seemed to turn around with one success after another."

Kaitlyn smiled and squeezed his hand, giving emotional support without saying anything.

"That happened to me also on the way from New York City to here when the weather was terrible. We almost had a wreck, but I was impressed by something—someone—to pray, so I did." He paused. "I think that may be what helped prevent us from crashing." He looked at her for any trace of doubt. "Do you think I'm crazy for those thoughts?"

Kaitlyn shook her head. "No, Iain. No, I don't. I've had some of those same feelings. I'm a scientist, and I believe in cause and effect, but I can't deny that something bigger—darker—was at play here."

Iain nodded. "Yes, I've felt the same. When this is over and we've all recovered, I want us to start attending church more regularly, and to pray together." He grimaced, unsure how she would react. "Are . . . you okay with that?"

Kaitlyn smiled. "Yes, Iain. I'm more than okay with that."

He squeezed her hand and kissed her forehead. "Good. Why don't you lie down again and get some more rest? I'm so happy you're doing better."

Kaitlyn laid back and closed her eyes. Iain went to step from the office but stopped at the doorway to look back at her. He thought back to how their lives had connected and intertwined. He wondered if all of that had been by divine coordination as well.

He turned and headed to where the others were working. He wanted to thank them for their work—especially following through with their efforts despite being quite sick. They were the heroes in this saga as much as anyone else.

* * * * *

Over the next couple of weeks, the deployment of the cure was carried wide. Distribution and administration centers were established across the United States, and progress was also made around the globe. It wouldn't be long before this nightmare would come to an end, but it also came at a great cost. More than five million people would succumb to the plague before it could be curtailed.

* * * * *

At the end of the month, President Vanderbilt invited Iain, Ted, and Kaitlyn to the White House Rose Garden for a ceremony where many were praised for their efforts; the three received special recognition. Amanda and Sam were awarded special accommodation as well. The President then invited the five of them, along with George Goldberg, to the Oval Office for a special meeting.

After they sat, Vanderbilt walked in front of his desk, then leaned against it while facing them. "I invited all of you here because our country still needs you."

They looked around at each other and then back to Vanderbilt.

"Dr. Sheridan, your new technology has brought with it new opportunities, but it has also raised the risk of new threats we need to guard against."

Kaitlyn nodded but also had a somber look.

"I have decided to create a new division under the National Laboratory for looking at not only the opportunities of this new technology but how to prevent it from getting into nefarious hands." He put his hands together and then pointed them toward her. "If you are willing, I would like you to lead this new division." He motioned with his hands for her to wait, that there was more. "This means you would have to relocate here, but I can't think of anyone more qualified to lead this effort. What do you say?"

Kaitlyn's eyes widened, and her hand went to her chest. "Well, I . . . I don't know what to say." She gestured to Vanderbilt. "That's certainly a generous offer . . . "

"But you don't want to take it, is that it?" Vanderbilt asked.

Kaitlyn's eyebrows raised. "Oh, no. I would love such an opportunity. But there are stipulations I would need assurance of."

Vanderbilt gave a wry smile. "So, because I want you, you're going to blackmail me now?"

Kaitlyn looked shocked, then grinned. "Well, not exactly."

Vanderbilt chuckled. "So what are your stipulations?"

"I need certain people to be guaranteed to be in this new department, and I need to be able to appoint who I feel is qualified to fill certain positions."

Vanderbilt's stance seemed to relax. "Dr. Sheridan, all of that is a given. I thoroughly expect Mr. Jordan and those you have already worked with to be on your team." He shook his head. "I'm certainly not wanting to break something that has produced such amazing results."

"And there are others in New Mexico I would like to recruit."

Vanderbilt raised his hands. "You recruit whomever you feel is needed."

Kaitlyn grinned and looked at Iain, who gave her a nod. "Then I accept," she said.

Vanderbilt stood. "Great." He turned to Goldberg. "Now, George, I will need people to investigate and vet those who would be interested in and trying to obtain this technology."

George nodded. "I know exactly where you are going with this, Mr. President. I know just the individuals who can do that." He gave Amanda and Sam a wink.

"Splendid," Vanderbilt said. He turned to Iain. "And that leaves you, Dr. Thornwhite. What am I going to do with you?"

"Sir?" Iain wasn't sure what to do with those words.

"Prime Minister Ezra Cohen spoke very highly of you. At first I thought you would make an excellent ambassador."

Iain's eyes went wide. "I'm not very politically savvy, sir."

Vanderbilt gave a dismissive wave. "Oh, that's stuff anyone can learn. Yet I think I need something else probably more valuable."

"What is that, sir?"

"You work for the Sloane Foundation, is that right?"

"Yes, sir."

"I've heard great things about it. We need someone to oversee all the clinical trials that will likely come forward because of this new technology. It's so new we need it to be coordinated. You would have to stop working for Sloane, but you could definitely utilize them for their expertise in this area."

Iain cocked his head. "You want me to give up my job, sir?"

Vanderbilt nodded. "Yes, so you can lead and oversee all clinical trials utilizing nanobot technology. I've spoken to the head of the National Institutes of Health, and he agrees that this is so new it requires its own department. It's yours if you want it."

Iain's eyes widened. He would be near Kaitlyn and doing what he loved. "Thank you, sir. It would be my honor to serve in that capacity."

Vanderbilt clapped his hands together. "Wonderful. I think that covers it for now. This is a thanks to all of you for your work in helping save our country. Few people will know all you have done and the contributions and sacrifices you made. I hope this makes up a little for all of that. Yet this also means more will be expected of you than before.

"This is a new age, a new world in which we are embarking. Dr. Sheridan, you have ushered us into a new century before our time. We are looking for you to help us catch up with where you have brought us."

CHAPTER 50

he wins in the end

Raphael looked at Mikael as Iain and his five friends stepped from the President's Oval Office. "It seems all has ended well." He shook his head. "Not well, but as well as could be expected given the circumstances."

Mikael nodded. "Yes, but it seems Lucifer gets more and more emboldened every time we encounter him. This is only the infancy of this type of technology. Think what he may do when this technology gets expanded."

"Yes. It's frightening."

Both turned to see . . . Lucifer himself, standing behind them.

"It makes my mouth water just thinking about it." The dark angel looked from one to the other. "Doesn't it yours?"

Mikael shook his head. "Lucifer, you are trapped in this time dimension. Our Lord and Creator is not. He has already seen the future for these humans. You ruling over them is not part of that future. He has already declared that."

"Oh, the Ancient of Days has already declared the future, has he?"

Mikael and Raphael both nodded.

"Well, I don't believe the future is defined. Look at each time I have almost gained my position. I come closer each time."

Raphael's eyes widened. "You think that because you are in the time dimension, you control time here?"

Lucifer shrugged. "It is the time dimension that I obtained from Adam. If the kingdom is mine, I would think that implies the time is mine as well."

"Okay," Mikael said. "Let's go with your analogy. You received Adam's kingdom, right?"

Lucifer nodded, and looked quite smug while doing so.

"But you didn't control Adam, did you?"

Lucifer gave Mikael a hot stare. "And what is *that* supposed to mean?

Mikael now shrugged. "Oh, just stating facts." He looked at Lucifer. "Do you control Adam?"

Lucifer shook his head. "No. You know he is now in Eden."

"Okay. Then what about Abel, Enoch, Abraham, Daniel, and a host of other individuals from this time dimension that you say you control . . . who you do not control?"

Lucifer was now livid, and his eyes displayed hot anger. "Get to your point, Mikael."

"It just seems to me—mind you, I'm thinking out loud here—that for someone who supposedly has control of the time dimension, he doesn't have as much control as he thinks he does. So, maybe—again, just speculating here—you don't really control the time of this dimension, either."

Lucifer took a deep breath and let it out quickly. "You are insufferable!" With that, he disappeared.

Raphael laughed. "I just love it when you get the upper hand when debating with him."

Mikael smiled weakly. "Yes, that did feel good, but it also only points out the inevitable fact."

Raphael sighed. "Yes. His stubbornness, determination, and pride will make him try even harder than the previous time to prove his point, the very point you just turned against him."

Mikael nodded. He put his hand on Raphael's shoulder. "Yet, we have truth on our side. Our Creator has made all, and he has seen the end of all."

"And he wins in the end," Raphael said with a smile.

Mikael grinned. "He wins big time." He looked at Iain and Kaitlyn as they left the President's office. "And so do they, and all other prayer warriors like them."

I hope you've enjoyed *The Luciferian Plague*. Letting others know of your enjoyment of this book is a way to help them share your experience. Please consider posting an honest review. You can post a review at Amazon, Barnes & Noble, Goodreads, or other places you choose. Reviews can also be posted at more than one site! This author, and other readers, appreciate your engagement.

Also, check out my website: www.RandyDockens.com.

—Randy Dockens

ERABON PROPHECY TRILOGY

Come read this exciting trilogy where an astronaut, working on an interstellar gate, is accidently thrown so deep into the universe that there is no way for him to get home.

He does, however, find life on a nearby planet, one in which the citizens look very different from him. Although tense at first, he finds these aliens think he is the forerunner to the return of their deity and charge him with reuniting the clans living on six different planets.

What is stranger still is that while everything seems so foreign from anything he has ever experienced . . . there is an element that also feels so familiar.

Available now!

THE STELE PENTALOGY

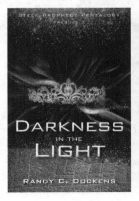
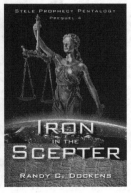

Do you know *your future*?

Come see the possibilities in a world God creates and how an apocalypse leads to promised wonders beyond imagination.

Read how some experience mercy, some hope, and some embrace their destiny—while others try to reshape theirs. And how some, unfortunately, see perfection and the divine as only ordinary and expected.

Available now!

THE CODED MESSAGE TRILOGY

Come read this fast-paced trilogy where an astrophysicist accidently stumbles upon a world secret that plunges him and his friends into an adventure of discovery and intrigue . . .

What Luke Loughton and his friends discover could possibly be the answer to a question you've been wondering all along.

Available now!

THE ADVERSARY CHRONICLES

Come read this exciting series where the many schemes of Lucifer are revealed and unfolded. Journey from when his pride first manifested itself separate from God's will and started our world down his same path, one of choice, to a path that seems could change even the prophecy of Scripture as we know it!

His schemes are always more devious than they first appear, with consequences that go far beyond what one would think. Despite his aims, he finds that God's unchanging promises always prevail no matter how well his schemes are crafted. Yet many are lost in the wake of Lucifer's lies.

The stories are as old as time but told in a new and exciting way. You don't want to miss them!

Available now!

Why Is a Gentile World Tied to a Jewish Timeline?

The Question Everyone Should Ask

Yes, the Bible is a unique book.

Looking for a book with mystery, intrigue, and subterfuge? Maybe one with action, adventure, and peril suits you more. Perhaps science fiction is more your fancy. The Bible gives you all that and more! Come read of a hero who is humble yet exudes strength, power, and confidence—one who is intriguing yet always there for the underdog.

Read how the Bible puts all of this together in a unique, cohesive plan that intertwines throughout history—a plan for a Gentile world that is somehow tied to a Jewish timeline.

Travel a road of discovery you never knew existed. Do you like adventures? Want to join one? Then come along. Discover the answer to the question everyone should ask.

Available now!